I took a last look around the front yard. Had Laura seen it coming? Had she known that the woman she lived with would turn out to be her killer? Had she felt any physical pain while Inez attacked her? Had she tried to fight back, or had she just surrendered, knowing she had no chance? Had this fight been the last of many similar ones before? Had Inez broken her spirit long before she finally killed her? Had Laura's last thought been I love you or I hate you?

I tried to shake off these obsessive thoughts and took a close look at the soil underneath the magnolia. The tree was throwing off its petals. Huge rosy and white leaves were covering the ground. They were turning brown at the edges, slowly decaying.

Of course there were no traces of what had happened under this tree or on the stone tiles that led up to the front steps of the building. Only later would I learn that it was on those steps that the police had found Inez. She had called 911 herself from inside the house. Then she had come back out, still clutching the knife, and had sat there, watching over Laura's body until the cops had led her away.

Visit

Bella Books

at

BellaBooks.com

or call our toll-free number

1-800-729-4992

LAURA'S WAR

URSULA STECK

Bella
BOOKS

2007

Bella Books, Inc.
P.O. Box 10543
Tallahassee, FL 32302

Printed in the United States of America on acid-free paper
First Edition

Editor: Cindy Cresap
Cover designer: Stephanie Solomon-Lopez

ISBN-10: 1-59493-090-2
ISBN-13: 978-1-59493-090-4

Acknowledgments

Once again, the people around me, my friends and family, have encouraged and supported me while writing this book. They have listened and given their opinions, and I want to wholeheartedly thank everybody who ever chatted with me about this book. Often it is the small comment, the occasional heads-up to the writer that steers a manuscript in the right direction.

Particularly, I want to thank my father, sister and my grandmother for their ongoing wonderful support and their interest in what I do. My writer friends Natascha Würzbach and Beate Sauer have again given invaluable tips and advice. Callie Silver and Kimberly A. Lucia, I'll be forever indebted to you for what you did to the manuscript. Thank you, thank you, thank you!

Cindy Cresap, my editor, thank you for the kindness and the beautiful work!

Linda Hill and the women of Bella Books, it has once again been the greatest pleasure to work with you.

And of course, my eternal love and gratefulness belong to my partner Yvette Fang, who has discussed every stage of the book with me, from the first fledgling idea to the last twists, who has read every draft of the manuscript, and most important of all, who never loses patience with me and is always ready to laugh away my self-doubt.

About the Author

Raised in Europe and the United States, Ursula Steck has spent most of her adult life in Cologne, Germany, until she met her partner, a resident of San Francisco, in 2001. For a few years she traveled between the continents and finally moved to Northern California in 2005. Ursula has published three mystery novels in German and numerous short stories in German and English. Following *The Next World*, *Laura's War* is her second American novel.

Possible existence of a parallel universe has been scientifically conceded.

—*Mr. Spock*
Star Trek, "The Alternative Factor," stardate 3088.7.

Chapter 1

She was lying in pools of blood. It had flowed from the countless gaping wounds that covered her whole body. Her clothes were torn. She lay on her back, her arms and legs extended in odd, crooked positions. Her eyes were wide open, glassy, yet lifeless—like the eyes of a stuffed deer, killed and gutted after a desperate, breathless, hopeless flight. Her long dark hair was tousled, caked with dirt from the ground beneath her and the fluids that had run from her body. Her cheeks were so pale they seemed almost green. The only thing that revealed that this dead person had ever been alive—had been breathing and feeling until only an hour before the picture was taken—was her mouth. The blood red lips were slightly opened, as though she had died while whispering a last unheard word.

I grabbed the next photo and placed it beside the ones I had already viewed. All of them showed Laura Cunningham after she had been stabbed to death in her front yard on a December evening last year, killed by her own lover. I forced myself to coolly scrutinize the crime scene photographs, tried to muster the calm of the determined, passionate, yet impassive investigator. I did not succeed.

Once more I stared at the picture her mother had given me of the living Laura. I took in the fine yet strong features, the narrow eyes, broad mouth, high forehead and angular jaw. I noted her smile, which was at once shy and challenging, and her gaze that could have belonged to a seasoned ballerina, hardened by pain, yet dreamy from the decades of music to which she had danced. Laura Cunningham had not been a classic beauty, but she had been striking in her own way, with a face that conveyed one very strong personal trait: courage—and the will to take on whoever was out there to get her. She had lost her last fight.

I was on a plane, thirty thousand feet above the Appalachian Mountains on my way into Laura's past. I wasn't supposed to dig into the reasons for Laura's death, and if Mrs. Marge Cunningham, Laura's mother, knew that I had gotten hold of these pictures, and was beginning to doubt everything that had looked so obvious about her daughter's murder, she would probably take me off the case. But the longer I studied the gruesome images from the police murder book, the more I became convinced that everything in this case was completely different from what I and many others had been made to believe. And the closer I looked at the crime scene photos, the more certain I was that these pictures had the power to save somebody, somebody Laura had cared for deeply.

In this moment on the plane I made a promise to the dead woman: I would uncover the truth about her murder. I had no idea yet that this unspoken promise would lead me close to my own death. And it would cost other people—people Laura had loved—their lives over the course of my desperate adventure.

❧

Marge Cunningham had only hired me to find something that had belonged to her daughter, something that had never surfaced in the course of the murder investigation by the San Francisco Police Department. It had been a short investigation. Laura's partner, Inez Belize, had been found at the crime scene, bloody knife in hand, and had confessed to the murder instantly. There had been no trial. Inez's court-appointed lawyer had gotten her a plea agreement, which placed her in prison for the next fifteen years on a murder two charge. The case was closed. Laura's mother knew whom to blame and hate for the loss of her daughter. All she wanted from me was to retrieve some of Laura's belongings which hadn't yet been handed over to her, but which she was sure existed.

My business partner Martha Bega and I had opened our private detective firm only four months ago. We had not hoped to be hired by such a high-profile customer so soon. We specialized in skip tracing. Finding missing people. I had experienced what it meant when somebody you cared for was suddenly gone without a trace. I knew the powerlessness, the existential feeling of betrayal, the devastating sense that this planet was a void that could just suck up a person and never spit her out again.

Mrs. Cunningham's request, therefore, did not fall into our specialty. But when Susan Bradley, one of the city's richest residents and an acquaintance I had met during a previous case, called and said she had referred us to yet another one of San Francisco's upper crust, of course Martha and I did not decline.

Marge Cunningham's residence was not as grand as I had first imagined when I heard the Pacific Heights address. It was located on Pacific, four blocks west of Fillmore. The whole neighborhood overlooked the bay, which on the day I first met Laura's mother, March 14, was covered by a layer of fog and gave the impression that the street hovered on top of a gray duvet. The air was heavy, wet, invading the lungs like a cold liquid.

Number 314 was a beige, two-story Edwardian with small

windows and a crescent driveway that seemed just a little bit too big for the size of the property. There was none of the wild, luscious green that overflowed the adjacent gardens. Only a few patches of small yellow mums huddled on the side of the gravel drive. Two cars were parked in front of the house: a white, brand-new looking Mercedes coupe, and a burgundy Ford minivan.

I rang the bell, and immediately there were steps behind the door. I ran my fingers through my inch-long hair, and found myself straightening my jacket, a blue silk thing in Mao style, which I had purchased in Chinatown the same morning, realizing that I might need to show up here a bit more dressy.

Despite the audible activity behind the door, nobody bothered to open it. I rang the bell once more. The eye of an automatic camera was circling above me. I would have loved to stick my tongue out at the lens. Just open the door, I mouthed instead.

Finally, my wish was granted. A rotund woman in a black dress and white apron stared at me with huge round blue eyes. Her gaze hooked onto the right side of my face where I wear an artificial eye. Today I had chosen the brown one, which matches my real eye. The woman had spotted my disability at the first glance. She looked like the stereotype of a servant from a British manor house of the beginning of the last century: obedient, naive, but inherently astute.

"I have an appointment with Mrs. Cunningham," I started.

"And who are you?" the woman inquired.

"Anna Spring," I continued. "Mrs. Cunningham is expecting me at two o'clock." It was three minutes before two.

"Are you sure?"

"Maybe I could speak to her myself, then we can find out."

Somebody appeared behind the woman. I hoped it would be the lady of the house who could save me from her factotum. But then I discovered it was a child in a wheelchair. The maid turned around, grabbed the handles of the chair, pushed it down a hall and signaled me to follow her. Like the house itself, the hall was a downsized version of something usually more glamorous. There were rococo armchairs, oil paintings in gilded frames and a petite sideboard on Chippendale legs. Everything was crowded together, though, and after a few steps we had already entered the next room. It was a kind of salon with leather chairs, a couch and an open fireplace over which hung a faded tapestry picturing a Victorian scene: a boy and a girl in a forest, looking into each other's eyes longingly.

Still there was no sign of Mrs. Cunningham. The maid placed the wheelchair in front of the window with its back facing me. The view from this window, which was much bigger than the ones in the front, was breathtaking. The city seemed to be rising from the clouds.

I would have liked to ask the child—I still couldn't make out what its age or gender was, as all I saw was a tiny back in a big wheelchair and curly black hair—where Mrs. Cunningham might be. But there was the maid who hadn't left the room yet. In fact, when I turned around I saw that she had placed herself in one of the armchairs and was pouring a drink from a carafe which stood on a side table.

Always expect the greatest possible weirdness, I reminded myself of the first commandment of the private investigator.

"So you are a detective," the maid stated, revealing that she was, in fact, informed about my coming, and that her incredulousness had been an act.

I only nodded.

"Don't you think two eyes would be of help in your profession?"

"Two eyes are always of help," I answered. "Just as an IQ of 210, a third eye in the center of your forehead or hair all over your body to keep you warm in the wind. As most of us don't have these kind of mutations, we have to work with what we've got."

"I've never heard of a mutation resulting in a third eye," the woman mused and took a sip of her drink.

"They happen," I said and placed myself in a chair opposite hers.

She took off her apron, straightened her dress, which, as I could now see, was made of a beautiful brocade, and looked me straight in the eye.

"You are Mrs. Cunningham," I guessed.

"I always like to see how somebody treats servants." She smiled. Her blue eyes had mysteriously gotten darker and less round. Her face had also lost the air of the peasant. Even her skin had taken on a different glow. Instead of a British maid she now looked like the apple-cheeked lady of the country estate. "I don't like to surround myself with people who think they are more valuable just because they don't have to clean up other people's messes."

So you always clean up your own mess? I would have loved to ask. But Martha and I needed every client we could get. Instead I said with a mix of admiration and irritation, "Have you ever worked as an actor?"

"Don't you want to know if you have passed the test?"

"Not particularly."

"Well, you did a good job keeping your composure, but I can tell you have an anger issue . . ."

"You said you wanted to hire our firm." It was time to get to the point or else my *anger issue* might truly take over. "In which matter did you want to see me?"

"It's about my daughter, Laura." Another astonishing transformation was taking place in Marge Cunningham's face. A deep, terrible sadness moved in, the outer corners of her mouth sank down, her skin paled, and tears appeared in her eyes. Before I had even heard her story, I felt sincere sympathy for whatever this woman had experienced. It took her just a few seconds, though, to collect herself. Her fingers continued to drum an unsteady beat on the glass she was still clutching.

She told me the short version. All I had to know was that Laura Cunningham had lived with her lover Inez Belize. Inez killed Laura. She went to prison. Now Marge Cunningham wanted Laura's possessions. The house the two women had lived in belonged to Inez's family, and Laura's mother wanted nothing to do with them. So it would be my call to contact them, get them to hand Laura's things over and bring them to Mrs. Cunningham.

It sounded like an easy task, more appropriate for a mover than for a private detective.

"Why did Inez kill Laura?" I asked.

"I don't think that is any of your business," Marge Cunningham said.

"I'd like to know what reaction to expect when I turn up on the Belizes' doorstep."

"To be honest with you, I don't even know who *the Belizes* are." Mrs. Cunningham spit out the name of Inez's family like a sip of wine in which she had detected cork.

"You never talked to Laura about the people she was living with?"

"Laura and I didn't talk much since she moved in with that woman."

"And during the investigation? Did anybody ever tell you more of the background on Laura's death?"

"Listen, this woman has killed my daughter. I don't want to know more about her or anybody related to her. And I'm definitely not interested in talking to you about the unfortunate affair. I think I made it very clear what I expect of you, and I will pay well for it. By the way, what is your fee?"

I named my hourly rate and asked for the address of the Belizes. Mrs. Cunningham said she did not know it, and it was part of my task to find out.

I rose from my chair. Then I remembered that Martha had

told me always to ask for a retainer.

"A retainer, aha," was Marge Cunningham's answer to my request. "But what if you are unsuccessful?"

"You will have to pay me anyhow for the effort. I'm not in the car repair business where you can expect guaranteed results."

Slowly she stood up and left the room. "Wait here," she ordered.

I sank back onto the chair. I would definitely have to get used to dealing with clients—particularly the difficult ones. So far I had tried to ignore this aspect of my new profession. Naively, I had imagined that a private detective would spend most of her time working alone, investigating on the computer, performing hidden surveillance, or at the most, questioning the occasional witness. The diplomacy necessary for talking to the people who paid you, no matter how undiplomatic they were, was something I had not taken into consideration. In my former professions I'd had endless time alone, as a security guard on night shift, and— seemingly many lifetimes ago—as a biologist in a gene lab.

Suddenly there was movement in the room. I flinched. I had completely forgotten the child in the wheelchair. It had been so quiet during the last twenty minutes that it might as well have been a statue, designed to decorate the salon. Now the wheelchair turned around. I still couldn't tell if the kid was a girl or a boy or how old it was. It had a narrow face the color of a roasted almond. Dark curls spun around its brow, and together with the amazing light-green eyes which looked into a far distance, the child seemed to belong to an imaginary tribe of fantasy creatures.

It pushed the rims of its wheelchair and fiercely rolled toward me until I called, "Whoa, slow down."

The child just stared at me, didn't break or turn, and eventually hit the armrest of my chair full throttle, banging its knees.

"Chhhh." Only a little sigh came from the kid's mouth, as if it were forcefully suppressing any louder expression of pain.

"Hey, you're set on self-mutilation?" I tried to joke. "You must have known you would bump into something."

Despite looking so petite, the kid must have been at least twelve. Its features were firmer and more determined than a young child's, yet more open still than those of most adolescents.

"I'm Anna," I said, looking the kid straight in the eye. And then I realized its pupils didn't meet mine, and the eyeballs wandered into two different directions. The child was blind.

"I'm sorry," I said. "I could have guessed it earlier, considering that I'm also missing an eye."

"She doesn't understand you." Mrs. Cunningham interrupted our one-sided conversation. "She only speaks Dari."

I didn't ask what kind of language that was, and Marge Cunningham didn't offer to enlighten me. I made a mental note to Google it later, though.

Mrs. Cunningham handed me an envelope. "Here is your check." Then she guided me to the door.

There was something else in the envelope, as I found out when I opened it back at the office: the picture of a young Asian woman, probably in her late twenties, whose face fascinated me immediately. On the back somebody had noted: *Laura, 2005*. The sum on the check was written in the same flowing longhand. It was double the amount I had asked for.

Chapter 2

The small office space in the Tenderloin that Martha and I rented for our firm was in a building across from the house on Geary where we both lived. Our area was centrally located, but that was about the only perk it had. Our apartment building radiated the charm of a former B-list film diva who was now drunk most of the time. During the day tourists wandered the street anxiously trying to avoid the panhandlers and droves of spaced-out homeless people. At night the tourists were gone, and the entrances to the buildings became the sleeping places for the street folks.

Martha and I had been neighbors for a little less than a year. Originally, I had mainly feared her and had hoped she would leave me alone. Despite being a wheelchair user, Martha was a towering presence: she was big, loud, commanding and gorgeous.

When I entered the office after my visit to Pacific Heights, she was sitting in front of her gigantic computer screen, her index fingers hammering the keyboard as if she were trying to poke them through somebody's skin and right into the jugular. Her thick black hair, which reached almost down to her waist, veiled her body. Her pitch black eyes were slanted in concentration.

"Hey, chicky," she called. "This darn machine ate my file with all the database links."

"What do you mean *ate*?" I had long given up asking Martha not to call me chicky. She was brighter than Einstein, but untrainable in certain aspects of life, one of them being the simple fact that brutality against your computer does not get you back lost files.

"It's just gone. See for yourself." Martha pushed her wheelchair into a corner of the room so I could squeeze by. Our office measured approximately two hundred square feet, one hundred of which were taken up by my partner, the other by the desk. I was supposed to work mainly outside the office, while Martha took care of all investigations which could be performed via the electronic networks. And that was a lot, especially in our field.

Martha was a retired police detective. She had been shot on the job, become a paraplegic, and since then had been bored to death, annoying her former colleagues who frequented the doughnut shop on the first floor of our apartment building, as well as her neighbors, myself included. When my best friend Jeff had been killed last year, and I had desperately tried to find out who had murdered him, Martha had helped me, eventually delivering the final clue, and saving a woman's life. After that, we had slowly become closer. I had gotten more used to her sometimes impertinent ways, and she began to respect me, little by little. When she suggested we open up a private investigation firm, of course I had originally hesitated, not knowing if I could take being around Martha day in and day out. She had quickly guessed the source of my indecision and had convinced me that we would hardly see each other, with me working out in the field and her specializing in cyber investigations.

As Martha was a trained police officer, she received a private detective's license immediately, and I was now her official apprentice. After two years I would be able to apply for my own license. We named our firm *Eagle Eye Investigations*, my lover Mido's suggestion. She was an advertising expert with an interesting sense of humor.

"Here's the file," I said. "You just put it into the wrong folder."

"As I said, he ate it."

"He didn't, you misplaced it," I stubbornly insisted, completely aware that Martha's brain didn't harbor many neurons capable of self-criticism. "And since when is the computer a *he*? Aren't we an all-female business?"

"He's a he when he kills my files."

"A transgendered computer who can switch sexes back and forth?" I joked.

"Does Marge Cunningham want you to look into the death of her daughter?" Martha changed the topic.

"So you already researched her."

"That was easy. There are articles on the Web. I printed them out for you. And then I made some calls. The case is as clear as an empty gin bottle. The gal's lover killed her. She confessed. The deal she got is good."

Martha quickly briefed me about Laura's murder case, and together with the information Mrs. Cunningham had given me, the events surrounding her daughter's death began to take shape in my head.

Laura had come home one evening, three days before Christmas last year. Her partner, Inez Belize, had waited for her and had seen through the kitchen window that she was approaching the house. Inez ran out to the front yard. For some reason she was extremely mad at Laura and confronted her immediately. At one point during their argument she lost control and stabbed Laura over and over with the humongous knife she still held in her hand from cutting vegetables for dinner.

"Mrs. Cunningham only wants me to retrieve Laura's stuff from Inez's family. She doesn't question the investigation," I told Martha.

"That's good. I'm sure the boys wouldn't like us to poke around in an obvious case like this."

With "the boys" Martha referred to her former colleagues from the homicide department. There were four female detectives working on the squad too, but for some occult police reason, they didn't mind being called boys as well.

"Does it say anywhere why Inez was in such a maniacal fury that she butchered Laura?" I didn't ask because I was looking for any kind of understandable reason, or even an excuse why somebody would kill her lover. I didn't think there was one. One person was dead and the other one alive. The power structure couldn't have been more obvious. But I was just plain curious what the energies at the core of their relationship had been.

"No," Martha said. "It seems that Inez never revealed what made her snap."

It was only four thirty. So I decided to look for the house where Inez and Laura had lived together. It was in the Excelsior district. One of the newspaper articles mentioned that it was located on Madrid and Russia, and even though there was no number mentioned, I was pretty sure I'd be able to identify it by the photographs the papers had printed.

I made my way there on BART and bus. I easily gained back the time that it took to wait for public transit by not having to search for parking. When I needed a car, I always just rented one.

I walked down Madrid Street, keeping my eyes open for a two-story clapboard house with a big magnolia tree in the front, and soon found the place. It looked uninhabited. The blue paint was peeling off the façade, the upstairs windows were dirty, the downstairs ones broken, the frames filled in with plywood. I had hoped that maybe the two women had shared the place with other members of Inez's family, who would still be living there. But when I recalled my conversation with Mrs. Cunningham, she had only mentioned that it belonged to the family of her daughter's lover—who obviously now wanted to get rid of it. A realtor's sign tagged it For Sale. I stepped through a low, wrought iron gate into the minute front yard.

"Do you want to buy the ghost house?" A voice sounded from the sidewalk.

I shot around. Not so much startled as feeling guilty for trespassing.

"I'm thinking of it," I answered the young woman who was standing on the other side of the fence. She was holding onto a stroller that had a toddler in it.

"It's about time someone moved back in there," the woman said. She had black curls, a friendly, broad face and wide hips. Her lips were glowing in a spectacular neon pink.

"Do you live around here?" I asked.

"Two houses down."

"So we'd be neighbors if my girlfriend and I decided to buy it."

The woman showed no visible reaction to the girlfriend part of my statement. She just rocked the stroller a little, as if contemplating what to tell me and what not. The toddler peeked out with huge nosy eyes.

"I know what happened here," I said. "It was on the news. But we don't have a lot of money, and with the real estate prices being so high this is quite a good deal."

Obviously the woman could relate to that. She smiled and said, "If you decide to buy, let me know. We can get together some time. It'll be good to have nice new neighbors." Then she lowered her voice a little. "And if you need somebody . . . for the spirits, you know . . . my mother-in-law has a gift."

It took me a moment to catch on that she wasn't talking about booze, and that her mom-in-law was no moonshiner but probably something like a psychic or a voodoo priestess or a similarly gifted person.

"Thanks a lot," I said. "We'll certainly get back to you. By the way, did you personally know the people who lived here before?"

"Inez and her father?"

"And Laura."

"Sure, I knew all of them, Inez since she was little. We went to elementary school together. We were never close friends. She was more the quiet type. But I always liked her. A good person to take care of her father and all that. And Laura was a doll. She once really helped me. I can't believe what happened to her. She and Inez always seemed so happy together."

"Did you ever hear them fight? Or did you see any bruises on Laura?"

The woman seemed puzzled. Then a male voice called from a few yards away, "Lucy, what's up with dinner?"

Lucy gave me a last smile. "I have to run. The man is hungry from work. See ya."

Her last words came out hurried, fearful.

I took a last look around the front yard. Had Laura seen it coming? Had she known that the woman she lived with would turn out to be her killer? Had she felt any physical pain while Inez attacked her? Had she tried to fight back, or had she just surrendered, knowing she had no chance? Had this fight been the last of many similar ones before? Had Inez broken her spirit long before she finally killed her? Had Laura's last thought been I love you or I hate you?

I tried to shake off these obsessive thoughts and took a close look at the soil underneath the magnolia. The tree was throwing off its petals. Huge rosy and white leaves were covering the ground. They were turning brown at the edges, slowly decaying.

Of course there were no traces of what had happened under this tree or on the stone tiles that led up to the front steps of the building. Only later would I learn that it was on those steps that the police had found Inez. She had called 911 herself from inside the house. Then she had come back out, still clutching the knife, and had sat there, watching over Laura's body until the cops had led her away.

Finally, I jotted down the realtor's number and left.

Chapter 3

When I walked up Geary a little later, I wondered if I should go back to the office and check if Martha had anything for me to do. After all, it was only seven, and maybe I could help her with some of our open cases. But then I remembered that I had promised Mido to have dinner with her tonight. The last weeks had been extremely busy for both of us. My lover had started an Internet advertising business a few months ago, and many nights we hadn't spent together but instead with our respective dark mistresses, the computers.

I slowly walked up the stairs to my apartment and got out my cell. There was one missed call. It must have come while I was on BART and had no reception. The display showed that the call had come from Mido, but she hadn't left me a message. So I speed-dialed her mobile number. She didn't pick up. I tried her home number, also without success. She was probably still in a meeting with a client. I spoke with Mido's voicemail and asked her to call me back when she had time.

For the rest of the evening, I waited for her to call me again, left her another message on her cell and her landline, but without success. Eventually, I popped a frozen dinner into the microwave, took a long bath and tried it again. I was just about to get seriously worried when Mido picked up the phone. It was ten thirty by now.

"You forgot our date?" I teased her.

"Sorry, Anna," she said. Her voice was as clear as always, but today it had an icy edge to it.

"What have you been up to?"

"Can you come over tomorrow night? I have something to tell you."

"Sure," I said.

I went to bed with a mean little worry pinching at the lining of my soul. I wished I had asked Mido what her news was. Something held me back from calling her again and finding out. Was it pride not wanting to appear impatient or overly curious? But wasn't Mido the person I should be able to ask anything? Share every worry with? Unfortunately, I knew that was not the reality of our relationship. We were both rather secretive, and one of our challenges was to open up to one another. I told myself that she was probably just stressed out from her job and was dying to get some sleep.

The real estate agent whom I called the next morning was a sugar sweet lady probably in her mid to late fifties. Her over-friendliness became annoying the moment she realized I was not a prospective buyer but merely wanted information on a house owner, "You have to understand," she crooned in an artificially polite tone, "this information is confidential. I cannot tell you anything about my clients."

"I'm not trying to bypass you," I said, attempting to sound equally sticky nice. "The matter is a personal one. My mother went to school with somebody who once lived in this house. Now she wants to organize a reunion."

"You can call 555-8342 and ask for Mr. Belize," Ms. Sugarsweet finally said.

I dialed the number. A woman with a strong, abrasive voice answered, "Public Guardian's office."

"I'm looking for a Mr. Belize."

"Nobody of that name works here . . ."

"Wait," I quickly said before she could hang up. "Maybe he's one of your clients."

"I can't give you that kind of information."

"Would it be possible to speak with his case worker?"

"One second."

She connected me to another line where the phone rang at least fifteen times. I was ready to hang up and dial the main line once more, when suddenly a male voice mumbled, "Pblc grdn's offce."

"Are you Mr. Belize's public guardian?"

The voice cleared up. "How can I help you?"

"I'd like to speak to him in a matter regarding his daughter Inez."

"That won't be possible."

"And why not?"

"I can't tell you more."

"Is there any other family I could contact?"

The man was rushed but not unfriendly. "I'm afraid not," he said. "But I'm representing Mr. Belize in all legal matters. Maybe you can tell me what it's about."

I quickly explained Marge Cunningham's request to him, and he said, "Most things that were in the house have been disposed of. Mrs. Cunningham should have contacted us earlier."

"Why didn't you get in touch with her? You must have known

that there were belongings of her murdered daughter in the house."

It was one of the days where I should have just Band-Aided my mouth shut in the morning. Of course such an accusation wouldn't make the man help me any further.

But he remained friendly enough. "When I took over Mr. Belize's case, the house was almost empty. There were a couple of misunderstandings after Ms. Belize's arrest, and we got called only some weeks later. Mr. Belize had been alone in the house until then. Believe me, Mrs. Cunningham wouldn't have wanted any of the things that were still left there."

I was smart enough not to question the public guardian's statement this time. However, when I asked him what he was referring to exactly, he became evasive, and only said that he couldn't tell me any more because it would reveal too much about his client's personal affairs.

Inez's former neighbor gave me a big smile when I showed up again at her doorstep. Finally, I had found somebody who was willing to tell me everything she knew about the Belizes.

"They took him to Laguna Honda, I'm sure," Lucy whispered.

"Laguna Honda?" I asked. "Isn't that a hospital?"

"No, it's the place where they send you if you don't have the money to pay for a private nursing home."

"What's the matter with Inez's father? Is he very frail?"

"He's a little . . ." Lucy's hand flew across her forehead like a small bird, indicating that something was wrong with Mr. Belize's mind. What it was exactly she couldn't tell me.

"I hadn't seen him in the year before . . . you know, the thing happened."

Lucy had not spoken much with Inez or Laura either. But every now and then the neighbor would witness them holding hands or exchanging a quick good-bye kiss in the front yard.

"They were so cute together." Lucy sighed. "Really in love. That's why it was such a shock, what happened."

"You mentioned that Laura once helped you."

For the first time, there was something like suspicion in Lucy's face. I should have just told her the truth about my interest in her former neighbors. But that's the problem with lies. Once you admit you used one, people won't be as open with you anymore.

Before she could become more suspicious, I said, "I was just hoping I could find Mr. Belize. You know it's such a big decision, buying a house, and my partner and I would really want to talk to one of the former owners."

"Try Laguna Honda."

The hospital with its beige stucco façade and little corner towers looked like a cross between a huge mission building and a prison. The receptionist didn't hesitate when I asked for Mr. Belize and sent me straight to the Alzheimer's ward. Here a buff, cheerful male attendant led me into a community room. There were at least twenty people in the huge room, some of whom didn't look older than forty, others who were possibly in their nineties. Most were sitting in wheelchairs, but some were wandering around. They all shared a certain gaze into a far empty distance. Nobody was smiling or laughing.

The attendant waited for a moment, of course expecting that I would know Mr. Belize and approach him. I admitted that I had no idea what the man I wanted to see looked like. "His daughter Inez and I are friends. She called me from jail and asked me if I could look in on her father, tell her how he's doing. It's my first visit."

The attendant pointed at a handsome, white-haired man and said, "This is Mr. Belize. And you can tell his daughter we're taking good care of him."

"I'm sure you do," I said with a smile, now waiting for the guy to leave me alone with Inez's father. But he stayed close by, watching my every move.

Mr. Belize was tall and broad-shouldered with long, strong fingers. He didn't look older than early sixties. His features were clear cut, conveying the intelligence of someone who could have been a professor of physics or a dynamic, successful contractor. He was staring out the window.

"My name is Anna Spring." I introduced myself to him, but he didn't even turn his head. I tried to talk to him for a while, mentioned his daughter, their house, Laura Cunningham, but the only reaction I got was a mumbled, "What?" in a high-pitched voice tainted with despair.

I finally asked the attendant if Mr. Belize ever had any other visitors. The man only shook his head. I was tempted to grab Inez's father and shake him to get at least some kind of reaction. Instead, I lightly touched his arm to wish him good-bye. This gesture triggered a powerful response. Mr. Belize jerked away from me with terror in his eyes.

"I'm sorry," I said, ashamed that I had involuntarily threatened him.

"He hates being touched," the attendant said. "It's always a struggle undressing him. We need three guys to get the job done."

Haunted by the image of three men as muscular as this one pulling the clothes off somebody as vulnerable in his confusion as Inez's father, I made my escape from Laguna Honda, hoping I would never have to enter this place again.

Chapter 4

I could only think of one more person to ask for information: Inez Belize herself.

"How can I visit a prisoner?" I asked Martha.

"You have to find out if the inmate is willing to see you and if she has visitation time available."

"And how can I even figure out in which facility she is?"

"Oh, that's easy."

My partner showed me how to enter the Web site of the state and federal prison systems. We only had to type in Inez's name to learn that she was in the Aldridge Women's Correctional Facility about two hours north of San Francisco. I called the prison's main line and was connected to visitors' services. I gave my name and the matter I was calling about, and the woman on the other end of the line assured me that the inmate would be informed of my request. She also asked me to print out the visitors' questionnaire from their Web site, fill it out and fax it to her.

I spent the rest of the day going through all kinds of records in a number of states searching for a deadbeat dad in a case Martha was currently working on. I wasn't very successful in my search for him and called it quits at five. Mido was expecting me at her house at seven.

I hadn't been able to completely shake off the feeling of dread which had accompanied me since our last, extremely short conversation the night before. But mainly I was looking forward to seeing the woman I loved. I longed to wrap my arms around her, kiss her, my whole body aching for the smell of her skin, the soft brush of her hair against my neck.

I walked up the street toward Mido's house carrying a bottle of red wine and a box of her favorite chocolate pastries from the French bakery at the Ferry Building, where I had made a quick stop. I was wearing a pair of faded, tight jeans, a white shirt and the bright blue cowboy boots Mido had given me for Christmas. She had explained that every real wild west dyke needed a pair of good boots. They were much more comfortable than they looked, and I had to grin whenever I caught a glimpse of my true wild west dyke feet.

Mido lived in a residential neighborhood twenty minutes by bus from downtown. The neighborhood had never been rich, and many of the small houses in her street still looked rather ragged. But Mido's own red house with the green vines embracing the front door was well kept, almost pristine.

My lover opened the door before I could even ring the bell. I leaned forward to kiss her, but her lips didn't meet mine. Instead she gave me a quick hug and led me into the kitchen. A big bowl of salad was sitting in the middle of the square white table.

I opened the wine while Mido was laying out forks and spoons. She asked me to take a seat and continued with her preparations. She wanted to know how work was, and I began to tell her about the Laura Cunningham case.

All the while, I watched her move around the kitchen, hoping to catch her eyes, to make her really look at me. She cut up some bread, heated a large pot of water on the stove, added pasta to the boiling water, stirred something that was simmering in a pan. It smelled great, of garlic and herbs and tomatoes. Still, I couldn't relax and just hang out peacefully.

Mido was as efficient about her cooking as she was about everything else in her life. Her movements were graceful with a certain athletic elegance. I had been intrigued by her face from the moment I first saw her. She had somewhat Scandinavian features, with deep blue eyes, high cheekbones, a straight nose. But then her mouth was that of a mischievous gangster, her teeth not quite as straight, and when she smiled, dimples moved on her face that disrupted the cool perfection of her lines.

Since we had fallen in love, I had caressed her face so many times, had kissed every warm, soft inch of her skin. I knew her body almost better than my own. Yet suddenly I didn't dare to just hug her from behind and press my lips against her neck as every nerve ending of my body twitched to do.

Instead I remained still on my chair and continued to talk about Laura and Inez.

"That's terrible," Mido said when I told her how Laura had died. She set down two plates filled with pasta covered in a red sauce.

"Let's not talk about murder and blood while we're eating," Mido suggested.

I nodded and realized I didn't know what else to speak about. The two things on my mind were the case and the question of what it was that Mido couldn't tell me on the phone yesterday.

"How is work going for you?" I asked.

Mido played with her noodles, creating neat little heaps of food on her plate. "I was super busy the last few weeks," she finally said.

25

"What is it you wanted to tell me?" I eventually mustered the courage to ask.

For the first time since I'd arrived, Mido looked me fully in the eye. Her blue gaze shone with the depth and turmoil of a glacier stream. She took my hand, swallowed visibly and stood up. I picked up the unspoken signal and rose, too. I was quite a bit taller than her, and as we were standing so close to one another I couldn't hold back anymore. I leaned forward, put my palms on her cheeks and pressed my lips against hers.

For the first second there was no response, then Mido's mouth melted, opened up a bit and made the connection. Before I could really comprehend what she wanted, she had already unbuttoned my shirt and was kissing my neck, then her hot dry lips were wandering down.

I sighed, leaned back against the kitchen counter and let my shirtsleeves slide down my arms while Mido pulled the sports bra I was wearing down to my hips. She began to kiss my breasts, letting her lips circle around my right nipple, then she flew over to the left one. I leaned even farther back and stretched myself out to her, the pulse between my legs growing to a hot, demanding throb.

But Mido took her time. All I wanted was to open myself to her lips, those agile, warm, teasing lips that stroked my body, nibbled and sucked on it. Mido's eyelashes were caressing the thin tissue right above my breasts. I couldn't suppress a deep moan, pulled up my arms and had to steady myself by holding on to the shelves behind me. My knees were getting soft, weak . . .

Swiftly Mido opened my belt, unbuttoned the jeans and yanked hard to pull them off my hips. She almost knocked me off my feet, but before I fell, she slung her arms around my waist and caught me. More gently, she pulled down my panties, waited for me to steady myself and pressed her face between my thighs. Her lips parted, and her tongue slid out. I didn't see it. I was floating in space, but every step the tip of her tongue took on its way toward my vagina seared right through the skin and into my core. The throbbing took on its own life. It let me move forward and backward and pressed high-pitched sounds out of me. Then Mido's tongue had reached its destination. It took only one last lick, right at my clit, to make me explode. A slow, strong wave of heat rose from my feet through my thighs, took over my whole body, let me expand, wiped out every thought and filled me with pure, vibrating, boiling pleasure. It pressed itself through my throat and out of my mouth in a loud groan. My lower body lost all strength, and I slowly sank to the ground.

Mido followed me, kneeled before me, and I pressed my forehead against hers.

When I could speak again I gasped, "Great dinner!"

Mido smiled.

I was still trying to catch my breath. But my desire hadn't been completely satiated. I longed to feel Mido move under the touch of my fingers. I pressed my face against her neck, began to lick her tender throat.

"Not here," she said and pulled me up with her.

She gently helped me put on my jeans and led me out of the kitchen. We passed the living room and walked into her bedroom. There was something different in the room. A new item of furniture was standing in a corner. But before I could get a clear view of it, Mido pulled me toward her. She was standing in front of her wide, low bed, and I began to undress her. All the while I was kissing every spot of her skin that appeared under her T-shirt, then beneath the wide khakis she was wearing. She was whimpering a bit, almost like a child, but I knew her so well, understood the sound as her melody of arousal. I laid her softly on the bed and sank to my knees. I wanted to kiss her mouth once again, but she pushed my head toward her lap. I let my nose wander through the light curly hair, opened her legs with my hands and buried my face in the place where it longed to be. Mido's hips pressed against my mouth, and I licked her carefully and thoroughly. Her clit was growing. I tasted wonderful salty liquid. She was dripping and moving and moaning underneath me. Then she tensed, became rigid. I stroked the sides of her thighs, pushed my tongue all the way into her wide open, totally wet, beckoning vagina. There was one strong upward movement of her body as she carried us both toward the sky, panted and groaned and finally, suddenly, became limp.

I rested my head on her stomach, and she stroked my hair.

"Lie next to me," she whispered, and I moved onto the bed.

We lay for a long time in each other's arms. I heard her heartbeat and felt I never wanted to go anywhere again, never wanted to leave this place next to the woman I loved.

But then Mido stirred, sitting up. "I have to go," she said.

Still lying down, I stared up at her face, her chin looked very determined from my position.

"Where to?" I asked and slowly sat up, too.

And then I saw it. The piece of furniture that had been added to the room since my last visit was a crib. Not the small, frilly kind for newborns. This one was wider, with wooden bars at the side, a no-nonsense bed for a somewhat older baby.

"What's that?" I asked.

"What do you think it is, Anna?" Mido said, the icy stream that was flowing behind her eyes seeping into her voice.

"Where do you have to go?" I said. "And where is the child who is sleeping in this crib?" Instead of the wonderful heat that had filled my insides just minutes ago, hard, aching despair was now beginning to spread through me.

"My adoption has come through. I'm flying to Guatemala tonight to pick up my daughter," Mido said. "I'll probably stay there for four to five weeks."

"Why didn't you tell me?" I stuttered. "You must have known this for a while."

Mido was standing in front of me, gathering her clothes. Through the open door to the living room, I now also saw the packed suitcases waiting there.

"You never asked."

I didn't know what to say. Last year Mido told me she had applied for an adoption. I felt threatened by it. I knew she wanted a child badly. When we had just met, she had once asked me if I wanted kids too, and I had said no outright. Since then, she hadn't talked with me much about her wish to adopt, and I had hoped it would take a long time before she would get a child.

"We were so happy together." I tried to defend myself. "I thought there would be a lot of time before you got a kid, and then we would figure it out."

"You knew how much I wanted it, and you never even asked if I heard anything about the adoption."

"And so you just stayed quiet, even now, prepared for your trip and never said a single word." My voice was loud, shriller than I wanted it to be.

"We haven't seen each other much lately." Mido sounded more sad than angry now. "I know you don't want to be a parent. This is my decision. I can't expect you to carry it with me."

She was still standing right in front of me. But it felt as if she had floated far away. Already now it seemed she was in a different world, and I was on the other side of a transparent, yet impermeable border. I could see her, but if I wanted to talk to her, I had to yell, and I couldn't touch her anymore.

"What does that mean for us?" I asked.

"I'm not sure, Anna. My mind has mainly been on Esmeralda in the last weeks. That's my daughter's name."

I should probably ask to see a picture. Mido must have been sent one. Instead I stood up, pulled my bra back in place and walked to the kitchen to retrieve my shirt. Mido didn't follow me. After a few minutes there was the sound of the shower from the bathroom.

We had hardly touched any of the food Mido had cooked. And now she would be gone for weeks. I didn't throw it away just yet, though, as it was not my food, and I didn't know what she wanted me to do with it. My main impulse was to leave the house, walk away and just keep walking, maybe until I reached the sea, let a sharp marine wind blow through my thin skin, to the core, rip out my worthless, confused mind. Instead I stayed and waited for Mido to reappear.

When she emerged again—dressed in a fresh white T-shirt and black jeans—I was leaning against the same counter where she had made love to me not even an hour ago.

"I'm sure we can work it out," I said. "I'll help you with the child."

"I don't think so." Mido was even more distant than before. "You know I love you, Anna. And we've been through a lot together. But I have to move on. This child needs me more than you do. And you and I, we haven't even figured out what we want from each other. You are such a loner, you throw yourself headlong into dangerous situations without thinking twice. Even before you started working as a PI you had a knack for getting yourself in trouble, but now—I can just see you jumping into the next snake pond with a splash, without thinking of your own safety or the feelings of the people around you."

"You supported me when Martha suggested we start our firm."

"I was completely infatuated with you then."

"And you're not infatuated anymore?"

I was still crazy for Mido. Just looking at her made my knees buckle all over again from desire. But she was right. We had never managed to blend our everyday lives together very well.

"You are terribly hot. The most attractive woman I know."

"And you love me, you just said." By now I was fighting for the very life of our relationship, and tears began to run down my cheek.

"I love you, but I can't be with you. Not with a child around. I can't explain you to her. You're just too wild."

I waited for an interpretation of this cryptic comment, but it didn't come. Mido began to putter around in the kitchen. She dumped the untouched bowl of salad into the garbage, poured the pasta sauce in a freezer container and collected the dishes.

I was still too stunned to help her. "Shall I take you to the airport?" I eventually managed to say.

Mido shook her head. "I've booked a shuttle. It will pick me up in half an hour."

I gave her a last quick hug. She hardly responded. And then I left.

I walked and walked. I couldn't stop my feet from making the same movements over and over again. Like a wind-up toy I walked on sidewalks, up and down steep hills, through dark neighborhoods. I didn't end up at the beach, but two hours later I arrived at my own front steps. Thoughts had come and gone, pierced through me like arrows shot from an invisible bow. I had never even known that Mido was so infatuated with me. She had always been rather reserved, and I had to initiate many of our encounters, had to court her. It had been a good lesson for me, because I was shy when it came to love. Mido eventually responded to my efforts: our first kiss, when I couldn't hold back anymore and had dared to press my lips against hers, our first sex, when I had not left after a dinner at her house but crawled into her bed.

I was too wild for her! What was that supposed to mean? And why couldn't I be explained to a child? I liked children. I was sure the girl and I could have a lot of fun. Or did Mido just not want her daughter to be under my terrible influence?

I stomped up to my apartment. A neighbor farther down the hall peered out her door, an old lady who looked like a white apparition, and whom I didn't know personally. Usually she barely greeted me when she saw me in the hall. Again she only glanced at me then quickly closed her door, and I could hear her lock it twice from the inside.

I slammed my own door behind me and sank down to the floor. I had no idea how long I remained crouched like that, sobbing, feeling like a pitiful, self-pitying, stupid, egomaniacal wimp, but eventually I must have just fallen asleep right there on the carpet, because that was where I woke up the next morning, sneezing when a ray of bright sunshine hit my face.

The thought of Mido painfully shot through me again right away, and I dragged myself to the bathroom. She was probably still in the air, and then she would be in a country where I didn't know her address, contact number, not even the city where she had flown. I couldn't talk to her, couldn't make her listen to me, beg her to give me another chance. After half an hour of wincing under the daggers my own mind drove through my heart, I realized the only remedy would be to think about something else. And so I got dressed, gulped down a pot of very hot, very bitter coffee, and went to the office.

Chapter 5

Fortunately, Martha wasn't there yet. It was only eight a.m., and she had probably worked long into the night. But there was already a message on our voicemail saying that I could visit Ms. Belize the same day.

On the prison's Web site I read that I couldn't wear anything made from blue cotton. My outfit shouldn't resemble the inmates' clothes. I looked down at myself. I had donned a pair of wide black pants and a green shirt. My denim jacket was probably too close to the prison wardrobe, so I went back to the apartment and put on a red sweater instead. I rented an Escort from the Hertz station at the Hilton a few blocks away, studied my Northern California road map and took off.

The drive led me through emerald hills powdered with white and pink wild flowers. The sky was a light bright blue, with mountains of clouds towering at the horizon and rows of giant eucalyptuses that bordered the road. For the final half hour I was driving along Highway One, the roaring Pacific to my left, throwing itself in heavy waves against the bottom of the cliffs. Then I had to turn inland again and pass through a couple of small, faceless towns along a very straight street, where eventually the walls, towers, razor wire and chain-link fence of a large prison complex rose against the backdrop of a barren hillside.

It was almost noon when I parked the car in the visitor's lot. The sky was overcast by now. The bulwarks of the prison reminded me of the border which had once run through my native country, Germany. Walking toward them weighed me down. Depression clung to my feet like iron shackles.

Little did I know about true depression, I realized, when I finally sat across from Inez Belize. We were separated by thick glass, only able to speak via telephone When she slowly walked toward her side of the glass, I noticed that Inez was tall. Taller even than me, and I'm almost six feet. She had big hands—like her father—and she resembled him in other physical features as well. She appeared to be muscular underneath the bulky blue jumpsuit. Her hair was short, unruly and completely white. Her face had the kind of deep paleness only people with naturally olive-colored skin can display, and which lets every shadow around the eyes and the temples look like a bruise. Inez's features were very even, her eyes were huge, her mouth expressive, and had she not so obviously given up on herself, she might have been a beautiful woman.

Her gaze was fixed on the tabletop in front of her. Before I began to speak, I cocked my head to get her to look at me. For a fraction of a second Inez's eyes caught mine. It was just long enough for her to register that there was something wrong with the symmetry of my own face and for me to get a glimpse of the utter darkness her eyes carried, both literally and metaphorically, as they were of a deep brown. This woman was living in hell.

"Did they tell you why I'm here?"

Inez nodded.

"I was hoping you could help me and my client with some information. I'm looking for Laura's things. Clothes, books, et cetera. Nobody could tell me where everything went. Maybe you have an idea where your father has put them. Or if somebody else, a friend or someone, took her stuff."

"Wasn't it in her room?"

Inez's voice was coarse, not accustomed to being used, but her inflection was soft, pleasant, cushioned by a natural friendliness.

This woman has slaughtered Laura Cunningham, I reminded myself. She has driven a knife over and over into the flesh of the person she claimed to love, a woman whose picture had etched itself into my mind, and which now flashed before me. I stared at Inez's hands. I had to push away the image of the smiling, happy Laura and tried to focus on my task.

"Your father's legal guardian told me that the house was practically empty when they brought your dad to Laguna Honda."

"They didn't listen to me. Didn't want to know that he needed help."

"That's ridiculous," I said with passion. How could anybody not see that Mr. Belize wasn't fit to be left on his own?

"What do you know!" Inez said. She thought I didn't believe her either.

"I'm with you," I quickly answered. "I met your father, and I can't understand why nobody helped him earlier."

"You met him?" Finally Inez looked fully at me, and there was a flicker of life in her face. I couldn't tell if it stemmed from agitation or desperation.

"Yesterday. I went to Laguna Honda to ask him about Laura's things."

"How is he? Do they treat him right?"

I certainly didn't have the courage to tell her that her father had to be undressed by three men. "He looked very well taken care of," was all I managed to say.

35

"Did he speak?"

"Not much."

"Look, I don't know what happened to any of the things in the house. If the guardian says that the place was almost empty, I guess my father burned the stuff. There's an old woodstove in the kitchen. Dad loves to start a fire there. Always has. As long as I was around I could watch over him so that he wouldn't burn down the place. I was scared that he would set everything on fire after they'd arrested me."

"What did you do when you had to leave the house for work or errands?" I was truly curious about the practical implications of living with somebody who had Alzheimer's.

"During the day I took him to a daycare center. At night I gave him a strong sleep aid. That made him conk out for eight hours and slowed him down in the morning so it was easier to dress him. The doctor prescribed it."

"Well, I guess then Laura's things have been burned in the kitchen stove," I finally said, wanting to get back to my original task. "But Laura must have had something like a bank account, something that would still exist, and that I could find for her mother."

"Her mother?" Inez asked.

"Yes, Mrs. Marge Cunningham. She hired me. I said so to the woman from the visitors' office."

"They only told me some private detective wanted Laura's stuff. I figured it had something to do with insurance or whatever. Laura didn't have any relatives. Her parents died long ago."

The photograph Mrs. Cunningham had given me showed a woman with Asian features. Until now I had assumed that Laura had a Caucasian mother and an Asian father, like me. But I had to admit that her face didn't look very much as if Marge Cunningham were her biological mother.

"Did Laura ever mention if she was adopted?"

"No. She only told me that her folks were killed when she

was little and that she had grown up in many foster homes, but that she didn't stay in touch with any of the foster parents."

"Hmm, but her last name was Cunningham."

"Yes."

Upon entering the prison, I'd had to hand over most of the contents of my pockets. They had allowed me to bring Laura's picture in with me, though, as it didn't pose any obvious threat. I now pulled it out of my pocket and showed it to Inez, mainly to point out to her the writing on the back. When Laura's former partner saw the photo, she stared at it with wide open eyes, shell-shocked. Then she buried her face in her hands and remained motionless.

After a few minutes the guard who had been watching us from a corner of the room pointed at her watch. I knocked lightly on the glass, hoping Inez would pick up the receiver again.

"Did Laura have any bank accounts, a safe deposit box, a storage locker, anything that might still exist?"

Inez whispered into the phone, "Her checking account was with B of A. That's all I know. Neither of us had any savings."

What was her job? I wanted to ask. And yours? What did you two live off? But on Inez's side of the glass another guard now came over to lead her away.

"Look in the basement," was the last thing Inez said. "He used to hide things there."

Then we got disconnected.

When Inez had taken her hands away from her face, I had gotten a glimpse of her palms. They were covered with wide red scars, as if somebody had cut them apart and sewn them back together. While I was driving away from the prison, I wondered if she used to work in a job where such injuries were common. The true answer, though, didn't dawn on me until Martha pointed it out some time later.

Chapter 6

It occurred to me to call the realtor with the sticky sweet voice and ask for the key to the Belizes' house. After all, Inez had given me permission to enter. But it seemed too complicated. A simple break-in would be easier, especially into an uninhabited house where the downstairs windows were already boarded up.

I drove back into the city across the Golden Gate Bridge. The sky had cleared up again, and the afternoon sun made the distant skyline sparkle like a pile of diamonds. My mind was still clouded over, though. As a molecular researcher, I had studied the biological complexities of life. I was forever in awe of the unimaginably intricate mechanisms that let us breathe and digest, think and speak. But as fascinating as the microscopic universe of genetics was, the big world had violently pulled me into it. The world of consequences, and feelings, and insanity, and nursing homes and prisons. I had become a private investigator because it involved the same skills you needed as a scientific researcher, but the problems Martha and I were dealing with were more concrete, personal and intimate. I had learned that what fascinated me even more than the workings of our genes were the conundrums of our minds. And now it bugged me that I had still not gained the slightest insight into the murderous mystery of Inez Belize's motives.

That was probably one of the reasons why I felt elated when I got ready to break into her house, forever hoping my curiosity could be stilled. Back in the apartment I put on black military pants, a black sweater and a dark cap. I packed pliers, a flashlight, a variety of other tools and a small rope ladder into a tote bag and searched for the white foldable cane I had purchased a few months ago to practice maneuvering without eyesight. If you have only one eye, it can be helpful to try out how it feels being fully blind, just to battle the fear of it.

The last item I packed was a pair of dark glasses, in case I had to follow through with the blind person act. I dropped off the rental car not too far from my destination and approached the corner of Madrid and Russia on foot. I tried to see if there was an alley behind the row of houses, but the backyards of one street directly touched the fences of the houses on the parallel street. I could only enter the property through the front yard.

Like last time, I walked through the gate. Today I immediately slipped around the house to be hidden from the street and studied the back windows. By now it was so dark that I needed the flashlight to make out anything. On this side, the ground floor windows were intact. I looked around for a while to see if I could find a separate entrance to the basement but had no luck.

On a hunch, I walked to the front of the house once more. And when I took a closer look at the door, I saw that it was secured only by a rather small padlock. Enough to discourage homeless people from entering, but nothing for the kind of serious burglar I was. It took one cut with the pliers and the lock was gone. I slipped inside and closed the door behind me.

A steep staircase led up from the front hallway. Inez Belize had said I should check out the basement, but of course I'd take a look at the whole house. The top floor consisted of two small rooms, both completely empty. I shone my light, looking for built-in closets or any other spots where something could be stored. The walls appeared to be freshly whitewashed. It smelled of dry wood dust. A floorboard creaked under my feet, and I kneeled down to inspect it, but it was not loose enough to lift up easily. I decided I was being unreasonably thorough.

The rooms on the second floor were equally empty and completely neutral. Every trace and sign of the people who had once lived, laughed and wept here was gone. The ground floor consisted of another set of two empty rooms and a kitchen with the infamous woodstove where supposedly most of Laura's things had found their fiery end. I inspected the inside of the broad white enameled stove, but behind the round door were only fluffy, sticky ashes.

So the basement was indeed my last hope. I finally detected a trap door in the pantry next to the kitchen. The door gave off a loud creak, almost like a baby's cry, when I pulled it open. I froze. For a moment I thought I heard a metallic clank from somewhere inside the house. I held my breath, but the sound was gone. I pulled the trap door closed behind me and climbed down into the cellar. Complete darkness surrounded me, only exaggerated by the wimpy beam from my flashlight. All I could make out was the very next step on the ladder, which may as well have been leading all the way to the smoldering core of the earth.

But after about ten steps, I reached firmer ground again, detected a light switch and sighed when the room lit up. Whoever had cleaned out this house had been a neat freak. The basement consisted of one large space, which was as freshly painted and empty as its counterparts upstairs. My hopes of finding any trace of Laura's belongings down here vanished. One could open a day spa in this cellar, but certainly not stumble upon hidden treasures.

Nevertheless, I looked around some more, touched the walls, knocked against some bricks. The bricks were all firmly cemented in place. But then, finally, in the corner farthest from the ladder, there was an irregularity in the surface of the wall. It looked as if somebody had applied wallpaper in a limited area of maybe three square feet and then painted it over. I began to poke at the paper with my nails, hoping that there was some sort of hole behind it. I scraped for a while, peeling off big shreds, and eventually reaching the raw brick. The paper had covered nothing but the firm wall itself.

I didn't want to leave any traces, so I began to gather the paper scraps, planning to dump them in the next garbage can. And then I saw that one of the pieces had writing on it. I could make out the drawing of a heart and the words *my . . . belong . . . always*. My interest sparked, I took a closer look at the other scraps and discovered that on many there were whole sentences. *You make me the happiest person, Lauri*, read one of them. *How could I have been so lucky to find you, Inni*, read another.

Hoping I had not destroyed too much of the correspondence, I carefully collected every last piece, placed all of it in my bag and climbed back up the ladder.

I was about to pull myself through the trap door when I heard a noise again. This time it sounded much closer than before. There were quick steps and something like a shuffle. And it came from right behind the pantry door. Now there was also the sound of a voice, "And this is the kitchen. Just look at this gorgeous original woodstove."

The real estate agent! Her gooey voice was unmistakable.

I quietly retreated back down the ladder and closed the trap door behind me.

The voices got louder. A woman with a piercing inflection asked, "Is there a cellar, too? My husband is a drummer, you know, and he needs to be kept behind closed doors in an insulated space."

Stickysweet answered immediately, "Of course, there is a full basement. You can keep your better half behind lock and key, if you want."

"Can I see it?"

Oh no! There was definitely no place to hide in that squeaky clean room below me. I had packed the blind person's costume out of a silly impulse, but now I actually fumbled for the cane. I couldn't find the dark glasses, hoped that I could look convincingly blind without it, opened the pantry door and stumbled into the kitchen. The two women jumped when they saw me emerge. I poked around in the air with the cane and said. "Finally somebody shows up. I think I got a bit lost here. Are you the real estate agent?"

I hoped the woman wouldn't recognize my voice. Startled, she just answered, "Yes, but this is a private appointment. The open house is on Sunday."

"I won't take the house anyway, too many stairs. But thank you."

With these words, I walked straight through the kitchen door, into the hall and toward the front door. All the while I was swinging my cane from left to right. I had made it almost down the steps when the piercing voice behind me said, "She must have been squatting in the basement. Let's call the police."

It was hard not to run, but I kept up my cane act until I was sure the women weren't following me. When I was definitely out of sight from the house, I slipped the cane and the cap into my bag. If they indeed called the police, the cops would only look for a stray blind person.

Light was still shining from behind our office windows. It was past ten p.m. At least five hours before my insomniac partner would call it quits for the day. I had taken BART back into the city center, and on the train my overly tense nerves had behaved like guitar strings strummed too hard. They wouldn't stop vibrating, and I wanted to laugh hysterically or cry, without an obvious reason. It was one of the moments where I wondered how other people in stressful professions—like real burglars, for example—survived the side effects of their jobs. I could practically feel my liver push out cholesterol. In this vein I purchased a big bucket of fried chicken and a bag of assorted doughnuts, then climbed up the stairs. Martha's face lit up when she saw me enter the office.

Food magically shut up my ever talkative partner, and we ate in quiet harmony, washing everything down with black dope from Martha's big coffeemaker. When we had devoured all of the grease sponges, my partner said that she urgently had to finish a search in a database where she had purchased access only for today.

I cleared some space on the floor behind her wheelchair and laid out the paper shreds from the Belizes' basement. Different qualities and colors of paper had been used. Some were yellow and lined, others were parts of old envelopes used to write down a quick note of endearment. I moved the pieces around and found many matches. It quickly became clear that all the shreds had once been parts of short notes. They contained everyday loving phrases on top of a shopping list or a reminder not to forget to pick up a prescription. The notes had been attached to the wall with clear tape. That was why I was still able to read most of them. Only the outer layer, to which the paint had been applied, was destroyed.

You are the bestest, xoxoxoxox L. read a typical note. *I'll miss you today, take care, I love you big time, Inni*, another one.

All of the short letters were signed either *Inni, Lauri* or just *L.* or *I.* Some even carried a date and time. The most recent one was from December 20, 2005, only two days before Laura had died, and it was signed *L.*

Nobody has ever been as good and caring to me as you, it read. *I am the luckiest woman. You make me so happy. Just remember, I'll always love you.* Underneath was a list of produce—*eggplant, tomatoes, garlic, etc, Remember, I want to make ratatouille*—and the reminder: *Don't forget dad's dental appointment at four.*

A picture began to evolve before my inner eye: two women deeply in love, living together in a house with one of their fathers who is demented due to Alzheimer's. Their schedules are different, so they communicate via short notes. Neither ever forgets to include a little expression of love. The last letter was signed by Laura—at least that was what I supposed L. stood for—but it referred to Mr. Belize just as *dad* not *your dad*. The image of a very close and committed relationship between the two women became even more vivid.

And then an unusual scene grew in my imagination of Mr. Belize taking all these notes, wandering to the basement and taping them to a defined spot on the wall, layer by layer. Had he gone down there daily, applying each note individually? Or had he only begun his project after Laura's death, when he was alone in the house? And what had made him do it when he otherwise liked burning things so much? Where had the notes been stored until then? Had the women kept them in a mutual archive of memories? Or had only one of them held onto the notes in a sentimental notion?

I could probably ask Inez this last question in person if I could get a chance to speak with her once more. Thinking of the incredibly sad woman I had visited this afternoon, and crouching over the letters she had exchanged with her partner, conjuring up their life together, a nagging little doubt crept into my brain: What if she didn't do it?

I quickly told myself to let it go. I had already looked deeper into Laura and Inez's life than I was supposed to. And I had become biased. Who isn't a sucker for sweet notes? But dysfunctional couples often utter the most extreme promises of eternal love, eternally betraying themselves, wanting to believe that they haven't long since jumped into the tar pits and gotten stuck in the deadly, stinky black matter of a hellish relationship, where violent struggling only pulls you faster into destruction.

"So how did it go today?" Martha's voice shook me out of my contemplation.

I gave her a summary. When I told her about my escape from the Belizes' house, she roared with laughter. I had promised her that I wouldn't break any laws in the course of a job without first conferring with her. After all, she was officially my job trainer. But tonight's little escapade didn't really qualify as breaking the law, apart from the destroyed padlock, and I knew Martha well enough to know she didn't care about a thing like that.

"So you put on your best blind ghost act." She chuckled. "Probably drove up the price of the house, too. The realtor can now advertise the place as one of San Francisco's haunted houses."

This remark brought back the memories of what had really happened there, and even Martha became silent for a moment and then said on a much more serious note, "So all that Belize woman told you was to look in the basement."

I nodded.

"Let me see the notes."

Martha studied the scraps for a few minutes. I waited impatiently for her to say something, but she just shook her head slightly.

"The scars you mentioned," she finally said. "On the Belize woman's palms. They're probably from the murder weapon."

I waited for an explanation. Martha asked instead, "What happens when you stab somebody multiple times?"

I hate educational questions. If somebody wants to teach me something, they should just say it. In an annoyed tone, I answered, "The person is likely to end up dead."

"Yes, but what happens before?"

"Save the didactics."

Unperturbed, Martha continued. "The victim is bleeding profusely. She is trying to fend off the knife as it comes at her. Her hands will be covered in defensive wounds, which are bleeding too."

"So Laura had a knife too, and Inez suffered defensive wounds?" I was getting a little confused.

"No. Defensive wounds would most likely cover the backs of her hands as well. If only the palms are affected, the scars probably stem from slippage. When the knife handle got so wet from all the blood that her hands slid onto the blade while she was stabbing and cut her palm. She must have alternated hands, as there are scars on both palms. Probably one side got exhausted. Pretty ambidextrous, your Inez."

I had to fight to keep down the food that still lay in my stomach in a heavy lump. I didn't ask Martha what she thought about the love notes. I just wanted to know if I could hand them over to Marge Cunningham.

"Technically, the ones that Inez wrote belong to Laura and therefore to her heir, Mrs. Cunningham," Martha said. "Laura's notes, on the other hand, are Inez's property. But still, it's private correspondence, so legally the ownership is a bit wishy-washy. Inez could claim that all the notes are really her own. The best is to ask her what to do with them."

I climbed the stairs to my apartment in deep thought. Inez's eyes haunted me while I contemplated what to tell Marge Cunningham. Then Laura's tough yet sweet smile flashed before my eye. It almost felt as if the images my brain produced had the capacity to talk to me, and I was waiting for them to open their mouths at last and tell me what had really happened.

46

Tomorrow I would trace Laura's bank account, then I would make copies of the love notes, send the originals to Inez, and take the copies to Mrs. Cunningham. I was sure Inez would not cause any trouble regarding ownership, and so I would at least have something to show Laura's mother for the fee she paid me. Then this case would be over, and the troubling images and questions it created in me would vanish. At least that's what I hoped and believed, naive baby PI that I was.

Chapter 7

The next morning I awoke under the influence of a dream that left its teeth marks in the soft tissue of my feelings for hours. Mido had been in it, smiling at me, her beautiful lips beckoning me to kiss them. But when I had come closer, her face had morphed into Laura's. The broad smile had transformed into a scream—a desperate cry for help. When I awoke and realized it was too late, that Laura had died before I had even known her, I had to struggle against an unspeakable despair.

I walked through my apartment in a daze, finally showered, had a cup of strong black tea and got dressed. Then I called Laura's mother.

"Have you found anything?" was Marge Cunningham's only greeting.

"Not much," I said, not wanting her to get her hopes up.

"What does that mean?"

"Only a few notes."

"Interesting. Come by in two hours."

I fought down my urge to lie to her and tell her I could only make it later. Who was she to take my availability for granted? But it felt too exhausting to spar with this woman over details, and I agreed.

I walked to the closest Bank of America branch where a skinny, nervous-looking woman in a gray pantsuit said she would be able to tell Laura's mother if her daughter had an account with them. Mrs. Cunningham only needed to show them the death certificate. But, sorry, no, she could not give *me* any information about any customer of the bank.

"I'd only like to know *if* Ms. Cunningham had an account with you. That's all. So that Mrs. Cunningham doesn't have to come here in vain."

I could practically see the cogwheels spinning behind the woman's forehead. She punched a few keys on her computer. Then she nodded conspiratorially.

"Mrs. Cunningham won't come in vain."

I thanked her for the wealth of information and left.

After I had made copies of Inez's and Laura's love notes, I still had some time before my meeting with Marge Cunningham and decided to spend it down by the bay at a place that usually gave me peace of mind and made me feel like I wasn't all alone.

I sat outside the Ferry Building in the chilly breeze. Tourists were rushing by, heading for one of the boats. Seagulls were hopping around them—hardworking creatures, eternally on the lookout for something to eat. As always, I purchased a mocha for myself and a cup of coffee in memory of my friend Jeff. Last year he had been killed on the Embarcadero, only a few yards from here, run over by a car whose driver wanted to send me a warning. I had not been able to protect Jeff, and this realization hit me today with more than the usual force when I stared at the tender white steam rising from his untouched cup. It was high tide and small breakers were crashing against the pier. I tried to remember how my friend and I had so often sat here together in happy silence.

But the memories were vicious assailants today, and after a while I surrendered, went over to California Street, boarded a cable car and let myself dangle off the train in good old break-neck fashion. On Van Ness I walked a few blocks, then caught a bus that took me right to the hilltops of Pacific Heights. Here the cold wind was even stronger. It felt like a wild beast trying to shove me off the surface of the planet.

Only when I had rung Mrs. Cunningham's doorbell did I realize I was wearing faded jeans with a tear above the knee and my oldest denim jacket. Also, this morning I had absent-mindedly inserted not my naturally brown artificial eye but the one which had the color of a green mamba. But Marge Cunningham actually gave me a smile when she opened the door and saw my outfit. "This is more what Susan promised when she recommended you," she said.

Instead of responding, I asked, "How are you?"

In return, Laura's mother led me into the little salon with the great view. I laid the stack of copies of Inez's and Laura's love notes on a side table and waited while Marge Cunningham looked through them. She had placed herself in the same chair as the last time, and I sat down in the high-backed leather chair opposite hers.

A long furrow deepened between her brows while she studied the notes. She also looked different today. She wore an ankle-length, elaborately cut, burgundy silk dress. It was gorgeous, resembling a classic Chinese dress of the nineteen forties with a high collar, short sleeves, a slim bodice and wide skirt. It made Laura's mother look younger than the last time, and more sophisticated. Even her face appeared narrower. Her sharp violet eyes now focused on me. "These are copies," she stated the obvious.

I told her the story of where I had found the notes. "The originals belong to Ms. Belize. I will try to contact her again and find out if she is willing to give them to you. Until then, I thought—"

"You actually talked to this woman."

"As I said, she was the only one who could tell me what happened to your daughter's belongings."

"And then you bring me their love notes." Marge Cunningham's lips were pressed together tightly, two angry red caterpillars.

"Look," I said. "I didn't think I was competent to decide which exact items you would want and which you wouldn't. I'm sorry for your loss and for the grief any memories of Laura may cause. But unfortunately these notes are all I could find. If you don't want them, I will destroy the copies and send the originals to Ms. Belize."

Mrs. Cunningham grew calmer as I spoke. I quickly told her about Laura's bank account. She merely nodded.

"I'd like to keep the notes," she said stiffly. "And I would appreciate getting the originals. At least the ones Laura wrote. To have a piece of her . . . something she touched . . . her handwriting . . . I just hoped there would be more of her things left . . ."

"I understand," I said. And I did.

It was time for me to say good-bye and leave. I would write a report for Mrs. Cunningham, reimburse the part of the fee I hadn't used, and this short, yet moving, case would be history.

But something told me to stay. Perhaps a flicker in the cool, albeit passionate gaze of my client. Or more likely just curiosity, which made me hope there was something more to this—an installment to the story which had already haunted me all the way into my dreams. Later I often remembered this moment and desperately wished I would have immediately stormed out of the room.

Chapter 8

After a long silence Marge Cunningham said, "I would like you to continue your work."

"I don't think—"

"I haven't told you everything."

She prepared herself a drink, poured brown liquid from the carafe sitting on the side table, then took tongs and dropped ice cubes from a small bowl into her glass. Today she offered me one, too.

"No, thank you."

"It's only iced tea."

Then I nodded, and she handed me a glass. It was lovely, lavender-infused tea, and I sipped it quietly while Mrs. Cunningham told me what I hadn't yet known about her daughter.

As suspected, she had adopted Laura as a baby. Laura's parents had been Vietnamese boat people who died during the escape from Saigon. Mrs. Cunningham had been unmarried and had raised Laura on her own.

"Laura was never an easygoing child," Marge Cunningham said. "Later I read that adopted children always carry with them the trauma of losing their birth parents, even if they were only a few weeks old when it happened. At first I was suspicious of this theory, but thinking back to Laura's childhood and teenage years, I have to say that it's the only explanation for the difficulties I encountered with her."

I had no idea what to think of the theory, as my experience with adopted children was nonexistent. Still, it seemed like a rather limited explanation. Aren't there oh so many reasons why somebody is difficult or perceived to be difficult, particularly as a teenager? Character incompatibilities between parents and children being only one of the myriad possibilities.

Marge Cunningham leaned back in her chair and elegantly crossed her legs. "But still, she loved me," she said. "There was no reason why she would disappear all of a sudden."

"When was that?"

"Thirteen years ago."

Laura had just turned eighteen when she left her family without notice. I asked Mrs. Cunningham if there had been any signals that something like that was about to happen.

"What do you mean?"

"Was there a fight? Any kind of falling out? Was she in a crisis? Or had she become unusually silent in the time leading up to her disappearance?"

"As I told you, Laura had always been sullen," she said. "It was never easy to talk to her, harder yet to make her understand what you were saying. She was very protective of her innermost self, possibly due to the early childhood trauma."

I tried to picture Laura as a little girl, as a teenager, as a young adult. Listening to her mother's description, I began to envision a tiny girl with a fierce expression, her eyebrows drawn angrily together. Then there was the image of an adolescent, the corners of her mouth pulled down, her gaze empty, unwilling to communicate with her desperate adoptive mother.

"You must have an idea what made Laura take such an extreme step," I insisted, knowing that I was much too close to the whole matter myself to stay objective. When a person breaks off contact with her family, with the people who are closest to her and most integral to her emotional identity, it never happens on a whim. I knew this all too well.

Marge Cunningham had a short fuse. Her chin moved upward, and her nostrils became wider. "None," she said with poorly concealed fury. "Laura had completed school the year before. She had everything a young girl could dream of: financial security, expensive hobbies. She liked sport shooting, and of course I paid for the best trainer and range time. Laura could have attended whatever college she wanted. But she couldn't decide what she wanted to do with her life. So I was preparing her to work by my side in our family foundation."

"What do you want from me?" I asked.

"I want to know where she was all those years," Mrs. Cunningham said without hesitation.

"Why?"

I received a gaze that clearly said I had asked an incredibly stupid question.

I just waited.

"Can't you imagine that I want to know more about my daughter? What her life was like? Especially now that she is gone."

"You could have hired me for that from the start."

There was another silence. Finally, she said, "You're right. I'm looking for something specific." She poured herself another tea, again with all the mannerisms that usually go into producing a hard drink. Then she continued, "Laura always wanted to be a writer. That was her way of communicating. As a little girl she would write me lovely notes for my birthdays or just in-between. To tell me I was the best mommy . . ." Another gulp of tea moved heavily down my client's throat.

"In high school Laura always won the creative writing awards. Her poetry was as good as her fiction. When she had finished school, I encouraged her to pursue a career as a writer. But no, Ms. Stubborn couldn't even make up her mind to apply to a junior college."

Marge Cunningham continued to tell me about her frustrations with her daughter for another half hour. I pulled out my notepad and jotted down the stations of Laura's life that her mother was aware of. Adoption, childhood, high school, shooting training, a supreme writing talent, disappearance . . .

"She told me she had her first novel almost completed. That she was looking for a publisher. I want to find the manuscript and save Laura's heritage." Mrs. Cunningham eventually leaned back in her chair and looked at me with expectation.

"When did she tell you that?"

"When we last spoke."

"When she was eighteen?"

"No, a few weeks before her death."

"So Laura got in touch with you again."

"Of course. I always knew she would come back."

Indeed, Laura had come back to her mother. But only after more than twelve years. When I pressed Marge Cunningham for more information, it turned out that Laura had only come to visit once. "What exactly did she tell you?"

"Mainly that she had worked on the book for the last years, and that she was extremely excited about it. She was certain it would be a success. And I was sure about this, too. Am sure about it."

"Did you ask her where she had been?"

"She made it clear that she didn't want to talk about it."

"And why did she suddenly resurface?"

"She missed me. Missed her family. She had clearly grown up and was sorry about what she had put me through. She wanted us to have a fresh start. And then this woman . . ."

"Did you talk with Laura about her partner?"

"Not much. Laura told me she lived with a girlfriend. She seemed shy about it. But she must have known that I'm no homophobe. I always had gay friends."

"After she left, didn't you try to find her?" I asked.

"Of course. But without result. The police registered her as a missing person, but that was about all they ever did."

Laura had not been a minor anymore. If there is no sign of a crime, police procedure doesn't allow for an intensive search for a missing adult.

"And private detectives?"

"I employed quite a battalion of them, but most just took my money and soon declared the search unsuccessful."

"And the others?"

"There was only one other. He sent me a preliminary report and then died of a heart attack. At least he never cashed his check."

"Do you still have the report?"

"Does that mean you'll help me?"

"Let me clarify what you want from me. I am supposed to find a manuscript your daughter wrote?"

Marge Cunningham nodded.

"It's likely it got burned with all her other possessions and we are just wasting our time and your money."

"But it's possible that somebody still has a copy. There must have been other people in her life apart from that woman. I'm interested in anything that belonged to Laura. Any writing, any note, even personal letters, if you find somebody who received them from her. She used to be an avid letter writer. It would be wonderful to find something that's left of her life. It would let me feel that she didn't just vanish from this earth without a trace. You must understand. I always knew that Laura was alive and that she would finally come back to me. And then she gets brutally murdered. She had such a short life, and I missed almost half of it. That's why I'm so keen on learning where she has been, whom she liked and loved, what adventures she has been through. And most of all, I would of course love to preserve her memory and have her book published."

My brain was already working full throttle. Mrs. Cunningham's hopes were not just castles in the sky. Means of tracking down people had changed dramatically in the last thirteen years. It had become practically impossible to go anywhere in the industrialized hemisphere without leaving electronic footprints. And there is hardly an author today who would refuse the protection electronic storage provides for their writings. There was indeed a chance that Laura's manuscript still existed somewhere on an Internet server or private computer where she had once stored it or sent it in an e-mail attachment to a friend, publisher or agent, even if every hard copy had been destroyed by the fires Mr. Belize had started in his kitchen hearth.

I nevertheless warned Marge Cunningham. "I can't promise you anything. Possibly I'll become just another one in your battalion of losers. What I can promise is that I will do my best and be honest with you. If I realize I am doomed to be as unsuccessful as the others, I'll let you know as soon as possible."

"That will do," Laura's mother said with a light yet determined nod.

Chapter 9

We spoke for another hour, and I let Laura's mother recall every detail she could come up with from the life of her daughter. I also asked her for pictures from the time around Laura's disappearance. It turned out that the photograph I already possessed had been taken during that one visit Laura had paid her mother shortly before her death.

I finally stepped out of the house with many pages of notes, a manila envelope with pictures, the old report by the dead private eye and another check. This time I hadn't asked for it. The advance my client had originally given me was not used up yet, but Marge Cunningham had insisted on paying me more. She was in a very good mood when I wished her good-bye, almost ecstatic. She smiled disarmingly and said, "I know you'll find something. Susan spoke so highly of you, and I can now confirm that you are so much more intelligent than all of the other private detectives before you."

With these words, she closed the door behind me. I walked a few steps down the driveway. Then I took the bag off my shoulder and stuffed the manila envelope in with the laptop. I was a bit absent-minded. The remains of my conversation with Marge Cunningham were drifting through my mind, and I was mulling over the weird compliment she had just offered.

I was trying to make space for my notepad in the cluttered bag, when a car entered the driveway. I stepped aside to let it through, but the burgundy minivan stopped a few feet before me. A man jumped out of the vehicle, opened the side door, pulled out a foldable ramp and helped the girl in the wheelchair who I had already met during my first visit here, out of the van. He parked her chair at the edge of the driveway and began to store the ramp. "How are you?" he called out to me.

"Fine. And you?"

"Not bad myself," he completed our nonsensical greeting typical of polite strangers.

I grinned at him, and he responded with a friendly smile. I gave up on fitting the notepad into the crammed bag, decided to carry it in my hand instead and walked toward the street. When I passed the van I realized the girl in the wheelchair was gone. The driver was still dealing with the ramp, so I looked for her behind the vehicle, wondering where she could have disappeared so quickly.

I found her on the street, sitting on the sidewalk, right at the point where it began its steep descent. I remembered that she was blind and the words DON'T MOVE thundered through my head. Before I could yell them, the girl pushed the rims of her chair and started rolling down the hill.

I jumped forward to catch her, but it was too late. She had already picked up speed and was out of my reach. For a second, her hands clutched the rims, trying to break the chair's movement, but then it became too fast and her palms whirled away.

I had already begun to run. I dropped what I was carrying and dashed down the sidewalk in a wild chase after the chair, which was of course much faster than I. I flew after the girl, tripping several times, having to catch myself from falling. All the while there was a strange sound in the air. At first it was low, but then it amplified like a siren, "Help! Help!! Help!!! Heeeelp!"

The girl was screaming in raw panic.

Fortunately she was approaching a stretch of sidewalk that was more even than the first forty yards of our chase. I managed to come closer, but the girl's chair was still racing at high speed. And there was a side street ahead crossing her path, with a high curb and passing cars. Even if she managed to get across, just past it, the incline became crazier again, so steep there was no way anybody on foot could ever stop a runaway wheelchair.

Now was my only chance.

My legs were moving faster and faster. I had almost reached the girl, when her chair jumped down the curb and began to topple over to the left. I made my last leap forward, caught the right wheel, pulled at it and then fell forward, landing right in front of the chair, which was now magically standing still and upright. It bounced against my thigh, using it as a final buffer.

Pain shot through my right leg. A bullet had fractured the tibia last year, and although everything had healed well, it was still a weak spot. And now I had twisted it badly during the fall. I bit on my lower lip, but a groan escaped from my mouth.

The girl whispered, "Help."

I was trying to catch my breath, holding my leg, when a male voice from above me said, "Shhh, Kali."

I looked up and saw the driver of the van gently stroking the girl's arm. "Are you okay?" he asked and offered me a hand to pull myself up.

The girl turned her face, and her amazing green eyes hit me. She looked unharmed. "Whoa," I mumbled, short of breath. "Always expect the worst drop in San Francisco," I joked, remembering at the same moment that the girl didn't speak English. Well, she had been able to say "Help," but now she didn't answer. She continued to stare at me, unseeing, her skin paler than the last time, her expression that of a very old person.

The man began to push the girl off the street. I limped behind them, and as soon as we had reached the sidewalk, the guy turned to me again and said, "You got hurt. I'm so sorry. She never endangered herself like that before, and when I realized what was going on, it was already too late. I only saw her dashing away and you running behind her."

The man's friendly face looked greenish. It was clear he had been given a major shock by seeing the girl race down the hill.

"Can you wait here?" he asked. "I'll just make sure she gets into the house safely. Then I'll come back and drive you to a doctor."

"That's not necessary." The pain was subsiding to a more bearable level. I could feel that nothing was severely damaged, even though it might continue to hurt for a while. "I need my stuff," I said and began to walk up the hill.

The man followed me, pushing the wheelchair as fast as he could. "I'll bring it to you. You dropped it in the driveway. It will still be there. Don't walk around more than necessary."

I was in fact glad to be left alone for a while and nodded. There was a low brick wall edging the front yard, and I sat down on it to stretch out my leg. Ten minutes later the man was back, carrying my laptop bag. He handed it to me and sat down beside me.

"Are you sure you shouldn't get this leg checked?" he asked again.

"Is she okay?" I said.

"Kalila? Yes, she doesn't even have a scratch. Thanks to you."

"I'm glad. I hope she overcomes the scare. It must be terrible to lose control of your chair. And when you can't even see where you're going."

The man quickly assessed my features. His own face was round and freckled, with pale blue eyes that were a bit milky around the irises. It could be a genetic discoloration or a very early onset of cataracts. Sunlight can damage your lenses, and in fact the guy looked as if he had been subjected to a lot of merciless UV rays. His hair was curly, white blond, definitely bleached by the elements. He could have been a sailor or a construction worker. But then his muscular build could also have been acquired in a fitness studio and the weather-beaten impression through some kind of outdoor sports. We were about the same age, mid thirties.

"Kali has survived more than an out-of-control wheelchair," he said. "She's a trooper."

"I can imagine," I said, when in fact I had no idea what this girl had experienced and what she was going through now.

"Can I at least treat you to a coffee?" the man asked. "By the way, I'm Leonard."

"Anna," I answered and stood up. On the one hand, I felt the strong urge to be left alone, but on the other hand, I was curious about the girl and what she was doing at Marge Cunningham's house.

We slowly walked down to Fillmore Street. I tried to suppress the limp but wasn't always successful. "I should have worn my eye patch today," I joked. "Then the stiff leg would make me a much more convincing pirate."

Not everybody can take this kind of humor, but Leonard laughed and said, "Actually I love your green eye. You remind me of a black panther with David Bowie eyes."

"It's called heterochromia iridium," I said. "When somebody is born with two differently-colored eyes."

At his puzzled look I just grinned and said, "I like the way it sounds. Like from a sci-fi movie."

"But your green eye is artificial."

"Exactly."

"Did you lose it in an accident?"

"No, from cancer."

"Your attitude about it is great. Rather than hiding it you show it off."

It's partly out of vanity that I like to play with the colors of my prosthetic eyes. But it's also self-preservation. If you don't hide your weaknesses, nobody can get a kick out of bringing them into the open.

We reached the first coffee shop on Fillmore Street. When we entered, there was a particularly strong smell of molten chocolate in the air.

"They specialize in chocolate treats here," Leonard said. "For me it's like an opium house."

We shared the same addiction. I ordered a brownie, a cupcake and a chocolate chip cookie and refused to let Leonard pay for them. "It's a coffee invitation, remember?" I said. "There was no mention of paying for fattening drugs."

Finally he stopped arguing, got three cookies for himself, bought me the desired cappuccino and an iced latte for himself and sat down across from me.

Again, I thought that he looked somehow out of place in this urban environment. He should be hunting bears in the high Sierra or riding around on a giant Appaloosa named Sitting Bull.

"So you are Kali's attendant?" I asked.

"I just help when my aunt needs somebody to drive her to the hospital."

"Your aunt is Mrs. Cunningham?"

"Exactly." He rubbed the back of his neck in one of these gestures that convey a thought process. "I never saw you around before. Do you work for the foundation?"

I wondered how honest I could be with this man. But if his aunt wanted him to know she had hired me, she would probably tell him herself.

"I'm looking into working for your aunt. She was so helpful

as to see me today." I had learned a bit from Mrs. Cunningham what the family foundation was about, so I continued, "I always wanted to find a job that matters and where I can visit foreign countries."

"Yeah, it's great work. I just came back from an assignment in Afghanistan myself."

"What did you do there?"

"I'm an agricultural engineer. I mostly work with small farmers in areas endangered by drought. We figure out ways of irrigating that don't lead to salinization of their fields."

I love such topics. Although I had given up my own research, I was still highly fascinated by complex scientific and technical questions. Still, today there were other matters that interested me more.

"Where does Kali come from?" I asked.

"Afghanistan. Actually, I accompanied her on the flight over. The foundation brings many child victims of war to the U.S. for medical treatment."

"So she stays with your aunt while she's here."

"Yes. Marge always has at least one child as a guest in her home. She's that type of person. Always lead by example."

There was deep respect for his aunt in Leonard's voice. But also something else. Maybe a certain weariness of her dominant do-gooder role.

Leonard didn't seem much older than his late cousin. I wondered if they had been close, and if he could provide me with a clue as to Laura's disappearance.

"Mrs. Cunningham mentioned that she is still mourning her lost daughter. I'm sorry that your cousin passed away."

Leonard's face looked as if a gray veil had been pulled over it. I realized when he began to speak that he was in deep grief. "It's a terrible tragedy. It broke my aunt's heart. And mine, too. Laura and I really loved each other as kids. Neither of us had any siblings, so she was like a sister."

Remember, you're just somebody interested in working for Marge Cunningham, I reminded myself. Don't go too far here.

"I lost my best friend last year," I said. "He was like a brother to me, too."

I couldn't coax Laura's cousin into talking more about her. He just nodded and then asked, "So do you know in what position you will be working for my aunt?"

"I'm not sure yet," I said.

"Well, hopefully I'll see you around. If you'd like to get involved with the kids who are here with the foundation, we're always grateful for volunteers. As I said, you have a great attitude about your own disability. I'm sure you could encourage the kids who lost an eye themselves. Or a child who has cancer."

He gave me his business card and said, "Call me if you have any questions about the foundation you don't want to ask my aunt, or if you want to get together for another coffee some time soon."

After a few more inquiries about my leg to make sure I really didn't need a doctor, I convinced him that I was fine and would be able to get home on my own safely.

Leonard was really a nice guy, a gentle, caring man, and I would definitely not mind getting together with him again and hearing more about his experiences working in arid parts of the world. For now, I was glad to be on my own again, not having to deal with the exhausting kindness of a stranger. I was frustrated that I hadn't managed to learn more about his relationship with Laura. If they had been so close as kids, maybe he had an idea where she had been after her disappearance, but I couldn't jeopardize the confidential nature of my work for his aunt. We wished each other a friendly good-bye, left the coffee shop together and walked away in opposite directions.

Chapter 10

Marge Cunningham had bought my exclusive services for as long as the job would take. I was to work solely on her case and brief her every night by phone. While I was riding home on the bus, I looked for my notepad. I wanted to jot down a quick reminder to ask my client about her nephew. I assumed that he would have told his aunt if he had known anything about Laura's whereabouts during the time of her disappearance, but wasn't certain. The bonds between teenagers can exclude adults completely. If Marge allowed me to tell Leonard about my true assignment, I might be able to receive valuable information from him.

The notepad was not in my bag. I remembered that I had tried to stuff it in, but before I succeeded I had run after Kali. When Leonard had brought me my bag, he must have overlooked it. I cursed and pulled out his business card. *Leonard*

Cunningham, Engineer, it read. There was no address on it, just a phone number. Maybe it was a cell.

I got my own mobile phone out and dialed his number. After the second ring, he picked up.

"Leonard, it's Anna again. Are you by any chance still near your aunt's house?"

"I'm right here in the driveway."

"Is there a yellow legal pad lying around somewhere, close to where you found my bag?"

"Let me take a look." A few seconds of silence passed, then Leonard said, "Good news! It was under some flowers. Sorry I missed it. It has almost the same color as these terrible mums my aunt seems to love. I'll bring it to you. I'm already in the car. Just let me know where you are."

I was about to get off the bus in front of our office. If I asked Leonard to meet me there, he would know what my true profession was. And I never give out my private address to strangers. "I'm on my way to a meeting with a friend. Can I pick it up from your place later?"

"I don't want to trouble you any more, and I'm about to leave the city for a few days. Why don't you give me your address, and I'll stuff it into your mailbox."

"My mailbox might be too small. But could you drop it off at the Thai place on the corner of Geary and Taylor? I'll pick it up later."

The restaurant was a few blocks from my actual home. I went there often, and the owner was a friendly woman. I quickly walked over and was assured that it would be no problem to hold onto my pad of paper until I could get it.

Taking all these precautions meant that I didn't have my detailed notes when I sat in the office and presented the case to Martha, but I managed to recall most facts.

Marge Cunningham had described the Cunningham Foundation as a charity whose main cause was to help children in developing countries. When her daughter couldn't come up with plans for her own life, her mother had thought it a good idea to get her an internship with one of the foundation's international projects. "Laura could have even chosen in which country she wanted to work," Mrs. Cunningham had said. "For an aspiring writer this would have been a wonderful life experience."

"But Miss Spoiled didn't want to get her hands dirty by touching sick little jungle kids," Martha mused when I quoted our client.

"Her mother didn't put it that way exactly," I said.

"Let me check what the foundation is into," Martha said, turning to her computer.

Meanwhile I dialed Marge Cunningham's number. I had to find out if I could ask Leonard some questions. Also, I wondered why she hadn't mentioned the nephew who had been like a brother to her daughter.

"I don't want the family involved in this quest," Mrs. Cunningham said.

She told me that Leonard had been at MIT when Laura disappeared. Over the years she had spoken with her nephew on many occasions about his cousin, and she was certain that, as he was getting older, he would have definitely revealed if he had known anything about Laura's whereabouts.

"He is very fond of me, and seeing how I was suffering, he wouldn't have left me in the dark," she said. "The poor boy went through enough last year when Laura died. I don't want to subject him to any more questions about her, or give him possible false hopes for finally having a sense of closure. When you discover something, I'll let him know. But for now I wish to keep it a secret from the family that I've hired you."

After I had hung up, Martha said, "You should take a closer look at this Web site. The Cunningham Foundation is quite an octopus."

"Meaning what?"

"That it has its long tentacles spread out all over the world."

I got my laptop out and logged onto the Web. The Cunningham Foundation's site described many projects aimed at children. There were initiatives to provide villages in remote areas in Africa with clean drinking water, local farming projects like the one Leonard was involved with, programs which made it possible for kids who had been injured by land mines or who had other medical conditions to receive treatment in the United States, like Kalila did.

The involvement of the original foundation was quite impressive. But when I clicked on the page with links to other sites, it turned out the Cunningham Foundation had many derivatives: charities that worked under different names, but when you looked at the lists of their sponsors, the Cunningham Foundation was always at the top. There was an organization for the elimination of land mines, another one that provided local initiatives in poor areas with trucks and other machines, a third one that gave out loans to women's groups in war-ridden zones and enabled them to purchase farm animals or looms in order to build independent businesses.

I wanted to find out where the original funds for the foundation had come from, and when I Googled Marge's and Leonard's names together, I found a family history that made me think of a miniature Kennedy clan. It turned out the Cunninghams had become super rich during the construction of the transcontinental railroad. Richard Cunningham, the great-great-grandfather of Marge, had been an engineer involved with the construction of the tracks through the High Sierra. Seeing firsthand what this enormous project really needed, he had begun to deal in explosives, and later, it seemed, in human capital.

At this point the family history became less detailed, but it looked as if Richard Cunningham had offered his services to Chinese immigrants who needed work permits, and had used his contacts to obtain the documents. He must have then sold the visas to the workers in exchange for a certain percentage of their wages, or so I figured. There was no precise information.

And after those golden days, the family's fortune grew and grew. Richard's two sons had dealt with whatever the market needed in terms of giant hardware: trucks, engines, railroad tracks. They had moved from being merchants to becoming manufacturers.

The family line had always remained small. None of the offspring had more than two children, some none, and Marge and her brother Stewart—Leonard's father—were the only two family members of their generation. After Laura's death, Leonard was the sole heir to the family name.

It seemed as if there was one more living family member: Leonard and Laura's grandfather, Alcott Cunningham, who must be ninety-three by now. I couldn't find an obituary anywhere, so I assumed he was still alive. He had started the foundation with millions he had made through the family corporation, a company called CBM—Cunningham Beams and Metal—which continued to deal in all kinds of specialized metal parts, manufacturing them all over the world and selling them globally. It seemed that one of their main lines of business was to build armored vehicles for money transports, for protection for heads of states in various countries, and for armored trucks and Humvees for the military.

In spite of all this enlightening information about my client's background, I still had no idea where to begin looking for Laura's tracks after her disappearance. I walked to the Thai restaurant where Leonard had already dropped off my notes. I picked up some food for Martha and me, coconut chicken and lamb curry, and went back to the office. I began to study what I had written down and compared it to the old PI report Marge had given me.

Laura's mother had told me that her daughter had left without warning on September 16, 1993. It had been a warm night.

Laura had asked if she could take her mother's car and drive to Stinson Beach where she wanted to meet some friends for a bonfire. Marge had agreed. When Laura didn't come back by the following afternoon, her mother got annoyed, mainly because she needed the car. Her daughter was eighteen and sometimes stayed with friends overnight, so Marge was not too worried at first. In the evening she began to call Laura's friends. Laura hadn't been particularly social, so there were really only one girl and one boy whom Laura had been close to, as far as her mother knew. Stacey Glum and Marcus Robinson. Neither of them had any idea where Laura could be, and they said they had never planned to meet with her at the beach the night of her disappearance. In fact, Stacey admitted that she and Laura had had a fight a few months before and weren't even speaking with each other anymore. Marge had never learned about this, and Laura had used so-called get-togethers with Stacey as a cover for other unknown activities a number of times since the girls had broken off their friendship.

Stacey, Marcus and Laura had gone to the same high school, a public school, albeit in lower Pacific Heights, so most of the students came from affluent households. Not Marcus, though. His parents owned an Indian takeout restaurant. He and Laura felt close because they were both adopted.

Marcus supposedly had a big crush on Laura. At least that's what her mother thought, and she was sure he was as shocked as she was that Laura had left without telling him. "This boy certainly didn't know a thing. Laura was much smarter and more mature than he was. She liked him because he was a sweet kid, but he was definitely not one of her confidantes," Marge had stated with conviction.

But then who was? Laura's mother had been unable to tell me. She assumed that her daughter had planned her disappearance all on her own. This was also the conclusion to which the now deceased PI, Miguel Santos, had come to eleven years ago, as his report confirmed. Santos had done quite a thorough job. He had questioned Marcus, had visited Laura's school, asked teachers and every fellow student he could still get a hold of. Some of Laura's former classmates had moved away, and he called and questioned them. He also talked to Stacey Glum, who had moved to North Carolina to major in premed. Stacey confirmed that she had never seen Laura or heard from her again since their fight shortly after high school graduation.

Santos had also checked with the DMV in California and the neighboring states to find out if Laura had applied for a name change, and he had asked a source at the Social Security office to find out if Laura had gotten a new Social Security number.

Santos's report was tagged as preliminary, and he had added a paragraph where he described what he was planning to do next. Mainly, he had wanted to extend the search in more states, trying to find out if Laura had left any administrative or bureaucratic footprints anywhere. And then his heart had let him down and the investigation came to a full stop.

Reading the report it became clear to me why Mrs. Cunningham hadn't employed a successor for the deceased Mr. Santos. He had worked well, and still he had come up with no clues. If a person cut off the ties to everybody who ever knew her, it used to be virtually impossible to find her. One can buy a new identity at a street corner and vanish into thin air without a trace. Santos's report reeked of the hopelessness of his quest, even though he had been determined to continue. It had promised to be a nice source of income for him for quite a while.

Martha and I had more to go on today. Otherwise, I wouldn't have accepted the job. We had the lead regarding the manuscript. And we knew that Laura had lived in the city for a while before she died. There were people who knew her recently, and it was possible she had told some of them about her life.

I studied the picture of Laura at eighteen, which I had requested from her mother. She looked oddly determined and lost at the same time, an imprisoned desperado intent on breaking free without knowing where to run to.

"The car turned up three weeks later?" Martha asked when I had given her my notes and the report. She had already finished her meal, while I was just beginning to eat. As usual, I had to suppress a cough at the first taste of the spicy Thai sauces, and my eyes began to water, but then my throat got used to the chili and I enjoyed the flavors.

"Are you crying?" Martha asked viciously.

"No, why would I?"

Martha put down the notes and looked me directly in the eye. Her gaze shot out like a pair of bullets from a double-barreled gun. "Because your leg is hurting, and your heart is sore, and you haven't slept."

My partner had this really annoying habit of speaking in non sequiturs. Often we hardly exchanged any personal information for days—which was exactly how I liked it—and then, completely out of the blue, she wanted to know how I was doing. I attributed this habit to her former interviewing techniques as a police officer and the power games she was used to playing.

"I'm fine," I said stubbornly, "apart from having an annoying partner, wanting to eat in peace, and then discussing the case."

"Where did you hurt yourself?"

I quickly told her the runaway wheelchair story, after which she began to rock back and forth expertly with her own chair, balancing the front wheels in the air. "The kid has to learn how to drive," she said. "Send her to me. I'll show her some tricks."

"She only speaks Dari," I repeated Marge Cunningham's original information about the girl. Now I knew that it was one of the two main languages spoken in Afghanistan.

"It's a nonverbal skill. I just have to show her."

"And she is blind."

"Well, that makes the job a bit more demanding."

Martha gave me another one of her piercing stares. Then she

said lightly, "How is Mido doing?"

"I guess okay," I said and stuffed the next forkful of food into my mouth. It no longer tasted of anything.

Martha's eyes seemed to change in texture, from rock-hard to almost velvety. Had I not known my partner better, I would have thought that she gave me a tender look of sympathy.

Yuck!

"Yeah, the car that Laura took was found later." I changed topics. "Actually, right in front of the driveway to her mother's house."

"Quite daring," Martha said, her expression back to its warrior queen self. "If the girl took it back herself, it means she might have wanted to be caught and brought back into the family."

"Or she just didn't want to leave any debt behind, any trace. Maybe she just needed it to transport a few of her things to wherever her first destination was. Her mother said that most of her clothes and many other personal items were taken from her room."

"Okay, so the girl planned this for a while. She needed a place to go with all her stuff. How about money? Did she have any? Credit cards?"

"No credit cards. Hardly any cash. Laura's mother only gave her money if she worked for it. So there was almost none in Laura's account."

"She must have had help then. Had she stayed in the city and worked under her real name, one of Marge's bloodhounds would have found her. She needed some cash to leave town, probably change her name."

"Inez should have learned something about Laura's past," I said. "And she must know about the manuscript. I have to talk to her again."

"That might be the easiest way," Martha agreed. "But you just visited her. I guess I have to pull some strings this time to see if you can get in so quickly again. Can't promise anything, though."

"Telephone?"

"Might be even more difficult. And I don't think you'll get much out of her on the phone."

I knew that Martha was right. And even though I itched to drive to the prison immediately and talk to Inez Belize, I had to remain patient—always a tough call for me.

Chapter 11

The Indian fast-food place owned by Marcus Robinson's parents still existed. It was located in the Western Addition, around the corner from the Fillmore concert hall in a rather ugly, though utterly alive, part of town. The Japantown mall, a nineteen seventies rendition of an Asian fortress, faced subsidized housing projects, as well as lower middle-class apartment buildings. There were drive-by shootings on a regular basis, yet it was not a particularly unsafe place to be, at least not during the day, so long as you were not a gang member somebody had a grudge against.

Taste of Cashmere was the name of the tiny takeout place. Behind the counter somebody had hung up an unframed poster of a Himalayan mountain range, with torn edges and greenish colors that looked like food gone bad. For a second, I believed I was the only person in the room. But then a tiny old lady in a pink sari rose from a stool behind the counter. She gave me a beautiful smile. "Want to eat?"

Had I not just stuffed myself with truckloads of another Asian cuisine, I would have definitely ordered something. The woman's smile had won me over instantly and convinced me that the food must be great. To hell with interior decoration.

"I'm actually looking for Marcus. Can you tell me where I can reach him?"

"You lucky. He here," she said and then yelled, "Maaarcus!"

A tall African-American man in blue jeans, a white T-shirt and a stained white apron emerged from the back room. He was very skinny and looked as if he had once worked as a boxer. The back of his nose was flattened and uneven, and one of his eyelids drooped lower than the other. He gave me a questioning look.

"Mr. Robinson," I said. "I'm here on behalf of Mrs. Marge Cunningham, Laura's—"

"I know who Mrs. Cunningham is," the man interrupted me. "What does she want this time?"

"She hired me to find out where Laura went when she disappeared," I said.

"What is the definition of stupidity?" he said instead of an answer.

I could think of an infinite multitude of definitions, but I was curious to hear what Marcus Robinson's was. "Tell me."

"To repeat the same thing over and over and expect different outcomes," Robinson said.

"I understand that Mrs. Cunningham has asked you before if you know where Laura went."

"She sure has. So have quite a few private eyes she hired over the years. And I still can't tell her or you anything else. I don't know where Laura is."

Don't know? "I just thought maybe Laura contacted you when she reemerged."

"When was that?"

"Last year. Or even sometime before." How long had Inez and Laura been partners? And had Laura been in California all along, maybe even in the Bay Area? Or had she only come back after many years of hiding somewhere else?

Marcus's face lit up. "The last time I saw or spoke to Laura was when we were both eighteen. But I'd sure like to hear from her again." A puzzled look took over Marcus's features and he said, "Wait. If Laura is back, why can't you ask her yourself where she's been?"

I could tell where the impression that this man was not particularly smart came from. His thought processes were visible all over his body and looked like hard work. His palms were rubbing up and down his thighs, his brows were moving across his forehead, and his eyes became empty while he was contemplating what he'd just heard.

"Laura is dead," I said carefully.

"Oh my god," Marcus mumbled. "I . . . I had no idea . . . how did it . . ."

"She was murdered. It was on the news."

"I was overseas," he whispered, shocked and slightly numbed, as if a heavy stone had struck his temple. "Deployed to Iraq. I only came back last month. Now I'm here to help my parents out for a few weeks. My father is quite sick. My parents didn't tell me. They don't read American newspapers. They will be so sad."

Marcus could clearly babble on for a while, so I interrupted him. "I'm really sorry you had to hear about it this way. Had I known, I wouldn't just have blundered in like this."

I sat with Marcus for a while. His grief was fresh and raw, and he asked me more details about Laura's death. I told him what I knew.

Even though I didn't think that Marge's assessment of his intelligence had been in the least correct—this man was as smart as she was, he had just never learned to show it—Laura's mother had probably been right about another thing: Marcus had once adored Laura.

"I really loved her, you know," he said. "And I always dreamed of seeing her again. When we were both sixteen, I professed my love. It took me more courage than I possessed. I took her out to Pizza Hut. And after we'd finished our pizza—I hardly ate, you can imagine—I told her what I felt for her. It almost broke me when she told me she didn't feel the same for me. I got beaten up quite a bit as a kid, and she used to protect me. I wanted to do the same for her when we were adults. And with all that pathos I opened myself up to her. She was really sweet about it. She said that being with her wouldn't make me happy, that my life had much more potential, and that I'd want to throw overboard who I was as a child, forget all about it. Today I know that she wasn't right. Sure, I'm not the tiny punching bag I once was, and I'm grateful as hell for it. But I would still love her, I know that. I will always love her."

The situation enabled me to stay serious. Otherwise I might have laughed out loud at Marcus's monologue. He sure had a sense for drama.

"Laura sounds like a great kid," I said. "And I'm certain she loved you, too, in her own way. That's why I thought maybe you know something about her that nobody else knows, that maybe you didn't even realize she told you."

"About her disappearance?"

I nodded.

"Believe me, I've racked my brain over this often enough, if only to get rid of Laura's mother and her questions. She never liked me as a kid. And then she was suddenly all over me, as if I possessed a holy map to Laura's whereabouts. At one moment Mrs. Cunningham was sweet, promising to reward me if I told her something, anything. Then she threatened to hand me over to the police if it turned out I knew something and didn't say so."

"And you really didn't."

"As much as I hate to say it, Laura was as big an enigma to me as to most other people. She was always kind to me. But if some-body pissed her off, she could be hell on wheels. Her victims always deserved it, though. There was this one boy at school who would relentlessly tease one of the girls. She was rather fat, not very attractive. And this boy would call her names. Your usual bully stuff. One day I saw Laura threaten him outside the school grounds. She had a hand firmly around his private parts. The guy was cringing in pain. Laura didn't know I saw her, and I never mentioned it to anybody. Now that she is dead, I don't think I can get her in trouble anymore. But Laura had guts. Just walked up to that guy, who was about twice her size, and squeezed the blood out of his balls. He never told anybody, of course. Too embar-rassing. But he left that other girl alone after that."

I asked Marcus if he remembered the names of these kids, but he couldn't come up with them. He also hadn't heard from Laura's other friend, Stacey, since the time around Laura's disap-pearance. I gave him my card, and he promised he would get in touch if he could think of anything that might be helpful.

"But only because you remind me a bit of Laura," he said.

"Yeah, don't we Asians all look the same?" I grinned.

"Same as us black folks." Marcus continued the oldest joke of ethnic minorities. "But I was talking more about your capacity to squeeze balls."

"See you," I said, unwilling to continue down that road.

Laura's old friend gave me a slow, lopsided smile. When I approached the door, the old lady who had silently listened to us all the while called after me in her high-pitched, sweet voice, "Be careful."

And I would certainly need her good wishes. I just didn't know at the time how much.

As I walked down Geary Street, the sun began to set. The bright white cathedral on the hilltop hovered before a sky that looked like it had been freshly water-colored in purple and rose. Then the aggressive red and orange city lights began to take over, dimming the sky to a dark blue. I was not yet ready to let the investigation rest for the night. Unanswered questions are bad sleeping companions, and I burned to do some more research. When I passed a coffee shop that offered wireless Internet connection, I quickly stepped inside, purchased a double espresso and set up my laptop.

There was only one listing for the name Glum in the Bay Area, and I called the number. When a man answered the phone, I introduced myself as one of Stacey's former classmates, looking for her because I was organizing a reunion. It was the oldest pretext possible, and since I had used it so often myself, I would probably never attend one of my own class reunions, eternally believing that every invitation was a scam.

Stacey's father—for it turned out that I had reached the right number—was quite careful himself.

"Who are you, please?" he requested in a harsh voice.

"Ani di Franco," I said. If you have no idea who you are supposed to impersonate, it's always good to choose a name of somebody a little but not too famous.

"I think Stacey once mentioned you," her father said hesitantly. "I'll give you her work number. She doesn't like me to give out her private information."

The number had an area code I knew very well. Atlanta, the city where my father lived. So Stacey had remained in Georgia.

It was unlikely I would reach her at this hour at work, especially considering the time difference, but I tried it anyway.

"Schaffner," a gravelly female voice answered despite my prediction.

"I'm looking for Stacey. Stacey Glum."

"That's me. Dr. Stacey Schaffner, formerly Glum. And who are you?"

"Anna Spring. I'm calling on behalf of Mrs. Marge

Cunningham, Laura Cunningham's mother."

"Yes?" The woman sounded as harsh as her father.

"I assume you know that Laura has died."

"So I've heard. Mrs. Cunningham sent my parents a note. I'm sorry for her loss, but what do you want from me?"

I repeated to Dr. Schaffner what I had said to Marcus and received quite a similar reaction. "I've already told Laura's mother and her detectives everything that I know. Just because she keeps asking doesn't mean I can remember more."

"I know that you and Laura had a fight a while before she left. May I ask you what it was about? You must understand, any little detail might give me a clue, even if you consider it unimportant."

"I don't even remember what we were fighting about. Something silly, the kind of thing teenagers bicker about. We were young. We took things much too seriously. Laura and I had just grown apart as friends and hadn't realized it for a while. That happens all the time when you're that age."

"Was it over a boy, or a girl, or a secret that one of you had?" I probed. Unsuccessfully.

"I really can't recall. And my beeper just went off. I have to run. An emergency. Sorry I couldn't help."

She didn't sound very sorry. She sounded stressed, almost anxious. She had been premed in college. Probably she had continued on that path and now had a life to save.

I called Martha, and it turned out she had been more successful than I. Through her law enforcement contacts she had somehow managed to get me another visitation with Inez the next day.

"Have I ever told you that I love you?" I said.

"Uuuugh," came her answer. "Body snatchers have devoured my partner's brain."

"Don't exaggerate. I won't go Stepford on you."

"You scared me!"

I called Marge Cunningham's number and was relieved when

82

I only reached her answering machine. She had asked me to leave her a voicemail if I couldn't get a hold of her personally. So I said I had just been tying up some old leads today and would probably have more interesting news tomorrow.

With the prospect of a meeting with our still most promising informant, I decided to call it quits for the day. Martha had agreed to do an extended database search, looking for every possible trace Laura may have left in the global electronic jungle. She had also offered to contact literary agents and publishers to find out if anybody had heard of Laura Cunningham and was maybe holding on to a copy of her manuscript.

I decided to walk home the last mile down Geary Street, to work off the caffeine that was palpably pumping through my system. On the last five blocks my leg began to yell at me that I had abused it enough for the day. I couldn't get myself to take a bus for one stop, though, so I slowly limped along the sidewalk, cursing the restraints our fragile bodies put on our lofty aspirations. When I had finally made it into the hallway of my building, I gave in and took the elevator up to the apartment. I stepped out of the small, rattling thing and almost tripped over the legs of somebody sitting in front of my door in the dark.

Chapter 12

"What are you doing here?" I gasped, partly startled, but mostly happy to see my friend Rita camped out here.

"Waiting for you," Rita said with a broad grin, her spiky hair over her thin face seeming to laugh at me as well.

"Why didn't you just call me?" I asked while I was unlocking the door. "Would have saved you the hard floor under your pretty butt."

"My butt is not pretty," Rita said. "It's big and flat, and you never call me back. Don't tell me you didn't get my messages."

I had gotten them. But I had forgotten them quickly amid the turmoil of the last days. And Rita was not only friends with me but was also Mido's best friend, and my only protection against my love sickness was to avoid all thoughts of the woman who left me.

"Your butt is not big!" I said with conviction.

Rita placed herself on the giant ugly couch, the only piece of furniture in my living room. "That's beside the point," she continued. "I was worried. I wanted to know how you're doing."

I escaped to the kitchen, ostensibly to get us something to drink, but mainly to give my anger a chance to boil down. Rita was a good friend, and it was not her fault that I simultaneously wanted to fall on my knees and beg Mido to come back to me, be with me, love me, forgive me—and scratch her eyes out.

I carried two glasses of Coke on a tray over to Rita, as well as a bottle of water and a bottle of gin. Rita downs water like other people do beer, and even though I usually don't care very much for alcohol, I wanted something numbing right now. I had once bought the booze for Mido, who liked the occasional gin and tonic, and I was determined to get rid of this vestige of her quickly. A generous splash of gin went into my Coke. Rita finished her soft drink, filled her glass with water and gave me a questioning look.

"You knew what she was planning!" I said.

"You knew it, too."

"What? That she wanted to break up with me?"

"She broke up with you?" Rita looked utterly surprised.

It fit Mido's personality that she hadn't even told her best friend what was going on.

I told Rita the story, confessed to her what an insensitive egomaniac I had been—not even asking Mido once about the progress of her adoption procedures.

"You know that Mido and I are like sisters," Rita said after I had finished. "But I didn't know any of this. She told me that her adoption had come through, and that she was planning her trip to Guatemala. But of course I assumed she had told you as well, and that the two of you were figuring things out together."

Rita looked contemplative. I wanted to shake her like a salt shaker, make her promise that everything would be okay, that Mido would come to her senses, that we would get back together. Eventually, she just said, "I didn't even know that Mido wanted a child so badly. But what happened last year changed her. I think she somehow lost the belief that she is inherently a good person. She has to prove something to herself with Esmeralda."

"I know what she has gone through in the last year," I said. "I've been part of it." It was weird thinking of those days. Immediately, the painful memory of losing Jeff took over. But then it had been the events around his death that had eventually brought Mido and me together. She still felt that she was responsible for the whole mess that had led to Jeff's death. But I knew that was not true. She had gotten herself into trouble, yes. But she wasn't the one who killed my friend. And in the end she had rescued me from the people who had.

Rita and I fell silent. Speculating over Mido's motives didn't get us anywhere. It definitely didn't make me feel any better to realize that I had no idea what really drove the woman I loved, what her innermost struggles and true desires in life were.

I leaned back and gulped down the whole glass of gin and Coke at once.

"Let's go out!" Rita suddenly said. "If you want to get senselessly drunk, at least use something that tastes good. Gin and Coke, shudder."

We ended up in the Valencia Bar in the Mission district. Rita, who was straight herself, had dragged me into one of the last true dyke dives in the city. I could care less where I was. My friend and I cracked silly jokes for as long as I could still think clearly. She brought me one crazy mixed drink after another— some were lime green, others tasted of chocolate, all of them were very sweet: the only way one can get me to drink more alcohol than I want. And of the rest of the evening, I have little memory.

I recalled that there were women around us, some of whom were trying to chat, others who just hovered quietly at the bar, drink in hand. They seemed to grow before my eyes—particularly a tall, muscular blond in a cowgirl outfit who held onto her beer for most of the night, staring into space. Before my intoxicated eye, she looked like the Statue of Liberty in drag. I tried to tell Rita the joke, but wasn't able to pronounce anything discernible anymore. Rita later told me that she and one of the other women had to practically carry me out to her car.

My next conscious thought occurred when I had to run to the bathroom at seven the next morning to throw up whatever was left in my stomach. Fortunately, I hadn't killed enough brain cells to not remember that I had to be at Aldridge at noon. I still had to rent a car and, if possible, get sufficiently sober to drive it. A gnome with a sledge hammer had moved into my head, and I was seeing double.

Stumbling into the living room, I detected Rita stretched out on the couch. She yawned, sat up and smiled at me.

"You could have stopped me," I said accusingly.

"You're your own woman," she replied. "You were determined to get drunk. I only steered you into the direction of getting happily drunk."

"We did have fun, didn't we?" I suddenly had to laugh, thinking about what a fool I had made of myself the night before. The movement of my face made the little pervert hammer down on my brainstem even more vigorously, and I cringed.

"You looked so excessively sad when you started to pour that yucky Coke stuff down your throat," Rita said and put an arm around me when I sank down on the couch next to her. "I couldn't stand it. I thought a real good hangover would take your focus off your lovesickness."

"Well, thanks," I said, giggling again, shocked back into pain by the monster in my head. "The only problem is, I have a really important date at noon."

"You travel fast," Rita said. "One night in oblivion and you're ready to start a new life with a fresh woman."

"She's in jail," I said. "For butchering her partner."

My friend immediately became serious. "A new case?" she asked.

I nodded extremely gingerly.

"I'll drive you there."

"Are you sure?" I knew it was the best solution—there was no way I could sober up in the next few hours—and a very generous offer. "Don't you have to work?"

"It's Saturday, Ms. Marlow. Normal people don't have to work today."

"Normal is the sickest word. And you'll get bored. It may take a while."

"That's fine. I'll bring a book."

I was wrong. *Normal* can be a beautiful word. As can *sane*. And that was what my friend embodied. I gave her a hug, still flinching with every movement, and she just said, "You can take a shower first. I'll make breakfast. And then off we go to Pelican Bay."

"Aldridge," I corrected her.

"Wherever it is you want to fly."

Inez looked even worse today than the last time. She shuffled into the room as if she were walking toward the electric chair. Her tall, strong frame seemed to have shriveled. She was extremely pale, and even though there was the thick glass separating us, I could tell her breathing was labored. Beads of sweat were glistening on her upper lip.

"Are you okay?" I asked, obviously a stupid question, but Inez Belize nodded, even gave me a little smile.

"I'm just a bit tired today," she said. "Probably the weather. But it's good to see you."

I looked around in the windowless room. The weather? Then I detected the quickest flicker of humor in Inez's face, like the flap of a butterfly's wing, and I smiled back.

"You look exhausted yourself," she said.

"I am," I admitted, forgetting for a moment whom I was talking to and why. "Laura's mother has extended my assignment," I said. "She knows that Laura was working on a book and would like to find the manuscript. As you suspected, none of Laura's belongings were still in your house."

Inez's eyes moved away from my face, sank to the floor again, and I was catapulted back to the realization that she was caged and that there was a reason for all this.

Remembering how quickly time had passed the last time, I continued. "Also Mrs. Cunningham wants to find out where Laura has been in the last twelve years. They haven't been in touch for all that time."

"Laura probably had her reasons," Inez mumbled.

Again there was this instant when I forgot to whom I was talking. Inez seemed just like any woman with whom I shared quite a similar outlook on things. But then the awareness was back. Who was she to judge Mrs. Cunningham's relationship with Laura?

"When did you and Laura meet?" I asked.

"July 14, 2004."

One and a half years before Laura's death.

"And where?"

"In Asheville. I was there for a conference. She was working in a coffee shop."

Inez's voice was barely audible. Her pallor was increasing. She looked as if an opaque film were covering her face. She lifted her head, stared at me suddenly in the eye. Frightened, silently screaming out for help.

For the first time I gazed uninterrupted into her face for longer than a second. And realized she was dying. Life was sneaking out of her features. Her full lips sank in, her irises dulled, then she slowly fell forward and dropped from her chair.

She was lying motionless on the floor. I jumped up, wanting to run over and help her, but there was the glass. And the next instant the guard on the other side had caught on to what was happening and stood over Inez.

"Backup!" the tall, broad-shouldered warden yelled.

I jumped back from the window, misunderstanding her order.

"I need backup!" she shouted again. "And medical."

"Feel her pulse!" I heard myself yell.

The CO remained standing, towering over the lifeless body of the prisoner in front of her.

"Step back," the guard on my side of the wall now ordered.

"But she needs help," I stammered.

"She will get help. But now step back."

I was led from the visitor's room. Nobody had attended to Inez yet.

"You can't just let her lie there like that. If she has a heart attack, she needs immediate help," I kept saying.

My voice echoed from the high concrete walls of the hall we were walking through. I realized I was screaming.

The guard, a small, chubby woman with a long brown braid, led me back to the reception area. "You better go home," she said in a patronizing tone. "You can call later and inquire about the inmate." Then she locked a barred door behind herself and left.

I collected my ID and cell phone from the front desk and stormed out of the building onto the deserted walkway outside the prison gate. Underneath my feet there was concrete. Left and right of the path was an eighteen foot wall topped with razor wire. A few yards ahead, the black glass head of a watchtower peeked over the wall. There was nobody to scream at, nothing to destroy anywhere in sight. And I badly wanted to kick some innocent, inanimate object. But not even a trashcan was in sight.

I grunted in frustration. The scene I had just witnessed replayed itself in my head, and I was still trying to understand it.

How could you remain standing over a person who was lying in front of you on the floor, unconscious, and basically do nothing to help her? Slowly, the reasoning of a prison guard crept into my thinking. What if she is only faking? What if she'll jump up and attack me the moment I bend over to feel her pulse? Why would I want to touch an inmate? What are the rules for such a situation?

Imagining what the guard had probably thought did not calm my rage. Inez was not faking. I had seen her face the moment she had passed out.

Dying from a broken heart. A line from an old song wormed itself into my ear while I walked back to the car. Rita had parked down the road, out of sight from the prison. She didn't want to have to stare at the walls while she was waiting for me.

I quickly told my friend what had happened. She fully sympathized with my reaction. That cooled down my own violent rage, and we drove back to the city in mutual contemplation.

Chapter 13

Rita dropped me off in front of the office. We had originally planned to have lunch together, but neither of us was hungry. I promised to call her in the next few days, and at that point I was determined to stick to my promise.

Of course, Martha was at her usual place in front of the computer screen. I filled her in on the events of the afternoon.

"Wherever you go, there's heartbreak, chicky," she said dryly.

Sometimes I'm just not up for banging against the bulwark of cool humor my partner likes to erect against the real heartbreak of human life. "She's still a person, isn't she?" I insisted. "And she deserves help when she's about to die."

"You haven't seen enough homicide victims yet," Martha said. "The close up, full color view of a human body torn to pieces by somebody else is a very successful remedy for your liberal compassion for the perps."

She was probably right, but also utterly wrong. I didn't agree with her hardball cop bullshit that you only know life when you've waded through the blood and gore of the darkest hells of humankind. Martha's view was as corrupted as that of a person who only sees love and peace everywhere.

Mainly to provoke her I said, "I'm still not all that convinced Inez really did it. What if she's just protecting the real murderer? Her father, for example. Maybe he snapped and stabbed Laura. Alzheimer's patients can be unpredictable."

So far I had found no indication that the relationship between Laura and Inez had been anything but loving and caring. The scars from Inez's hands could have another explanation. And her confession would make sense if she were covering for somebody she loved, and whom she perceived as more vulnerable than herself.

"You think us cops are idiots?" Martha said, and there was no trace of humor in her voice anymore.

"You know I think you're the brightest person I've ever met," I said with sincerity. "But, yes, I do think that there are cops who are idiots or just plain sloppy or overworked or whatever. You're too smart not to agree with me on that. And we both know that there are quite a few cases where people have been convicted based on false confessions."

"Inez Belize confessed after twenty minutes in police custody. They didn't even have time to question her, much less apply *unlawful pressure*." Martha put an ironic emphasis on the last two words.

"That's what I mean. If Inez is covering for somebody, the police wouldn't be to blame for her conviction."

"They would," Martha said. "They still have to take the evidence into consideration. Look at all the facts." With these words she turned away from me and continued to torture her keyboard with her forceful fingers, punching the life out of every single little key.

I had no idea what to do with my suspicion apart from outright asking Inez Belize. As if she had read my thoughts, Martha turned around again and promised she would make some calls later to inquire about Inez's condition. There are moments when my partner's heart suddenly shimmers through like a silver box at the bottom of a muddy lake. She also agreed to search the databases to see if there was any trace of Laura staying in the Asheville area before 2004.

I had hoped to find out from Inez what her profession was, if Laura really had worked on that manuscript, if Inez had ever read it, who Laura's friends were, if she had any kind of day job—and, of course, I had hoped that Laura had told Inez in detail how her life was and what she was up to in the last thirteen years. The only other person I could think of who maybe had a few of the answers to these questions was Lucy, the neighbor.

So I climbed her front steps once again. Before I had reached the door, there was a loud noise from inside the house, a dull yet sharp bang. I rang the bell a few times, then I hammered against the door. Finally, somebody opened. It was a dark-haired man with a broad smile. He was very muscular and handsome in a conventional way, with a set jaw and narrow, expressionless eyes. "Can I help you?"

"I'd like to talk to Lucy."

"She's not here. You have to come back later."

He didn't close the door fast enough. I could see a shadow move in the hall behind him.

"Lucy," I quickly called.

The man banged the door shut. "I'll call the police!" I yelled.

A few seconds later the door was opened a crack, and Lucy's nose appeared. "Everything's okay," she whispered. "It's just not a good moment."

"Can I see your face, please?"

She fully opened the door, and I could see that she had been crying. Her face looked unharmed, though.

"He beats you where nobody can see it," I said.

"He doesn't beat me," Lucy insisted. "We had a little argument. All couples fight sometimes."

"I can take you to a shelter, and your kid, too."

"I told you, it's okay. I'm fine. What do you want?" She didn't sound unfriendly, just distraught. But even that impression was already vanishing. She was bouncing back as quickly as a piece of stepped-on latex foam.

I tried to focus on the reason I had come here. "I'm not really planning on buying Inez's house," I said. "I'm sorry I lied to you, but I work as a private investigator and it's sometimes necessary to act incognito. But I know I can trust you, and I have some important questions to ask."

"Just a second."

Lucy disappeared inside the house and soon came back with her toddler in the stroller. "We can go for a walk."

I helped her carry the stroller down the steps, and we started out into the blazing afternoon sun whose glory belied the craziness of this day.

The toddler, a little boy with auburn curls and the mouth of a cupid, was unusually quiet. He just stared straight ahead from his position in the stroller without turning his head or making any sound.

"I can't stay long," Lucy said. "I told my husband you're an old friend from school who just dropped by. He doesn't like me to socialize too much."

"Okay." I cut to the chase. "Did Laura ever tell you anything about her life? Where she grew up? Where she lived before she moved here? What her job was?"

Lucy didn't even ask why I needed to know these things. Her former friendliness was gone. She just wanted to get the situation over with and get rid of me. By acknowledging my profession I had clearly changed sides in her eyes. She probably associated me with the cops.

"I think Laura didn't have a steady job. She stayed at home a lot. Picked up Mr. Belize from daycare. She told me she was an editor, a freelancer. But really, we didn't talk much. I don't know where she came from. I assumed she had always lived here in the city like Inez and myself."

"And Inez? What did she do?"

"She's a professional chef. She used to have her own catering business."

"I have one more question, and please be honest with me."

Lucy's smooth features tensed. She gave me an angry stare.

"Did you ever witness any violence between Laura and Inez? And by violence I don't only mean yelling and hitting each other. Were there snide remarks? One of the two running out of the house crying? Any unusual bruises on the arms or face?"

Lucy didn't hesitate. She looked at me openly, her face more relaxed again, and said, "No, and I have to say I almost envied them."

We walked back to the corner of her street. We had slowly rounded the block, and the little boy had become a bit more lively. He was whining softly now, repeating, "Cook, cook."

"He wants a cookie," Lucy said with a smile, pulling a package of graham crackers from a bag connected to the stroller.

"He threatens to take your son away if you leave him, doesn't he?" I said.

She handed the toddler his cookie, her features frozen.

"And you know he'll find you wherever you go. If he can't get custody, he'll kidnap him and run, at least that's what he says."

Lucy nodded lightly, with a certain astonishment in her gaze.

I had never experienced domestic violence myself, had never even assisted a friend through it. But the mechanisms were so well-known, so universal that I was utterly surprised this poor woman obviously thought her story was unique and I must be clairvoyant to guess it.

"You're not alone," I said and wrote down my cell number

and the office number for her. "Call whenever you want." I sounded more assertive than I felt. If this bastard was really intent on harming her, snatching the child, or anything of the like, I wasn't sure I could protect her or that she would even be safe in a shelter. But I was sure Martha had more ideas and resources in such a case than me.

"What did Laura do for you?" I finally asked. "You mentioned before that she once really helped you."

"I can't tell," Lucy said. "I promised her."

"Did it have something to do with a gun?"

The muscles in Lucy's neck tensed like a bow string. I waited at the corner until she had made it back to the house. It would have been polite to help her carry the stroller back inside, but I didn't want to enter her possessive husband's field of vision again. I hoped to spare Lucy further questions about my visit.

I was also somewhat distracted. A truck had parked halfway down the block from where I was standing, a dark blue Dodge Ram with tinted windows. It had pulled over and stopped shortly after Lucy and I had walked by. Nobody had exited the vehicle. I had the strange sensation that the car was watching me, its headlights odd space alien eyes. I walked down the street, away from Lucy's house. The car didn't move.

On Mission I entered the next bus going downtown and got off by the BART station. There was a long line of cars waiting at the intersection. The fourth truck was a dark blue Ram. This time I memorized the license plate. Flagging a taxi would have been the fastest way to get to my next destination. Instead, I ran down the stairs to the subway. A train was just about to close its doors when I reached the platform and jumped inside. Nobody entered after me.

Three stops later I got off the train, surfaced on Market Street, hopped into a cab and enjoyed the luxury of a chauffeur for whom Marge Cunningham would have to pay.

Chapter 14

It was just getting dark when the cabby dropped me off at the shooting range in Golden Gate Park. Mist was crawling through the tree trunks, and the taxi's lights were swallowed instantly by the milky dusk.

The driver was a quiet, cranky Middle Eastern guy. He waited impatiently for me to close the door behind myself, then he stepped on the gas and pulled out of the parking lot with squealing tires. I couldn't tell if he was just eager to pick up his next fare or if the place spooked him.

Shots were sounding from behind a wooden bungalow at the far end of the lot. Mrs. Cunningham had given me the address of this shooting range where Laura used to come as a teenager. I was hoping she might have shown up here as an adult, too. Gigantic oaks hovered at the fringe of the premises. It seemed they were slowly and very silently stepping forward.

The front door of the building was unlocked. I entered a brightly lit, small room furnished with file cabinets, some chairs and a desk. Behind the desk sat a red-haired woman, almost a girl still, with wild curls, freckles and a friendly grin.

"Want to check in?" she asked.

"Not really," I said. "I just have a few questions about somebody who used to come here many years ago."

"I've only worked here for a year."

"Is there an old-timer around?"

"There are quite a few folks who look pretty old to me," the girl said mischievously. "But I wouldn't know exactly how long they've used the range."

"Anybody out there right now?"

"You wouldn't want to interrupt them when they're aiming. They might just turn around—and boom."

She was an interesting pick as an employee at a shooting range. I returned her grin and pulled from my bag the photo of Laura from last year.

"Have you ever seen her around?" I asked the girl.

"Is she dead or something?"

"How do you know?"

"No, seriously, I was just kidding. You come in here like some movie detective and ask me, *Have you seen this lady*?" she mocked me with an artificially deep voice. "I was just making a joke. So she's really dead?"

"She is."

"What happened?"

"You don't really want to know."

"Did she get shot?"

"No."

The girl uttered a sigh of relief. "Good. I always think I shouldn't work here, you know? Guns freak me out, bad karma and so on."

Wouldn't life be boring if we didn't all harbor these absurd inconsistencies and contradictions?

I just asked the girl once more, "Do you remember seeing her around last year?"

She concentrated on the picture. "There are not a lot of Asian women who come here to practice," she finally said. "She's not a regular, but her face somehow looks familiar. You know, I might have seen her once or twice."

"Do you remember when that was?"

"Sorry, not really."

"Maybe you could help me look up her name in your files?"

There was a sign saying that you had to show a valid ID if you wanted to shoot here. I hoped that the range kept records of the customers' log.

"Of course you know I'm not supposed to do that." The girl smiled as she turned to her computer screen.

I figured I really deserved somebody like her today. I hoped I wouldn't get her fired.

"What's her name?"

"Laura Cunningham."

The girl typed it in, clicked on the mouse a few times and shook her head. "She didn't check in last year, and she's not a member."

"And 2004?"

After another series of clicks the freckled face looked as disappointed as I felt. "Nope."

"Shoot," I said, and received a little smile in response.

A door to my left opened and a man entered the room, a gnarly-looking guy with a mean face. He pulled off protective earmuffs and goggles and immediately stared at Laura's picture, which was still lying on the desk. "Who are you?" he asked in a drill sergeant's voice.

"And who are you, please?" I purred back.

"That's none of your business."

The girl gave me a warning look. She probably expected he'd

pull a revolver and shoot me. She really needed a change in work environment.

"You looking for Laura?" he asked. His curiosity had beaten down his gruffness quickly.

"You know her?"

"I used to. She was the biggest talent I ever trained."

Marge Cunningham had not been able to recall the name of Laura's shooting trainer. She had given Laura the money for her lessons, and Laura had chosen and paid her own coach, this guy, probably, if he was speaking the truth.

"Have you been in touch with her lately?" I asked.

"She just up and left one day. Didn't hear from her again."

"So you have no idea where she was in the last twelve years?"

"Only saw her again once. Last year. She lost her aim, though. Couldn't hit a target for all it was worth. I almost didn't believe it was really her." The drill sergeant's tone had vanished from his voice. Even the meanness in the man's features had softened like the ridges on a thawing ice sculpture.

"Could I treat you to a drink, sir, and ask you a little bit more about Laura?" I asked with the most respectful tone I could muster.

"I don't drink, and I'm not done with practice. I just need to get something from the car."

"Then maybe later."

He was visibly struggling, his curmudgeonly self-image fighting a deeper, stronger urge.

"Is there a table where we can sit down for a few minutes?" I asked him.

"Come with me."

He led me through a side door down a long, poorly-lit hallway and unlocked a heavy steel door. Behind it was a room full of guns. There were precision rifles locked up in glass cases, air guns leaning in a corner, and some historic-looking, long-barreled pistols hanging on the walls. At the far side of the room was a row of metal lockers. Unlike those in athletic locker rooms, these cabinets didn't have holes for air to circulate. It smelled of cold concrete and oil.

There was no other furniture in the room, nothing to sit down on, but after the man had closed the door behind us our need for privacy was fulfilled.

"I'm Anna Spring," I volunteered in order to break the ice. "Laura's mother has asked me to find out where she was after she disappeared."

"Mother can't ask her herself?"

"Laura's dead."

"Accident?"

"Murdered."

The man didn't ask any more questions. He slowly moved his head from left to right, as if by just thinking hard enough, he could find out what had happened.

"You didn't read about it in the papers?" I asked softly.

"I don't read newspapers. Don't watch the news either. Makes me a happier person."

"I figure you were already asked a few questions after Laura disappeared when she was eighteen." I tried to segue to my cause.

"No."

"None of Mrs. Cunningham's investigators came to see you?"

"It wasn't my happiest time back then. I was in and out of rehab for a few years."

"Did Laura ever confide in you?" Something about the old guy told me I didn't have to beat around the bush with him. "About having trouble at home? Or at school, with a boyfriend, a girlfriend, anything like that?"

"No. She wasn't much of a talker. But I could tell how she felt from how she shot. That was all the language we needed."

"Did she shoot better when she felt better?"

"Just the other way around. She'd come in with this angry,

searing fire in her eyes, and I knew she'd hit the mark with every shot that day. Keep that anger up, I told her, and you'll make it to the Olympics. But she didn't even want to go to county tournaments. She liked to shoot for the sake of shooting, like a meditation. I'm the same way. That's why we got along."

"Was she angry often?"

"Most of the time."

"Couldn't have made it easy to work with her."

"As I said, she shot all the better for it. And she was good at containing her anger. That's all that counts in a shooting range. If you blow up, you get kicked out. Laura learned that at an early age."

"So she did sometimes blow up?"

"Tried it once. When she was still really young. Got suspended from the range for a few weeks."

"What happened?"

The man shook his head again in contemplation. Then he said, "Pointed her air gun at another girl who was teasing her. You know how kids are. The girl had gone pretty far. Aimed at Laura's target. Got suspended, too."

"Do you remember who the girl was?"

The guy pondered my question for a few seconds, then he shook his head. I could tell he wanted to add something.

"Did she get shot?" he finally asked.

"No."

"Who killed her?"

"Her lover confessed to it."

"Do you know why he did it?"

"She. And I have no idea why."

The old guy looked puzzled for a moment then he processed the information and said, "But her mother thinks you'll find out."

"Sort of."

My vague answer seemed to satisfy the man perfectly. "We were

103

friends," he finally said. "As strange as that may seem in your eyes. Even when Laura didn't really need me as a coach anymore, we used to get together for practice regularly. She gave me as many tips as I gave her. Shooting was something like a life philosophy for her, and we would often talk about it. Over the years she tried all kinds of weapons, even archery and crossbow. She was really good at free pistol. As I said, Olympic caliber. But as she grew up she liked bigger calibered handguns. Her favorite was a Smith and Wesson 38 revolver. Very traditional. She said she liked the sound of it."

"But then last year, when you saw her again, she'd lost her aim?"

"She only fired a few shots. Maybe it just wasn't her day."

"So she just suddenly shows up here again, without contacting you first?" I didn't take pleasure in rubbing salt in the old guy's wounds. But some people need to talk about their injuries in order to soothe the pain.

"She didn't have to. We were both gone for a long time. Then we're back. No big deal. But she didn't even want to know me anymore. Or herself. Even changed her name. And pretended she was someone else."

"She didn't acknowledge knowing you?"

"Nope."

"But you're sure it was her."

"Cheap whiskey may have done its thing with me, but I still know who I am and who I once knew."

"Do you remember the name she used?"

"She didn't tell me. But when I called her Laura, she said I must have mistaken her for somebody else."

We were standing in the middle of the room facing one another like duelists. The guy looked more frail than at the beginning of our conversation. He was slight, a little rodent of a man, smelling increasingly of cold sweat.

"By the way, what is your name?" I asked with a smile, attempting to ease the situation.

"You can call me Al."

"Paul Simon fan, huh?"

But Al's unknowing stare told me he wasn't.

He stepped toward one of the metal cabinets and unlocked it.

Handguns were hanging at the back of the locker. I felt the urge to run for the door. But then Al pulled out an empty leather holster and held it for me to look at. It was made from shiny brown leather, obviously well taken care of, and embroidered with thin, lighter colored leather bands. "Laura gave me this once," Al explained. "For my birthday."

The embroidery read: *No. 1 Cowboy.*

"She was only fourteen. Spent her allowance on it."

The holster showed that Laura had not only been an angry, sullen teenager, but she also possessed a sweet, loving side.

"And she never even gave you a hint what made her so angry?" I tried my luck once more.

Al shook his head in contemplation. "She did look different when I saw her last," he finally said. "Not just older."

I was wondering if it hadn't been Laura after all whom he had seen.

"It was her," Al said, piercing my forehead with his little black eyes. "But her face was somehow crooked. You can't see it in the picture because it shows her in profile. Her right side was different from her left. Just a bit. As if it was lower than the other side, you know what I mean? The eyelid coming down a bit more. The mouth also."

A stroke? I wondered. It almost sounded like the effects of one. That would possibly also explain Laura's bad results at shooting.

"And she had this scar. I only caught a glimpse of it. When she pushed back her hair to aim. It was right at the hairline. A pretty long, nasty, red thing."

The scar could have stemmed from brain surgery. Maybe she had an aneurysm removed. Maybe there had been another source of hemorrhaging of the brain. There were many possible reasons for such a surgery. And all of them could have caused the facial asymmetry described by Laura's old coach. I wanted to ask Marge Cunningham if she had noticed any of these symptoms. And why she hadn't mentioned them to me if she had.

But I had one more question for Al. "Is there any way I could find out which name she used? Did you see her talk to anybody else on the range?"

He remained silent for almost a minute, his face motionless, as if in deep meditation or near coma. Then he said, "Maybe."

He led me back to the front desk.

"Look up who checked in November twenty-second last year between two and six p.m.," he ordered the red-haired girl who was watching a video on her iPod.

The girl looked questioningly at me, and I gave her a nod of encouragement. Al didn't seem to have any administrative authority over her, but he clearly made up for it with his fear-inducing air.

He looked over the girl's shoulder while she operated the computer. When she had opened the file he was looking for, he moved his lips as if talking to himself.

"I don't think it was Lynn Crooper. I'm pretty sure I know her," he finally mumbled. "The only female name on the list I don't recognize is Rosanna McQueen."

"Thank you very much," I said with sincerity.

Al merely nodded and walked toward the door we had just come through. I recalled that he had wanted to get something from his car and then continue his shooting practice. Well, he must have changed his plans. Before he vanished back into the dark halls I said, "How come you remember exactly the date you saw her?"

"It was my birthday," he answered in his drill sergeant voice and left.

Chapter 15

The last light of the day had died, and the parking lot lay in deep darkness. I turned on my cell phone to call a cab. The display lit up and a sharp beep sounded. I had received two voicemails. The first one was from Martha. "Hey, chicky, I found three Laura Cunninghams who lived in and around Asheville in the last decade. But none fits our Laura. Two are much older, and the one I talked to on the phone was happy and alive. Oh, speaking about alive, the Belize woman is still with us. She's in the prison ward at Aldridge hospital. As you suspected, she had a heart attack, but she's stable now. Call me later."

She was still alive! The news lifted a load off my heart that had been heavier than I would have liked to admit even to myself. And the relief stemmed from more than professional interest in knowing an integral witness to my case was still there.

The second message came from Marge Cunningham, and it

had been received ten minutes ago. "It's five minutes past our agreed time. Call me immediately."

It was a quarter past six now. My client had asked me to call her at six every evening. I had told her I couldn't promise such an exact time. Once again I was wondering if I should just let her wait a bit longer, just for the fun of it, and once more I decided against playing games, reminding myself that she paid well and was entitled to her eccentricities.

There was a bench at the far end of the parking lot, next to a lone weak streetlight, and I sat down and dialed my client's number. She picked up after the first ring. She only said, "Good to hear from you. Where are you?"

I told her and also reported many of the other events of the day. Well, the version I wanted her to know. I didn't mention Lucy's distress, and also left out Inez Belize's breakdown. Somehow it seemed obscene that Laura's mother would possibly be happy about Inez's heart attack.

Mainly I reported that Laura had probably lived in Asheville before she had come to San Francisco, and that I had learned from her old shooting coach, Al, that she had at one point used the name Rosanna McQueen.

"Asheville, North Carolina?"

"I'm not sure. But that's the most known one, isn't it?"

I informed my client that I might have to go there if it turned out Laura had really lived in the South.

"You can go tomorrow. Sundays are good travel days. I'll book you a flight. I have a myriad of air miles. You just have to pick up the ticket at the airport. I can get you a rental car and a hotel room, too."

Whoa.

"Maybe I should look into it some more," I finally said. "Make sure that the lead is really hot."

"Call me as soon as you know."

It felt weird that Mrs. Cunningham wanted to take over my

travel arrangements. But there was probably not much I could do if I didn't want to pay for the trip out of my own pocket. Her suggestion had caught me off guard, and I had forgotten to ask her about Laura's scar. Begrudgingly, I pressed the redial button.

"I realized her face was different," Laura's mother said. "But when I asked her, she just waved it off, said she'd had a dentist appointment in the morning and those were still the effects of the anesthetics."

"You didn't see a scar at her hairline?"

"No. She was wearing long bangs, and her hair looked perfect. Do you think she could have been seriously ill?"

Laura's mother sounded worried about this idea but also somewhat relieved. Maybe she felt that a brain injury would be some kind of explanation for all the heartbreak Laura had put her through.

"Hopefully, I'll find out," I said.

My next calls went to a number of cab companies. Most lines were busy. The one where I got through wanted to know the exact address of where I needed to be picked up. On a bench next to a streetlight under an oak tree in Golden Gate Park didn't qualify, obviously, and the dispatcher had never heard of the shooting range in the park.

I wandered back in the direction of the range's entrance in order to find out the official street address. But when I passed the driveway to the parking lot, I decided to walk down the street which would lead to the park's exit. Again, there was not a soul anywhere near, and the natural darkness of the surroundings made me feel invisible and safe.

Apart from the occasional car slowly driving by, I didn't encounter anybody on the way. Everything was strangely quiet. I missed the sounds of animals, an owl's cry or just the shuffle of a mouse's little feet. But the fog sucked up every noise, even muffled the sound of my own steps on the damp pavement.

I finally exited the park close to Irving and 9th Avenue and realized I had made a long detour. At least it had led me to a lively neighborhood full of cafes and small restaurants. I needed food. But I needed caffeine more, so I stepped into a big coffee shop right across from the park which beckoned with its colorful artwork visible through the glass front.

I ordered a quadruple espresso and earned a broad smile from the boy behind the counter who looked like he had materialized from one of the blown-up Manga panels hanging on the wall behind him. "My grandmother had a quadruple bypass," he teased me.

"I'm working on it." I grinned back, carried my cup to a table and became one of the many people in this place who were sitting by themselves bending over their laptops.

An online search for *Ashville* told me that there was a city of that name in Alabama, as well as in Ohio. Both were too small to ever have hosted any type of bigger conference. My search engine graciously informed me, though, that I was probably looking for *Asheville*, and after I had corrected the spelling error, it turned out that the city in North Carolina Marge Cunningham and I had thought of was probably the right one. It had a well-known university, all kinds of sights and a convention center.

I checked the phone book as well as a few other online address directories for a Rosanna McQueen in the Asheville area. There was none. Also no McQueen with any other first name. In all of North Carolina there was no Rosanna McQueen. But then these were current listings. If Laura had lived there until approximately two years ago under this name, it would be hard to find a listing at all. I would need old phone books, assuming she even had her number listed. Considering how thoroughly she had orchestrated her disappearance, it seemed futile to expect I would just find her alias in some public database.

To channel these frustrating thoughts, I clicked around some more and performed a search for Rosanna McQueen in all of the

United States, and got one hit, right here in San Francisco.

At first this puzzled me. But then an idea escaped from my entangled thoughts like a little firefly. I typed in the name Lynn Crooper, and the only hit I received was in Asheville, North Carolina, 24 Mountain Road.

Just for fun I Googled Lynn Cooper and quickly realized why the name Lynn Crooper had rung familiar for Al. There were over four million hits for the first name variation, many of them for a popular Christian singer-songwriter.

Nobody picked up at Lynn Crooper's number, not even an answering machine. After the thirtieth ring, I pressed the disconnect button on my cell phone and pondered the implications of my finding. It was still a long shot, but I finally decided it was the best I had. So I called Marge Cunningham, told her that Laura's alias had probably not been Rosanna McQueen but Lynn Crooper, and that I would indeed like to travel to Asheville the next day. She said she'd have her assistant arrange my trip. I looked at my watch. It was 7:44 p.m. Mrs. Cunningham must have a very diligent assistant. Or maybe the foundation had administrative personnel on weekend late night shifts.

Then I spoke to Martha and let her know about my plans. She agreed with me that it was worth a try, especially as my trip would not impoverish our client. The alternative would be to contact a PI firm in Asheville and ask them for assistance, which would make Martha and me lose money and not necessarily save Marge Cunningham much. And to pursue the lead just from here, to look for possible neighbors whom we would have to reach and ask for information about Lynn Crooper, would prolong the proceedings and probably not lead to conclusive results.

Travel fever, together with the last big sips from my espresso, let my stomach dance a little, and it was clear it was a hungry dance. Raw fish sounded like a great way to stuff the beast, and I remembered there was a good sushi place just across the street.

When I stepped outside, the mist had become even denser. It

had assumed the thick, opaque quality of fog I was used to from Europe and which hardly ever occurred here. San Francisco fog usually comes in high and hovers like a cloud cover just above your head. But now I could hardly see the cars driving by on the street next to the sidewalk. Only their headlights shone through the mist—the eyes of melancholy ghosts.

I missed the entrance to the sushi restaurant. Not until I reached the next street corner did I realize I had walked too far, and I turned around. I wouldn't have noticed the car had it not performed a strange maneuver. There it was, a few yards down, halfway pulled out to the street, turning its headlights on just now. As I came closer, it turned its lights off again and moved back into its parking spot. I gave the dark blue truck a close look—particularly its license plate. Then I stepped around it and approached the driver's door.

"It's hard to shadow somebody who's on foot when you're in a truck," I said after I had pulled open the door.

It was a stupid thing to do. The person inside could have had a gun. But most of the time we don't survive because we are particularly smart, or well-armed, or careful, but because we are lucky. The woman who was staring back at me from inside the truck didn't point a gun at me. She looked somewhat surprised. Not too much, though. I knew her. I just couldn't tell from where.

"Why are you surveilling me? Who gave you the job?"

"Nobody," she quickly said.

As if I had caught her naked, she grabbed a hat which was lying next to her and put it on her head. She had pretty hair with long blond curls. Her face was even with high cheekbones, smooth skin—pretty but rather boring had it not been for her eyes. They were either pale blue or pale green—it was hard for me to say in this light—and quite big. But most of all, she was cross-eyed. Her right eye went in a different direction than her left, which was now focusing on me. I finally recognized her.

"You were at the bar last night," I said. She was the woman who had reminded me of the Statue of Liberty in a cowgirl outfit.

She nodded.

"Why are you following me?" I repeated my question.

"Because you're cute."

"Bullshit," I answered.

"You *are* cute."

"And that's why you've been shadowing me all day?" I asked incredulously. "Anyhow, how did you find me here? I was pretty sure I'd managed to lose you on Mission."

"You went down to BART. There were only two directions you could have gone. I took my chances and spotted you back on Market Street."

A car whose driver had overlooked her opened door drove by and almost hit me, and I had to step closer to her.

"Do you like sushi?" I asked the woman.

"Sure. If it's not raw."

For me there is no real purpose in eating cooked sushi, but, of course, she was entitled to her taste. We entered the restaurant, were placed at a small table for two, and before we even ordered, I had to ask her another question that still bugged me. "So what was your plan? To just follow me around and get a kick out of knowing where I went?"

"You did go to strange places."

"When did you start trailing me?"

"Last night. When you and your friend left the bar."

"And you waited in front of my house all night long?"

"No, after I knew where you lived I went home."

"And came back early in the morning?" It was just too ridiculous that this woman had decided to waste her Saturday by following me around.

"I came back at noon. Figured you wouldn't be up so early after what you drank last night. You lovesick or something?"

Wow. Did I have it tattooed on my forehead for every weird stranger to read? But I was relieved she had at least not followed me to the prison. My fledgling PI honor would have suffered learning that she'd been behind me for such a long trip without me noticing it.

The waiter came, and I absentmindedly ordered a spicy tuna roll and a few pieces of uni nigiri. I love uni, sea urchin. Although it's somewhat sad to think about the prickly, dangerous shell this creature has developed through millennia of evolution just to have its soft insides slurped up by me after all. Evolution should have made it less tasty.

The cowgirl ordered an unagi, a vegetable roll and a seaweed salad on the side.

"So what else have you learned about me today?" I asked. Who knew? Maybe she was even private eye material. Or maybe she was already one herself. But then who would hire another PI to shadow me, and one who let herself get caught as quickly as this one to begin with?

"I know that you have a friend in the Excelsior who has a small child and that you probably like shooting practice."

"That's all?"

"That's all. But why do you want to know, anyway? It's not as if I wanted to spy on you."

Now I was really incredulous. "But what was the whole thing about then?"

"I just wanted to see which bar or pub or restaurant or whatever you'd maybe go to tonight. So that I could show up as if by coincidence and get a chance to chat with you before you got as wasted as yesterday."

"Why not just go back to the Valencia Bar and wait for me?"

"I never saw you there before, and I didn't want to take a chance."

Our food arrived, and I let the information sink in while I swallowed the first piece. This woman was really something else.

But I had to give it to her. She didn't spare herself the trouble when she wanted to meet somebody.

"So tell me about yourself," I finally said. "First of all, what's your name? I'm Anna."

"Jasmine."

"Beautiful name."

"Thanks," she replied with a smile. It was sweet but also somewhat weird. As if she was very pleased with herself. Well, she had achieved her goal for today. Here we were, having dinner together. The oddest first date I ever had.

I didn't want to reveal too much about my life to this stranger, so I wasn't sure what to talk about, but we managed to chat easily for the next half hour. It was one of those conversations where in the end it's hard to say what it was about, but it had been fun. Jasmine told me she was from Minnesota and that it got so cold there in the winter you ended up with icicles under your nose. I talked about Germany and how people wore beer glasses around their necks in weird crocheted contraptions during Carnival in Cologne.

"Are the glasses full or empty?" Jasmine asked.

"First full, then empty, then probably smashed."

"Just like their owners, huh?"

We left the restaurant giggling, and Jasmine asked me if I wanted to have a drink somewhere. I knew it was not a good idea. I had to try to call Lynn Crooper's number another few times tonight to make sure I hadn't just missed her. That was, of course, no guarantee that it was really Laura's place, but it was the best I could do. And I had to get ready for the trip.

But that wasn't all. As Jasmine and I were facing each other in the fresh air, the intuition that I'd had about her from the moment I first saw her got a chance to grow. She was in her own way endearing, sure. And she seemed perfectly friendly, albeit quirky. But I'm seriously quirky myself, as Mido liked to tell me more than once, knowing full well that she was a distinguished member of the quirky tribe, too.

But there was something else about this cowgirl. There was mockery behind her features. I like mockery, I like teasing. But Jasmine's was different. She gave me the feeling she knew something I didn't know, and was oh so secretly making fun of me, while at the same time she couldn't help herself but let me feel that she was playing with me. I'm not into this kind of power game. On a certain level Jasmine seemed unstable, and I had the strong impulse to run away from her. Or was I the unstable one? Anyhow, right now I didn't want to hang out with this woman.

"Sorry," I said. "I have stuff to do tonight. It was great talking to you, but I think we should leave it at that."

"Sure," Jasmine said, unfazed. "But let me give you a ride. That's the least I can do after you took me out."

I had paid for our dinner. It had been my suggestion, after all. She seemed very intent on driving me home now, and since she already knew where I lived, I finally agreed.

In the truck, Jasmine continued to chat. She didn't seem to notice or care that I had fallen silent. In front of my house I wanted to jump out of the Dodge, but she spotted a parking space almost in front of the door and began to pull in.

"That's not necessary—" I protested.

"Come on," Jasmine said. "It was such a fun evening. Let's just talk a bit in the truck."

Then she turned off the motor, leaned over to me and gave me a light but long kiss on the ear.

She smelled a bit like the eel she had just eaten, but also of rose shampoo and sandalwood cream. Her beautiful silken hair brushed my cheek, and I turned my face to her. I'd like to say in an attempt to talk sense into her, but when her lips fully embraced mine, I responded to them quickly.

The human heart is unpredictable and fickle. Lust is its playful sister, and Jasmine was an incredible kisser. Her lips were like gentle hands cradling my mouth, the tip of my nose, my cheeks, my chin, and then they moved back to my mouth, from the corner inward until I opened it and let her moist warm lips enter, and finally her muscular, salty tongue.

My hands wandered down her shoulder blades. They were unusually strong and broad. Her fingers did something to the nape of my neck, and I could feel cool liquid trickle from between my legs. I sighed.

Jasmine giggled. Then whispered, "I knew I'd get you."

These words broke the spell. I pulled myself away from her, opened the passenger door and jumped out of the truck, which was so high my knee protested with an angry shot of pain.

Jasmine didn't follow me. When I reached the door to my building, I turned around, but again I couldn't make her out behind the tinted windows of her truck.

Chapter 16

Martha must have seen the light come on in my apartment. I had just closed the door behind me when the phone rang.

"I have something for you, chicky. You want to pick it up or shall I bring it over?"

"What is it?"

"A little surprise."

Martha wasn't in the habit of surprising me with unexpected gifts, so it had to be work-related. And I could tell she was dying to show me whatever it was she had found.

"Did you manage to get a hold of Laura's manuscript?" I asked.

"Not quite as good, but you'll like it, too."

I could have begged her to tell me what it was. Or I could have rushed over to the office to retrieve it. But I sometimes need my fun as well. So I said nonchalantly, "Just leave it on the desk. I'll pick it up in the morning. Or does it have anything to do with my trip?"

"No."

Even though she tried to suppress it, it was clear that my partner was disappointed. Maybe I would let her dangle for just a little bit, and go to the office later tonight.

For now I needed a shower. Then I called Lynn Crooper's number again—again without success. My own phone rang once more. It was Mrs. Cunningham herself, informing me that her assistant had booked me on a flight to Atlanta with connection to Asheville for eight o'clock the next morning. A Hertz rental car would be waiting for me at the airport, and a room was reserved at the downtown Marriott. I began to pack, needing to keep busy.

I had escaped from the cowgirl's truck. But the image of her smug little smile still made me cringe. And the warm softness of her lips was burning up my own mouth. I had run from her because of the triumph she displayed when she thought she had won, had gained control. But I also had to run because when I had closed my eyes, enjoying the kiss, all of a sudden Mido's small, fine boned face and her dimpled smile had appeared before me.

I gave up, unpacked my laptop, let it connect to the wireless router I had set up in the apartment, and sent my lost love an e-mail. *How are you?* I quickly typed. *How is your daughter? Anna.*

I clicked the *Send* button before I could change my mind, and sat in front of the computer with my face buried in my hands for a long time. I didn't expect or even hope for a quick answer. But I was just too heavy to move. The beeping of the cell phone startled me out of my depressed contemplation. I picked up the phone and pressed the receive button. "Hello!"

At first there was no response. Then I heard a low breathing—not the nasty, fast breathing of a lewd call. It sounded delicate, interrupted by somebody clearing his throat. There was also a suppressed sob.

"Who's there?" I asked.

Then the connection was broken.

I studied the little screen of my cell phone, trying to find out the caller's number. But caller ID had been disabled by the owner of the other line. When I punched *69 a phone rang, but nobody picked up.

Finally, it was almost midnight. I left my position on the couch, made it to bed, and quickly sank into the sweet unconsciousness of sleep. The first thing on my mind when I woke up to the beeping of the alarm five and a half hours later was Martha's mystery finding. The curiosity I couldn't muster the night before had me in its happy grip now.

I showered, donned comfortable travel clothes—a pair of wide black corduroys, and a long-sleeved blue T-shirt—and applied a self-adhesive matching blue eye pad over the orbit of my missing eye. The dry air on planes can make it uncomfortable to wear an artificial eye. I was already carrying my duffle bag over one shoulder and my laptop case over the other when I passed by the office. There was a green, bleached-out looking folder on the desk.

Hi, chicky, read a yellow Post-it note on top. *This material is confidential. Maybe it can clarify a few things for you.*

Inside the folder were color photographs, together with a few pages of computer printouts. The picture on top showed a knife. Red stains covered its blade and most of the handle. Next to it lay a piece of plastic with the number one on it. I looked through the other photographs. There were more of the knife. But then came those of Laura, dead, and twisted into a position that made her look as if all limbs had been pulled from their sockets. She was lying in puddles of blood which spread around her like a distorted lacquer painting of her mangled body. Martha had managed to get a hold of the crime scene pictures.

I quickly closed the folder and stuffed it in my bag. I would take a closer look at its contents later. I had to rush to the airport. There was not enough time left to take BART, so I flagged the next cab passing by on Geary and made it to SFO in half an hour. My ticket was indeed waiting for me at the Delta domestic counter, and after I had checked in, I had time for a quick breakfast.

There was only one place close by that was open at this hour, a mix of sports bar and fast food restaurant. The few tables were taken, so I slid onto a barstool at the counter. Other patrons were sitting close by. I was burning to open the folder again. I knew how gruesome the images were, but the first glimpse had left me with the sense that they contained a secret. I didn't want anybody to sneak a peek at the pictures, though, so I had to contain my impatience for the moment. Once my breakfast of bacon and three eggs over easy arrived, I was glad I hadn't just refreshed my memory of the photos. Instead I stared at the TV hanging from the ceiling.

The news was on. Reports of car bombs in Iraq. Three American soldiers had died last night. And then the local news. A man had been shot dead in Golden Gate Park. The police suspected it was a mugging gone bad. The victim had been seventy-two-year-old Albert Burns of San Francisco. He had been killed in the parking lot of a shooting range. His body had been found by patrons of the range who had walked to their cars after practice. Because of the shots fired from the range, nobody had noticed the shooting in the lot. Mr. Burns had been shot twice, once in the abdomen, once in the neck, sometime between six fifteen and seven o'clock Saturday evening. His wallet was lying next to his body, cash and credit cards gone. Witnesses to the crime were asked to contact the police.

The picture of Albert Burns showed a much younger man than the one I had met the day before, but it was Al. There was no doubt. In the picture, he had fewer wrinkles, but the same tightly set black eyes that looked like the tips of cold cigarette stubs.

So he had walked out to the parking lot to get from his car whatever it was he wanted in the first place. Before he had met me and been interrupted.

I made a quick calculation. I had called Marge Cunningham at six fifteen, had left the lot approximately twenty minutes later. Nobody had been in sight. In my sight, anyway. There were endless possibilities for a mugger to hide in the bushes around the lot or between the cars, or even in a car. But wouldn't a possible attacker have tried to mug me first? I must have made quite a tempting target, sitting alone on a bench, then walking off into the dark. So the perp must have arrived only after I had left. That meant there was a window of about twenty-five minutes before Al's body was discovered.

Was I a witness who probably had something to tell the police? I hadn't seen anything. But I knew the officers would have a lot of questions for me when they found out I had been one of the last people to talk to the victim, and if I gave them a call now, I would have to postpone the trip. I hadn't given the girl from the range my name, but she had other information that would lead diligent police officers to me. I would worry about that when it was time. For now I could only hope somebody or something else would lead them to Al's killer.

I hardly touched my breakfast. My stomach was in knots. It was time to board, and I walked down a very long hallway to the gate. Had I really come that close to my own death the night before? Or was there some kind of master plan? Had it been Al's turn to die and was the mugger just some sort of cosmic tool to get him? Unfortunately, I didn't believe in cosmic tools all that much, which left me with the troubling idea that I had merely been luckier than the old guy. Al had most likely fallen victim to a random, albeit particularly brutal, junkie, delirious for the next fix. I couldn't tell what made me shiver more, the fact that I had so closely escaped the ultimately unpreventable dive into darkness, or that a man I had talked to just last night, and who had been his very alive, grumpy self, was now gone, just like that. I was deep in thought, and only when the plane was slowly taxiing toward the runway did I realize I had the whole row to myself. That meant I would be able to finally look at the contents of the folder without freaking out a seat neighbor. Only later, when I talked to Martha about this folder did I learn it was called a murder book, and that one of her buddies at the homicide department had given it to her at her request. As the case had been an open-and-shut one, it hadn't cost Martha much convincing. She had declared to the detective that she needed it for educational purposes to teach her apprentice a lesson.

And I was learning my lesson with every second I spent with the material in the book. Hanging in the sky, thirty thousand feet above the ground, I realized once again that even when we think we walk on firm ground, even when our heart is beating strong and steady, we are still just little spiders anyone can step on and squish at any moment. What I didn't learn from the pictures or the police report was how to accept that Inez Belize was Laura's murderer. Actually, while Martha had intended to convince me of Inez's guilt, she had achieved just the opposite. After I had looked at each photo for as long as I could bear it, I was even more inclined to believe that Inez hadn't killed Laura—and neither had her father, even though Inez possibly thought he did. I couldn't come up with any other reason why she would take the blame for her lover's murder.

The police photographer had done a good job, much better than the other crime scene experts. The pictures were clear and comprehensive, and they told their own story. I would have to do some more research, piece things together, fill in gaps, ask the right questions, but I was hopeful that with the help of the photos, Inez's case could be reopened.

In her confession, Inez had claimed she'd been in the kitchen cutting vegetables for dinner when she saw Laura come home.

Inez also said that she left the house carrying the knife she was using with her and met her partner in their front yard, where she stabbed Laura. The picture of the murder weapon did show a blood-smeared knife. But what professional chef like Inez would cut her vegetables with a hunting knife with a gut hook? This was the weapon depicted.

The pictures of the kitchen showed the veggies—some bell peppers and a zucchini—lying partly sliced on the counter. Next to them lay yet another knife, a small paring knife. Again not a knife a professional chef would use to cut up her ingredients. And she wouldn't cut them into such crude, irregular shapes as the veggies on the photo.

The murder weapon, whose handle was so covered in blood that the camouflage pattern it bore was hardly visible, didn't have barriers to protect your hands from slipping onto the blade if you brutally stabbed somebody with it over and over. It was meant to be used to slice open the belly of a dead deer and pull out its intestines. Not a particularly cultivated task in itself, but a much less bloody one. Ideally, the prey had already been drained before it was gutted. So Martha had been right. The murderer's hands had probably slipped off the handle down onto the blade and cut his own palms.

And here lay the main inconsistency of my reasoning, which was still fed by intuition, a certain common sense and very weak evidence. Assuming Inez hadn't killed Laura, then where did the scars on her hands come from? Her father's palms had been uninjured. I had seen them when I had visited him. Had he snapped, after all, and stabbed Laura in some sort of Alzheimer-related psychotic episode, it wasn't very likely that he would have put on gloves first to protect his hands. But if Inez was indeed not the killer, maybe the real murderer's DNA could still be isolated from the trace on the knife—if the police had preserved it as evidence, and if she'd be willing to revoke her confession.

The manner in which Laura had been murdered was an

incredibly personal one, another reason why the cops had accepted Inez as the killer immediately. But if it hadn't been Inez or her father, then who had done it? Who had been so close to Laura, so infuriated by her, that he had not only killed her, but cut her to pieces, virtually destroyed her?

As soon as the plane had touched down in Atlanta, four and a half hours later, and I was allowed to use my cell phone again, I called Martha.

"And has it enlightened you?" she asked after I told her I had already looked through the folder.

"It has," I said honestly.

"Good."

I wasn't ready to tell Martha that the pictures she had given me in order to convince me of Inez's guilt had in fact done exactly the opposite.

"Can you do me another favor?"

"Any time." Martha clearly sounded elated thinking she had pulled me onto her hard-boiled, seen-it-all, former homicide detective side.

"I need to speak to Inez Belize again. Do you think you can find out when she will be ready to have a visitor?"

"Why don't we just wait and see what you'll find in Asheville? The case may be solved once you've discovered Laura's manuscript all neatly typed and lying on the desk in her apartment there."

"You must be kidding. Life is never that easy."

"Sometimes it is. Like when you have a murderer who confessed without pressure and never tried to revoke her confession."

"So you won't help me."

"I'll always help you, chicky. You know that."

Chapter 17

It was already late afternoon when I picked up the car in Asheville. The flight from Atlanta had only lasted forty-five minutes, but the time difference had eaten up three hours of my day. Filling out the rental car forms swallowed another half hour, and when I finally checked in at the Marriott, it was already seven p.m. But I was eager to take a look at 24 Mountain Road, and the evening darkness was just what I needed.

I dropped off my things in the hotel room, picked up a map at the front desk, studied it inside the rental—a small white Honda—and quickly found what I was looking for. Mountain Road hit the fringes of downtown Asheville and then led in the direction of the surrounding Blue Ridge Mountains. I had only caught a glimpse of the gorgeous Appalachians from the window of the plane, but I looked forward to getting a better view in the morning.

Mountain Road itself wasn't hilly at all. It was a winding street, bordered by houses made of gray rock. Number 24 had four floors and no front yard. The neighborhood looked like it could have once been working class, but had somehow lost all sense of belonging, and was now just a faceless habitat. There were new-looking medium sized sedans parked along the street, as well as dirt-crusted pickups.

Four brass mailboxes were attached to the wall near the front door of the building. One of the names read *Crooper*. The mailbox was empty. The position of the bell button indicated that Ms. Crooper's apartment was on the top floor of the building. No lights were visible behind the windows. I pressed the button. Nothing happened. I rang the bell another time, and another, and finally held my finger on it for twenty seconds. Only then was I convinced that nobody was there.

On the second floor, light shone from behind yellow curtains. The name tag for this unit read *Delaney*. I rang the bell.

A window opened right above my head, and a man's voice sounded, "What's up?"

I tried to make out the guy's features, but there was only a silhouette. "Do you know Lynn Crooper?"

"She's not here. She's on a trip."

"When was the last time you saw her?"

"You're a cop? Something happened to her?"

"I'm here on a family matter. I just want to make sure this is really her apartment. Can you take a quick look at a picture?"

"I'll be right down."

The man who came out the door a few seconds later looked like a soldier. He was not wearing a uniform, but his whole appearance, from the shaved black scalp to the upright posture and the way he scrutinized me with polite but somewhat exaggerated self-confidence, spelled military to me.

I showed him Laura's picture, and he confirmed that, yes, this woman was Lynn Crooper, his neighbor.

"I'll have to enter her apartment," I said. "She has passed away, and her family has employed me to take care of her matters. Can you tell me where I can find the landlord?"

"Wait a sec."

The man disappeared into the house and reappeared with a little notebook. "You have something to write?"

I copied the number and address of a housing agency in Asheville.

"One more question," I said. "Do you know who has been emptying the mailbox since she was gone?"

"No idea."

I thanked the guy and wished him good-bye.

"Tell her family I'm very sorry," he answered. "I didn't really know her, but it's always bad when somebody passes away too young. Especially a fellow veteran."

Laura had been a military veteran? Back in the car I whispered, "You never cease to amaze me," to her spirit that seemed to hover very closely right then. Although Laura was dead, she became more vivid to me every day that I was following the elusive threads of her life.

For tonight I had done all that I could. I wasn't planning to call the rental agency, Singer and Partners, and deal with all the paperwork they would probably ask me to submit—a letter from Mrs. Cunningham, Laura's death certificate, and so on—before they would hand me a key or grant permission to enter the place. And how could I even prove to them that Laura Cunningham was really their tenant Lynn Crooper? Now that I was certain that Laura and Lynn had been the same person, I had no inhibitions against entering her place. The easiest thing would be to come back the next day with a few tools. If any of the neighbors asked me what I was doing, I'd tell them I had already called Singer and Partners. I hoped everybody would be at work on a Monday morning anyway.

Asheville had a busy downtown area with restaurants and cafes that reminded me of San Francisco. There were vegetarian places, sushi joints and coffee shops overflowing with crowds that looked like a mix of university students, aging hippies and tourists. Singer and Partners had their office next to a tiny Italian place, where I ordered a dish of spaghetti putanesca. I finished the meal with a cappuccino at a pastry place next door, collected a number of flyers and free papers on Asheville culture, made sure my little digital camera was ready to go and snapped a few pictures of the surrounding buildings. The rental agency kindly had its logo displayed on its door, and I managed to get a good shot of it.

Back at the hotel I asked the receptionist if there was a place where I could print out a few documents.

Yes, they had a printer I could use in their business center. I had taken the pictures of the Singer and Partners logo just in case. But, of course, it hadn't even been necessary. The rental company had a beautiful Web site, and I could easily piece together a letterhead by using the JPEG image of their logo. Now I only needed to compose a few lines allowing Ms. Anna Spring to enter the late Ms. Lynn Crooper's apartment at 24 Mountain Road in Asheville, NC 28804 on behalf of her mother, Marge Cunningham, and I was prepared for a nosy neighbor demanding to see my credentials.

Before disconnecting the computer, I quickly checked my e-mail. Rita had sent me a sweet message saying that she always enjoyed hanging out with me. I wondered if she was referring to the part of our get-together where I had gotten senselessly drunk, or the next day when I made her drive me to a state prison. She was really a treasure of a friend, and I quickly mailed her back. The e-mail from Mido I had secretly hoped for had of course not arrived.

I was back at the gray building the next morning at nine o'clock hoping that all the tenants who had a day job would have left by now. The front door was easy to open. It had an old-fashioned, single bolt lock that was no match for my credit card. Martha had given me intensive lock picking training. Cops are not necessarily great at opening doors without damage, but lock picking was one of Martha's favorite hobbies, and she had been delighted to show me her tricks. A major lesson of the course had been that there are many locks which are impossible to pick even for the most advanced burglar or private lock buster.

The lock on Laura's apartment door belonged in this category, unfortunately. She had an up-to-date security lock installed, with a high-end cylinder aligned with the door. My heart stopped for a moment when I saw it. The quality of the cylinder indicated there was also metal paneling inside the door and multiple bolts. To break into such a door, you practically need a hand grenade. But these contraptions were expensive, and many people went for the cheaper, fake ones. I would only know after drilling off the lock, and so I began to drill away filled with dread over the possible futility of my efforts.

But once again Laura's ghost was on my side. Nobody came to find out who was creating a ruckus in the stairway of their apartment building, and after some more drilling and a few jerks with my handy crowbar, the lock panel came off, the cylinder gave way to my prying, and it turned out Lynn Crooper, alias Laura Cunningham, had gone for the make-believe version of the medieval fortress door.

I had also purchased a few new lock cylinders of different sizes, one of which I inserted before I reattached the panel. Now the keys to this castle were mine. I slipped into the apartment, closed and locked the door behind me and inhaled deeply.

I was standing in a spacious studio. My quick tour of the place revealed that there was a small bathroom, and otherwise all amenities were to be found in the huge main room. A kitchen corner was separated by a breakfast counter. Behind a wooden screen stood a queen-sized futon bed, and the center of the room was occupied by a large orange armchair and a TV. A thin layer of dust covered everything. The air smelled dusty as well but otherwise not bad. There was not much decoration in the room. Its most enticing feature was the large window front facing the mountains. The windows were dirty. Many rainfalls had left a gray, streaky film on the outside, but that couldn't diminish the beauty of the scenery outside. The trees on the steep hillsides had just acquired a light green hue, and in the morning sun, still covered with dew and veiled by the faintest mist, they were glowing in such primeval bliss that I almost gasped.

I had to tear myself away from the view to start searching the place systematically. There was one bookshelf and a wide chest of drawers. The drawers contained bed sheets, a small assortment of women's underwear, socks, a few T-shirts, four pairs of jeans and three wool sweaters. A green down jacket hung on a hook attached to the wall. Underneath were a pair of hiking boots and a pair of sneakers. On the shelf stood a little collection of mystery novels, a few lesbian classics—*Desert of the Heart, An Emergence of Green*—and a number of videotapes. They were store-bought movies, *Shrek, Monsters, Inc.* and a few romantic comedies.

I took a closer look at the clothes. The shoes were particularly peculiar. The sneakers were at least five sizes larger than the hiking boots. The jacket would have fit me, but when I compared the sizes of the jeans, it turned out that two pair were 30 inches long and 31 inches wide, and the other two pair 30 inches long and 36 inches wide. Had Laura undergone rapid weight changes? But that wouldn't have affected her shoe size. Or had Inez come here with her? The sneakers were at least size fourteen. Inez was tall, but I was pretty sure her feet were not that big.

I tried to imagine what Laura had used this apartment for. Inez had said that Laura had worked at a coffee shop when they had met. The man from last night had mentioned she was a veteran. The last one and a half years of her life, Laura lived in San Francisco, at least mostly. Had she come to Asheville often, to her old place, maybe to go hiking in the mountains for a few days? The apartment did have the feel of a vacation home—somewhere that isn't the center of your life, but where you keep a few things for the weekends and holidays that you spend there. But why had Inez not mentioned it when I spoke to her about Laura's belongings during my first visit? Did she even know Laura had kept the apartment after they had moved in together? And if Inez hadn't come here with her, to whom did the other clothes belong?

The bathroom was almost empty apart from an old piece of soap lying by the shower and two toothbrushes by the sink. There was no drawer or cabinet here, and on the only shelf lay three neatly folded green facecloths and two bath towels.

My search of the kitchen revealed equally nondescript items. There were pots and pans, a few pretty yellow plates and mugs, some old looking packages of salt and pepper and mixed herbs, and a drawer filled with silverware. The fridge was almost empty apart from a container of ground coffee, which smelled like wet sand, a pack of teabags still in its cellophane wrapping, some sweetened condensed milk and three Styrofoam cups of dry instant noodle soup. Just enough to fix yourself a hot drink and a snack when you arrived here at night after a long flight.

A boom box sat in the corner of the kitchen counter next to a coffeemaker. The tape in the recorder was homemade, and its label read: *Mix from Stu.*

When I pressed the play button, sweet jazz music sounded, a Cole Porter song.

There was a telephone but no answering machine. I picked up the receiver, caught a busy signal, the sign that a digital voice-mail system had recorded a message. When I called Lynn Crooper's number from this phone, an electronic voice asked me to enter my pin. I tried a few combinations, the first digits of the phone number, Laura's birth date. Each time the system told me I had the wrong pin, and finally I gave up.

I began to take pictures of the apartment. Sometimes looking through the viewfinder of a camera lets you discover details you haven't noticed before. Was there a loose edge to the carpet? I tried to poke at it, but it only came up an inch. The rest was tightly glued to the floor. I searched and searched but couldn't detect anything in any of the usual secret hiding places: toilet water tank, under the mattress. I looked for a second bottom to a drawer and inside the stove. I even studied the ceiling inside the apartment and outside on the landing. The structure of the house indicated there was an attic, but I couldn't find a door leading to it.

Finally, I played each of the videotapes in fast forward to see if there was anything on them apart from the movies they claimed to contain. My efforts were in vain. None of the cassettes had a secret message on them.

After that I took the books out of the shelf. They were paperbacks. All of them looked read, and there were no hidden banknotes, love letters or manuscript drafts between their pages. The last one I picked up—*The Hours* by Michael Cunningham—had a bookmark stuck in it. It had the size and firmness of a postcard, and when I pulled it out, I expected to see the logo of a bookseller, but it turned out to be a photograph.

It showed Laura and two other people, a man and a woman. Laura and the man were wearing uniforms, some kind of military gala outfit. Laura held a flower bouquet in her hands. The man was maybe an inch shorter than her with crew cut reddish hair and an extremely muscular build. Both Laura and he were smiling impishly, while the woman on Laura's side bore a more serious expression, albeit with a little smile in the corner of her mouth. Her features looked Italian or Middle Eastern. She had brown eyes, curly brown hair and an oval face. Her face was a bit too stern to be conventionally pretty, too intelligent and serious, but definitely intriguing. I had seen her somewhere before, and after a minute of racking my brain, I pulled out the envelope Marge Cunningham had given me, which contained the pictures of the young Laura.

In one of them was the woman as a teenager. She had an arm around Laura, but Laura wasn't smiling at all. She appeared as furious and unhappy as her mother had described her to me. On the back of the picture it read: *Laura and Stacey, April 1990.*

The picture had been taken three years before Laura's disappearance when the girls were fifteen. The photo from the book showed people in their late twenties. Laura's old friend Stacey had lied. The women hadn't broken off their contact forever before Laura's disappearance.

I pulled out my notebook and cell phone, found the number I was looking for and dialed it.

Chapter 18

After at least thirty rings, somebody picked up. "Atlanta Medical Center, Emergency Department. How can I help you?" an unfriendly male voice blasted into the phone.

"I'm looking for Dr. Schaffner."

"She's not available. You have to try again."

"When can I reach her, please?"

"Later."

Before I could ask if he could give me any other number to call, the man hung up.

I continued my search of the apartment. I knocked on the walls, looked in every hole, every gap, every crevice I could detect. Two hours later, I couldn't think of anywhere else to look, short of tearing out the carpet and scraping off the wallpaper.

At twelve forty-five I decided it was now *later* and called Stacey's number again. There was another long series of rings.

The people at this ER were certainly not ready to respond to an emergency by phone. Then a squeaky female voice answered. Yes, Dr. Schaffner was in. She would try to locate her for me. Finally, the gravelly voice I had already spoken to two days ago answered, "What is it?"

"This is Anna Spring. We spoke on Friday. Please listen to me for a moment. I know that you've been in touch with Laura long after she had disappeared from San Francisco. Could you please answer a few questions that I have? I won't bother you long."

"You won't go away if I tell you to just piss off, will you?" Dr. Stacey Schaffner barked into the phone.

"I'll go away quicker if you talk to me," I said, trying to sound as amiable as possible. Telephone lines are bad places to create trust.

"I can't talk now."

"Can I call you later . . . or . . ." my thoughts took a quick turn. "How about if I come to Atlanta? It's always easier to speak in person."

"You want to fly in from San Francisco?"

"I'm in the South already. I can drive down and meet you later today."

"Where are you?"

"In Asheville."

"You've found her after all," Dr. Schaffner said with a deep weariness.

"I've found her old apartment."

There was just a sigh on the other end. Eventually Stacey Schaffner said, "Do you know the Firestone Restaurant on Brillard Street?"

"In Atlanta?"

"In Asheville."

"I'm sure I can find it."

"Meet me there at seven tonight."

"You want to drive all the way here?"

"I don't want you anywhere near my workplace, my family . . . and I don't want to discuss any of this on the phone. See you tonight."

The restaurant was not far from 24 Mountain Road. It was located on an access road into Asheville. I followed the road out of the city for another two miles and found the entrance to the Biltmore Estate, the city's major attraction. For lack of anything else to do with the afternoon, I drove through the brick gate-house, passed a beautiful bamboo grove, paid my entrance fee at the next gate and slowly continued in the direction of the mansion. I had noticed a vehicle behind me at a distance, just before the first gate. Now, I looked for it in the rearview mirror. I wanted to enjoy the drive without having to worry about a faster driver trying to pass. But it was gone. Only when I turned the last curve before the mansion did I spot it again farther down the road, maybe a mile away. It was a big pickup. It reminded me of Jasmine's Dodge, except this one was dark green. Obviously its driver wanted to go even slower than me and study the scenery.

There was a café next to the entrance of the manor house. I purchased a sandwich and a coffee, devoured both quickly and then looked around. I didn't feel like going on a tour of the house.

There were beautiful gardens close by, and then the land-scape opened up to meadows and parklands. The mountains guarded the estate, a promise of wilderness once you escaped from the fairy tale hills dreamt up by the super rich builder of this place. Mist was rising from the tree-lined slopes of the Appalachians like smoke from a hidden dragon's nostrils.

Questions gathered in my head, but the answers were as eva-sive as the mist. What did Inez really know about Laura's past? Had she ever been to the Mountain Road apartment? Who had paid the rent since Laura's death? And why had Laura kept the studio in the first place after she had left North Carolina? Were there bank accounts in the name of Lynn Crooper? And obviously, Laura had been in the military. But when, and in which division?

I told myself that Stacey could probably answer some of these questions tonight. If she made the three-and-a-half-hour drive from Atlanta.

Who was the man in the picture? I pulled the photograph from the book out of my bag. I didn't know anything about the military, so the uniforms told me nothing. But they certainly were festive, and the flowers in Laura's hand gave the scene the feel of a wedding.

I suppressed the sense of urgency these unanswered questions created in my chest and tried to focus on the hope that the uncertainty would soon be over. What I couldn't suppress, though, was the feeling that underneath Stacey Schaffner's anger something else had reverberated in her gruff tone: a strong and old fear, one that she had become extremely frustrated with but one she couldn't shake off. I knew that she had agreed to meet me mostly because she needed to exorcise this fear. But all I had to offer her was my curiosity.

I went back to the parking lot. A security guard informed me that I was the last visitor of the day. The guard at the last gate gave me a friendly nod and closed the gate behind me. I drove back to the hotel, showered and then called Marge Cunningham.

I told her about the apartment and the photo I had found there.

"The military," she said. "That's interesting. Do you know where she was stationed?"

"I'm working on it."

"I would like to see the photo as soon as possible."

"I can scan and e-mail it. But you'll have to wait until later tonight or tomorrow. I have to run to a meeting now."

"Whom are you meeting?"

"Stacey Glum. She's in the picture as well. She must have been in touch with Laura long after her disappearance."

"Where are you meeting her?"

"Here in Asheville."

"Good work. Let me know immediately what she tells you. You can call me anytime tonight."

Chapter 19

The Firestone Restaurant's best feature was its huge parking lot. Otherwise, the place was a nondescript flat building that looked about as inviting as a freeway truck stop. Inside, it radiated the charm of a Swiss log cabin gone Chinatown. The walls were cheap wood, the tablecloths red and white checkered, and before it had become a steak place, it must have served some kind of Asian cuisine because the lamps were fake paper lanterns made from plastic. It was almost endearing in its clear resistance to fulfill anybody's expectations.

Dr. Stacey Schaffner was already waiting for me. I spotted her black curls in a booth at the far end of the almost empty restaurant.

I introduced myself and slid into the bench across from her.

"It used to be a more lively place," the woman greeted me apologetically. "I guess its best times are over. Probably changed the chef or something."

"You know Asheville pretty well," I said after we had placed our orders.

"I went to school here."

"Is that why Laura came here, too, to be close to you?"

"The story is much more complicated."

"I'd love to hear it."

Our steaks arrived, and we both worked hard to cut the veiny, tough slabs of meat into bite-sized pieces, which we then had to chew hard in order to get them down our throats. After a while, Stacey laid down her fork and knife and said, "I give up. Maybe the dessert here is more edible."

"It can by no means be as hard to cut."

To be on the safe side, neither of us ordered pie. Stacey went for ice cream, and I tried the chocolate cake.

"So you used to come here often, Laura and you," I said, trying to lead back to my quest. I pushed the cake plate away after the first few bites. It tasted too much of old grease. The ice cream must have been better. Stacey finished her dish slowly.

"Let's get some coffee. Then I'll tell you the whole story."

Our coffee came.

"So you work for Marge Cunningham," Stacey finally said.

I nodded. "She has employed me. But to be honest, the case has begun to develop its own dynamic."

"How so?"

I knew I still hadn't won. Stacey still didn't trust me. But I had spoken the truth. My interest in Laura's life had long exceeded the job description Marge Cunningham had given me.

"I don't think Inez killed her."

Stacey's hair looked almost blue in this light, as if an electric current were running through it. It was now spreading out to her charcoal eyes, making them spark with interest. "Can you prove that?"

"Not yet, but I'm working on it."

"What does Laura's mother say to this?"

"I haven't told her."

Stacey looked at me intently. I waited for her to ask how I had come to the conclusion that somebody else was behind Laura's death, but she didn't. Instead she said, "Laura loved Inez. I never met her, but from what Laura told me, she sounded wonderful. Caring, gentle. I couldn't believe it myself when I heard what happened. But didn't she confess?"

"Yes, but I think I know why."

Again Stacey didn't ask me for details. "If I tell you what I know about Laura, will you tell Marge to leave me alone for good?" she said.

"I promise to let her know. And I promise to make it very clear to her, in my report, and orally, that you don't know anything else apart from what you told me."

Stacey looked neither relieved nor convinced. She had only agreed to this meeting because she thought there was no way around it, that I, or the next one of Marge Cunningham's bloodhounds, would continue to bother her.

"You helped Laura get away from home," I probed.

"Yes. I was just about to begin school down here. She brought her few belongings over to my parents' house, and I packed them in with my own stuff. I gave her some money and held on to her things for her."

"I take it she didn't stay with you here in Asheville."

"No, of course not. Much too dangerous."

"Where did she go? And how did she manage to change her identity?"

"She didn't. She basically lived without any paper trail for many years. In the beginning she was so scared they would be able to track down a fake identity that she basically became undocumented."

"They? You mean the Cunninghams?"

Stacey nodded. "She moved around, became a migrant

142

worker. Never stayed anywhere for long."

"Did you see her in those years?"

"Hardly. She would sometimes call me. A few times, when she felt very daring, she would drop by. Then I took her here to this restaurant. It was cheap and good then. Buzzing with students. We could hide among the crowds."

I didn't want to interrupt Stacey's flow, but the question was so burning, I couldn't keep myself from asking it. "Do you know why? I mean what happened? What was she so desperately running from?"

"Laura never told me any details. She said she wanted to protect me."

I knew Stacey was telling the truth.

"You must have had a suspicion, an educated guess. Was she being beaten? Sexually molested? By her mother or somebody else in the family?"

"I have no idea, and of course it bugged me. When we were teenagers I once even asked Leonard what was the matter with Laura. She was just so extremely moody, and as her friend I could tell she was suffering. After I asked him, I could have bitten my tongue off. Leonard just stared at me. Then his eyes got wet. He was about to cry, but he just turned around and walked away. He and Laura were extremely close. One time Laura told me that she was glad she was adopted so nobody could later give them trouble for being cousins if they ever wanted to marry. She was joking, of course. But there was some truth to it. They loved one another deeply."

"What did their parents say about their relationship?" I wondered.

"Laura hardly ever talked about her mother. I have no idea if she or Leonard's father even knew exactly how they felt for each other."

Probably not, considering Laura's basic secretiveness, I guessed. "How about Leonard's mother?" I hadn't read anything about her in the family history.

"I don't know what happened to her," Stacey said. "He never spoke about his mother, and as far as I know she wasn't present in his life."

Leonard had also changed, a while before Laura left, Stacey told me. He didn't hang out with Laura anymore. But then he was a few years older. He finally moved away to go to college, and Laura was left behind. She became more and more anxious, and furious, and shortly after graduating from high school, she told Stacey that she had to get away from her family.

"We were teenagers, you know? I sensed that she was really in trouble, and it felt great to help her, to be her best friend and only confidante. It never occurred to me that she was probably creating an even greater problem for herself and that there might be other ways to work things out."

Or not. Laura's fear of whatever it was she was leaving behind must have been extreme, otherwise she wouldn't have chosen to lead such a difficult and lonely new existence.

"You're still scared of the Cunninghams yourself," I said.

"I know. I keep telling myself I probably osmotically inherited Laura's fear, but there is something else there. The way Marge has hunted me down with private detectives. Threatening to drag me to court if I knew something and didn't tell."

"She didn't believe your story that Laura and you had broken off your friendship?"

"It was the best we could come up with. Laura even had the idea to tell her mother that she was meeting me the night of her disappearance. If I later contradicted her and told Marge that Laura had lied and we hadn't been in touch for a while, it would ring more true to her mother, who was used to Laura lying. For that reason, we hoped Marge would leave me alone. It didn't work all that well."

"Marge never won, though. You never told her anything."

"I didn't. Until now."

"Now Laura is dead, and you can help me find her murderer."

"I know there's no foundation for this suspicion, but from the moment I heard Laura had been killed, I couldn't help but think they did it. They finally found her and did it."

"Actually Laura showed up at her mother's house of her own volition shortly before her death," I said. At least that was what Marge claimed. Stay objective, I told myself. So far it's Stacey's story against Marge's.

"I never knew she got in touch with her mother again. I already thought it was quite daring of her to move back to San Francisco."

It almost seemed as if Stacey's vicarious fear had in the end surmounted Laura's own feelings toward her family.

"Did you talk about her move? And why she risked living so close to the Cunninghams? She even used her old name again."

"Really? I never met Inez, so I didn't know if she called her Laura or Lynn."

"When did she change her name, anyway?"

After about five years of moving around the country, always avoiding the west coast, Laura had felt the need to settle down, Stacey explained. She was in her mid twenties by then and felt as if her existence were that of an apparition. One day she was there, the next she was gone. Nobody knew her. Nobody remembered her. She was morbidly lonely and wanted a life at last. So she picked up the papers Stacey had kept for her, her birth certificate and her passport, and applied for a name change. Laura felt that the long gap in any paper trail which she had created, together with the new name, would be enough to keep her family from finding her.

"Laura hated to be scared. Fear was nothing she could easily accept as part of her life. She felt insulted by it," Stacey said.

"Do you think that's why she moved back to San Francisco?"

"It might have played a role in it. But only a minor one. She definitely wanted to be with Inez. More than anything else. And

Inez had her life there. Her business, her father, whom she couldn't uproot in his condition. But it also had something to do with Afghanistan."

"With Afghanistan?" I had no clue what Stacey meant by this.

"Laura was deployed to Afghanistan. She got injured there and was different after she got back."

"I think I'm a bit lost here," I said.

Stacey smiled. "Laura would always tease me that my stories were really long-winded and full of non sequiturs. I guess she was right, huh?"

I just smiled back.

"Okay," Stacey began. "After Laura became Lynn she needed a job."

For a while Laura had basically continued along the same line of work as when she was undocumented. Hard, poorly paid, back-breaking labor. She worked as a fruit picker, factory worker, waitress. She had settled down in Asheville not too far from Atlanta where Stacey had moved by now. She wanted to be close enough to her only friend to be able to see her sometimes, but not too close, still protecting their secret pact. Laura soon realized that nothing much had changed, now that she had an identity. She still couldn't make ends meet. Stacey helped her with the deposit for an apartment, but she was only an intern at the hospital herself, had to pay off student loans and couldn't do much more financially for her friend. Laura knew she couldn't save up any money. She didn't even get a credit card due to her lack of any financial history. She wanted to get an education, some sort of training, but she had to work most hours of the day. And in this situation she came across an army recruiter. The military promised her a steady income, the prospect of help when she wanted to go back to school after her service, and a sense of belonging and purpose.

"That was before nine eleven," Stacey said. "Before you'd have to immediately face being sent to a senseless war. I advised her against enlisting, nevertheless. As a doctor it's hard to accept people killing and injuring one another for whatever purpose. For me it's just plain stupid. But something about the military struck a chord with Laura. She told me she liked the idea of being able to defend herself and others who are weaker. And I think she just needed a home badly, whatever kind of home. And she was always fascinated with weapons and guns."

I nodded. "Yes, I've learned that."

After her basic training Laura had been assigned to an army unit, where she was trained as a gunner. She had been stationed at Fort Foberland, about an hour and a half from Asheville, and Stacey hadn't seen much of her in those days.

I pulled out the photograph that showed her with Laura and the mystery man and said, "Sometimes there were occasions when you could get together, though."

Laura's friend stared at the picture. "That was at her wedding," she finally said, brushing her curls back from her forehead only to let them fall back into her face.

There had never been many patrons in the restaurant, and by now we were the last remaining. It was almost nine p.m., but I was determined to learn everything Stacey knew about Laura. I signaled the waiter and asked for a serving of ice cream. Stacey ordered a beer, and I said, "Make that two and cancel the ice cream."

"Who is the groom?" I asked and pointed to the red-haired guy in the picture.

"Stu," Stacey said. "Stewart, I guess is his full name. Laura called me two days before and told me she was getting married. I was kind of excited—annoyed, too, that she hadn't told me she was seeing somebody, but she said it was for reasons of protection."

"He's gay," I guessed quickly.

"You are way faster than I was when she told me that. Laura never explained to me exactly what she meant, but I figured it out for myself in the end. At least about him. I didn't know about Laura's own feelings for women then. And we never talked about it until she met Inez."

"So you don't know if she had a lover in the army?"

Stacey shook her head.

"What happened to Stu? Do you know where he is?"

"No. I only saw him once at the wedding. And I had to leave shortly after the ceremony. I had to get back to the hospital."

"And you never talked to Laura about him?" I asked incredulously.

"We didn't have many occasions to chat then. I was in residency, had to work faster than I could breathe. I met my husband, became pregnant, and then Laura was sent to Afghanistan. She sent me e-mails from there every now and then, but that was about all the communication we could muster."

"Do you still have the e-mails?"

"I always wanted to print them out, but before I got around to it, my computer crashed, and they were all gone. After Laura's death I was particularly sad about that."

"What did she write about?"

"Mainly her life in camp, what they did all day long. Laura saw a lot of combat. Fortunately, the initial battles against the Taliban didn't last all that long."

"But she got injured."

"I only learned about it when she was already back in the U.S. She called me from Walter Reed and I flew there a couple of times to visit her."

"What had happened?"

"She was in a Humvee on their way to a combat zone. They were targeted by a sniper. Bullet grazed her forehead. Fractured part of her skull but didn't enter the brain. Nevertheless, she suffered brain trauma."

"How bad was her injury? I mean from a medical point of view."

"There had been hemorrhaging to the brain. With these kind of injuries it's usually hard to predict the long term consequences. Her speech and coherency of thought didn't seem to be affected. But she had persistent headaches afterward. She didn't want to take painkillers, though, said the pain was bearable, but . . ."

"But?"

"I'm not so sure. I think they were pretty bad. And there were also other consequences. Although I don't even know if Laura was aware of them herself."

"I heard she couldn't shoot very well afterward."

"That's very possible. Aiming a gun is a complex task of hand-eye coordination. If some of your neurons have been damaged or if you just can't focus because of pain, it can be hard to do. She was retired from the military due to her injury, so it's clear the doctors there thought she had a lasting disability."

"What did you think?"

"I believe her frontal lobe was affected, probably also her amygdala."

"Did she show any sociopathic tendencies?" The only consequences I had heard about injuries to the brain's frontal lobe were loss of empathy and compassion, the trait that marked sociopaths.

"Not really. She was still capable of love and friendship. But she had changed. There was this jumpiness. She always seemed on the edge. Even when you were sitting calmly at a table with her, it felt as if she wanted to hop up the next moment and run somewhere. When she spoke there was a sense of impatience or a lack of focus. She would often not finish a sentence, or she would hint at something she wouldn't explain fully. And I believe she finally achieved what she had secretly always longed for: to overcome her fears. But not in a natural, healthy way. It seemed that she had just become a renegade. She'd always had this tendency. Stood up for the weaker kids in school, got into fights with the bullies. I loved that about her. But now it seemed she was picking fights without reason. To let off steam or to prove to herself that she could take on anybody. She had just left the hospital and was still pretty weak when we got together. We were walking down a street here in Asheville when she saw a guy reprimand his kid. A tall, strong man, his son was around ten, but he stood up for himself pretty well. The father didn't slap the child or do anything else that was off limits. But Laura still walked up to him, told him to leave the boy alone, and when the man asked her to mind her own business, she showed him her fist and walked off."

"It sounds like she was on a path to self-destruction," I said.

"That was maybe part of it. But for me it felt as if she had somehow liberated herself from her fears, but now her anger was taking over."

"That must have been hard on you."

"She wasn't like that to me. I could sometimes sense her irritability when we talked, but she never took it out on me."

"So she could still control it," I said. "Doesn't that sound more like a psychological than a physical thing then?"

"The brain is still such a mystery. How its physiology interacts with the psyche is so hard to examine, and probably ineffable anyway."

"Anyhow, you said that her injury and its consequences made it possible for her to go back to San Francisco to live with Inez. Because her old fears were gone."

"That was certainly part of it."

"And the other part?"

"There was something else. It's hard to grasp. She came to the South every now and then after she had already moved to San Francisco. If I could make it, I would meet her in Asheville. She never wanted to come to Atlanta. She hasn't even met my husband Mark or my children. She still felt that it was better if nobody really knew that we were in touch. But when we met she told me about Inez, how happy she was with her, how she enjoyed finally having a home. I asked her if she wasn't afraid to run into one of the Cunninghams in San Francisco and if she had ever tried to get in touch with Leonard again. Her eyes turned somehow glassy and she mumbled, 'I don't know what to do, Stacey. I just don't know.' Then she fell silent and never brought up the topic again."

"And you never asked?"

"I knew I wouldn't get an answer. But I felt that there hadn't been closure yet for her when it came to her family. I felt that part of the reason she was in San Francisco was because she needed to be close to them. She was on to something there."

"On to something?"

Stacey grabbed a small purse that was lying next to her on the bench. From it she pulled a wallet.

I searched for my own wallet, thinking that Laura's friend was ready to leave. But then she pulled a piece of paper from the bill compartment of her wallet, unfolded it and laid it on the table.

"Laura gave me this on her last visit," she said. "Only two weeks before her death. She asked me if I could make sense of it."

It was a photocopy. The original must have consisted of two different sheets. On the top one was Arabic writing, the typical smooth mountains and little hooks, interspersed with numbers. Underneath were some words in English and the same numbers. It looked like a kind of lab result. When I studied it for a moment certain phrases rang familiar.

"A blood test," I said.

"Yes. The lower is the translation of the upper. It's a regular ABO test, determining that the patient has blood type AB negative."

"Who is the patient?"

"Laura didn't tell me. Maybe she didn't know. She just asked if I knew any Afghan doctor, who could tell her what the writing meant. I asked one of my colleagues. The translation is from him."

Stacey pointed at a thick black bar across the top of the Arabic page. "He said this blacked out part must have been the patient's name. Before I could get back to Laura about it, I heard that she had died."

"Maybe it was Laura's own test result. From when she was in Afghanistan."

"Laura had blood type O negative. I know that because she once donated blood to me."

Of course I was curious under which circumstances, but I was too shy to ask. However, Stacey seemed almost eager to tell me.

"We were teens. I got into trouble. I didn't even know I was pregnant. We were camping up north, close to Eureka, and suddenly I had terrible stomach pain. Laura took me to a small clinic in the next town. It turned out I had an ectopic pregnancy and my tube had burst. I lost a lot of blood. Laura immediately donated some. It was fortunate she had this blood type. She was a universal donor."

"You went through a lot together."

"We did. She saved my life. But I couldn't save her in the end."

"You protected her as best you could over many years."

Stacey turned around and signaled the waiter to come.

"Can I keep this?" I asked her, pointing at the photocopy.

She nodded and pulled some bills from her wallet. "I still have a long trip ahead," she said almost apologetically.

"You've really helped me," I said.

"I did it for Laura," Stacey said. "Find out what happened to her."

Chapter 20

We exited the restaurant together, and I asked Stacey where her car was.

"I came by cab. I'll just call another one to pick me up."

"By cab from Atlanta?"

"I flew here. I have a pilot's license. It will be good to put in some night hours. To keep my license active."

I was pretty astonished that Stacey volunteered all this information. She seemed relaxed now, less wary.

"I'll wait here with you until you're safe and sound in the taxi."

"I'd rather you just take off already. It won't be long anyway."

"Are you sure?"

She motioned me to get to my car, one of only three left in the lot. It didn't feel good to let Stacey just stand all alone in the empty parking lot, but I followed her wish. At least she was still close to the restaurant door where it was well lit.

I drove off and checked the rearview mirror. Stacey was talking on her cell phone. She was a slim woman in well cut jeans and a white trench coat. Her dark hair blended in with the night, and only her face, which was a little bit too long but whose brilliance I had admired while we were speaking, was visible against the background.

I had to turn right to get onto the highway. In order to get back to Asheville I would have to take a U-turn soon. About half a mile down the road was an intersection, and I turned the car back toward the city. Once more, the neon sign of the Firestone Restaurant appeared in the distance. The road was empty, so I slowed down before the entrance to the lot to check and see if Stacey was still there. It was too fast for a taxi to have already arrived., She was standing in the same place as before, looking up at the starry sky. Then she lowered her face and looked straight at me. The next second her head jerked to the side. Her knees buckled as if her body had been kicked by a giant invisible foot. She fell to her left and lay on the ground, motionless.

I stepped on the gas, pulled the car across the double line and sped into the lot. A few yards before I reached Stacey's body, I braked the car, shot out and ran over to her. And then I heard it—the sharp, high pitched whistle of a shot. I let myself fall to the ground and waited for the next whistle, the hit. But everything remained silent. Only a few branches were cracking. Somebody was running away along the edge of the lot. I struggled to my feet and began to run as well, into the direction of the sounds, into the sheer blackness. Whoever had been there was sucked up by the night, lying in wait, invisible, close by. And he had a gun.

My senses transformed back from animal to human. I ran over to Stacey. I was shaking, breathing against the vigorous pressure of what felt like lead plating around my chest.

I kneeled down beside Stacey and lifted her head gently. A

hot, sticky liquid poured onto my fingers, caking her curls into a gooey mass. Her eyes were open, her face waxy. I felt for a pulse at the side of her neck. There was none. Her gaze was broken. And then I spotted the entry wound—a smaller, bleeding hole beneath the curls. The bullet had been a through and through. When it had exited, it had torn off the side of her head.

There was no hope. I tried to exhale and could hardly force my own breath out of me. It finally exploded in a sound I couldn't control, a hard, gasping howl. With it, unconnected thoughts began to shoot through my skull like ricocheting bullets.

Try to resuscitate her . . . you have no chance . . . she's gone . . . she trusted you . . . no chance . . . she was Laura's only friend . . . you killed her . . . who killed her . . . try to resuscitate her . . . whoever did this is connected to you . . . this was no mugging . . . Al's death was no mugging . . . get away from here . . . call an ambulance . . . call the police . . .

I knew she was dead. From the extent of Stacey's wound, she never had a chance of surviving. I closed her lifeless eyes and stood up. I tried not to touch anything anymore, tried to leave the scene intact for the forensics team.

I picked up my jacket, walked back to the car, got inside and drove off. There was a pay phone a short way down the road. At the bottom of my bag I found a box of latex gloves. I put on a pair, walked to the phone, called 911 and whispered into the receiver that they should send an ambulance and a police car to the Firestone Restaurant.

I was sure there was nothing the paramedics could do, but I didn't have it in me to announce Stacey's death by not asking for them.

I knew I should immediately drive back to the scene myself, wait for the detectives and tell them everything I had seen. And everything I knew. But I had seen nothing. And I knew too much.

With the clarity intuition brings in the moment of emotional trauma, I knew that whoever had shot Al two nights ago had now also killed Stacey. Somebody was murdering my informants immediately after I spoke to them. The only person who knew that Al had given me information and that I would be meeting Stacey to speak with her about Laura, was Marge Cunningham.

My neurons were firing away while I was driving. I couldn't help the police. If I talked to them, they would have too many questions. The restaurant staff had seen Stacey and me together. In order to explain reasonably my connection to her, I would have to reveal my whole case to them. And then they would take over. And never find out anything.

It must have been a hired gun who had shot Stacey and Al. Even if they could track him down, there would be no traceable connection to Marge Cunningham. If I ever wanted to get to her, I would have to discover what lay behind the killings on my own.

For a moment my mind took a quick detour. Laura had been injured by a sniper in Afghanistan. She had led a whole life between the day she ran away from Marge Cunningham and the day she reappeared on her mother's doorstep. What if there were people from that other life who wanted to kill her, who had finally gotten to her, and now had reasons to murder first Al and then Stacey in order to shut them up? Neither Al nor Stacey knew much about that life. But they had both talked to Laura after she had come back from Afghanistan.

My hands, jacket and T-shirt were covered in Stacey's blood and brain matter. I couldn't show up at the hotel the way I looked. I had almost reached Mountain Road. Laura's apartment was a possible hiding place. It had a shower and hot water. I parked the car a few blocks away, glad its interior was deep burgundy. A passerby wouldn't detect the blood on the steering wheel and seat.

While I was walking up the stairs, Stacey's dead features stood before me, but she looked different, somewhat Asian, as if Laura's face was mixed in with hers. Marge Cunningham hadn't employed me to honor her daughter's life, I realized. Marge wanted me to find everybody in whom Laura might have confided. There was the old story which had made her run away from them in such tremendous fear. But then there must also be something new Laura had discovered. What was so much worse about the new information on the Cunninghams that made it necessary, in Marge's sick view, to silence Al and Stacey only now? This was true madness! But I felt that in order to stop it I had to find out what was at the bottom of it. I had to uncover the Cunninghams' secret.

Still deep in thought, I stuck my key into the lock of Laura's apartment. Something was wrong. It didn't fit. The lock didn't look any different. The scratches on the metal cover stemmed from my own tools. I leaned down to examine it more closely. In that moment the door opened. Before I could step back, there was a blow to my head. It felt as if a locomotive had hit my forehead and split the skull in two. My legs melted, my spine crashed, my brain blew up. Then gentle night moved through me and took away the pain. I felt myself go limp and sank to the ground. The world turned black.

Chapter 21

When I came to, my face was freezing, my vision blurry. I touched my artificial eye. It was still in place, undamaged. I couldn't easily adjust the focus of my seeing eye, though. Water was dripping into it. There was a cold, wet cloth on my forehead. I pushed it away, wiped the liquid from my face and struggled to sit up. My hands were tied behind my back. My feet were bound, too, with duct tape. I was sitting crookedly, leaning against a wall. Nausea set in, grew and tightened my throat. I fought against its vicious force, tried to swallow it, but it won. I had to throw up. Somebody shoved a bowl underneath my chin and pulled it away after my stomach had emptied itself. The smell was bad and almost made me sick again. I wanted to turn, wanted to see who was there and kick the life out of him.

"You probably have a concussion," a cheerful male voice said. "You should lie down."

I could see better with every second. I was in Laura's apartment, half sitting, half lying on the futon. The wooden screen had been taken away. A man was standing in the middle of the room, examining me, a short, red-haired guy with big feet and the overly serious expression of a concerned toddler.

"Take off that damn tape," I whispered, then cleared my throat and managed to say louder, "You broke into my client's apartment. If you don't want a lot of trouble, you'd better free me quickly."

"I broke into the apartment?" the guy asked incredulously, blasting out a short, not so amused laugh. "You tried to break into my place. I didn't even want to knock you out. It was an accident. But when I saw you were all covered in blood but clearly not bleeding from any wounds yourself, I got scared for my life. That's why I restrained you."

I recognized him now. It was the groom in Laura's wedding picture, Stu.

"Let's cut the crap," I said resignedly. "I know who you are. You're Lynn Crooper's husband, Stu. I'm Anna Spring, a detective. Lynn's mother hired me to take care of Lynn's estate."

"Lynn's mother is dead."

"Lynn's mother may be, but Laura's isn't."

The man was thrown off. His forehead crinkled in thought, pushing his freckles into a chaotic pattern. *Marcus*, shot through my head. Had they killed Laura's old friend Marcus Robinson, too? I had to make a number of phone calls ASAP.

"I'll explain everything if you untie me."

Curiosity clearly won over the man's caution. Anyway, I was a physically weak opponent. No match for the muscles that bulged underneath his T-shirt like violent, twitchy boxer pups.

Stu cut the tape around my wrists and ankles with a kitchen knife, and blood whirled into my limbs with a strong but comforting pain.

I leaned forward on the futon, balancing myself in a better

position.

"You want some chamomile tea?" Stu asked. "It will help your stomach." He handed me another cold towel for the bump on my forehead, and I had to giggle uncontrollably at the absurdity of the situation.

The guy seemed relieved he could let me free, and I said, "Tea would be great."

"Then I have to tie you up again while I make the tea. Can't risk you jumping me from behind."

"Listen, I promise I won't jump you from anywhere. I'm harmless. I've seen your wedding picture. I know Stacey Schaffner was there. I know Lynn was in Afghanistan and suffered a head wound. I'm from San Francisco where she moved after she got released from duty."

"What else do you know?" Stu walked over to the kitchen counter and began to prepare the tea.

"I know you're probably gay, and Laura—excuse me—Lynn and you married for protection."

The man gave me a long, anguished look.

"I'm gay myself," I said. "I understand why you two did it. And it's none of my business."

"There was this officer," Stu mumbled. "He made a pass at me. But I wasn't interested. Then he started to bully me, threatened to get me exposed. I didn't have anything I could use against him. It would have been his word versus mine, officer against enlisted. Lynn and I met on the base. We were friends. I confided in her. She suggested we get married. It wasn't hard to pretend I was in love with her. She was great."

"You know that she's dead, don't you?"

Stu nodded. "After I couldn't reach her for a few weeks, I searched for her. I had her address in San Francisco. I flew there while I was on leave from Iraq last winter. Went to the house. A neighbor told me she had been killed. By Inez. The neighbor also referred to her as Laura. But I knew it was Lynn."

160

"Do you know Inez personally?"

"I only know her name. I was deployed to the Middle East most of the last two years. I haven't been in touch with Lynn all that much. We e-mailed, sometimes called each other. We were good friends but led pretty separate lives. We kept this apartment as our mutual address."

"So you're the one who picked up the mail?"

Stu nodded. "I've been back at the base now for a while. I check in here frequently. But usually I live with Gerard, my partner, when I'm not on watch duty."

"Where are you stationed?"

"Fort Foberland, still."

I wanted to ask Stu many more questions, but I also had to make those phone calls. I checked my watch. It was almost midnight. Still evening on the West Coast.

Stu handed me a cup of steaming tea. "I'll be back in a minute, but I need to use the restroom," I said and set the cup on the carpet.

My bag containing my cell phone was lying in a corner, and I grabbed it while I slowly walked toward the bathroom. My knees still felt as though they were filled with strawberry jelly, but I made it through the room. When Stu looked questioningly at the bag I mumbled, "Feminine protection products."

He had certainly searched it for weapons already and now let me take it without protest.

"Listen, Martha," I whispered into the receiver, crouching on the toilet. "Somebody just shot Stacey right after I spoke with her. And I'm very certain they killed Al, the other contact."

"Did they shoot at you, too?"

"No, it was a coincidence I even saw the shooting. The plan was to have no witnesses."

"And you're still at the scene?"

"I'm not. I have to figure out what's behind all this. I couldn't wait around."

"Where are you?"

"Back at Laura's place. Trying to come up with a plan."

"And you're not alone."

"No. I found her husband. Maybe he knows something."

"Go to the cops, chicky. This sounds bad."

"I can't, Martha. The Cunninghams are somehow behind all this. I have to find out why. The police in Asheville are too far away from them to get results quickly enough. I have to keep up the cover for Marge. I have to pretend I'm still working for her and that I don't know what she's up to. Otherwise she'll go after you and me and whoever else."

Martha sounded far from scared when she said, "Let her try."

"You're no match for a sniper."

There was no more time to bicker, and I just asked her to do me a favor and contact Marcus Robinson. I mainly wanted to know if he was still alive, but had no idea what to tell him if he was.

"I'll tell him to be careful," Martha said with a very cynical edge.

"Oh great," I said and hung up.

The next call I made was to Marge Cunningham. I had promised to inform her after my meeting with Stacey. And I knew I had to keep up the pretense if I wanted to stay out of her line of fire for now. I gave her a very condensed and censored version of what Stacey had told me, just enough to sound believable. Mainly I told her that Laura had changed her name after a few years on the road, and that she had eventually joined the army and gotten deployed to Afghanistan.

"That's interesting," Marge Cunningham said, but she didn't sound all that interested.

After we had said good-bye, I was left to wonder who was chasing whom in our little game of tag.

"Who did you talk to?" Stu greeted me when I exited the bathroom.

Of course he had heard me through the thin bathroom door. "Who do you think?" I replied. "Didn't you eavesdrop?"

"No, I just heard you mumble. Figured you were on the phone."

"Good for you."

My tea had become lukewarm by now, but I took a seat at the breakfast counter and slowly sipped it anyway. It was actually soothing. And drinking it gave me time to reflect on this weird situation. Was I Stu's prisoner? Or could I just walk out the door? But then I didn't even want to leave. Not without having shaken him down good.

"Would you mind if I took a shower and borrowed some of Laura's—sorry—Lynn's clothes?" I asked.

"How did you get so bloody, anyway?"

"I'll tell you when I'm cleaner, okay?"

He nodded.

I grabbed a T-shirt and a pair of jeans from one of the drawers, answering Stu's questioning gaze with, "I've been here before, remember? Changed the lock and so on," and took off again into the bathroom. I locked the door behind me, trying to chase the shower scene pictures from *Psycho* from my mind's eye.

I took out my artificial eye because it had started to itch like crazy, and used one of the skin-colored patches I carry in my bag to cover the socket. Then I showered until my skin burned from the heat of the water.

Laura's T-shirt was a size too small, hugging my chest tightly. Her pants fit around the waist and were only a little too short.

When I stepped out of the bathroom Stu was sitting on one of the barstools from the counter, which he had pulled over to the apartment door, blocking the exit. I placed myself in the orange chair across from him, stretched out my legs and tried to look nonchalant. His curiosity had by now had time to grow and blossom. He quickly assessed my eyepatch and then said "Who is Lynn's family? I never even knew she had one."

"She was adopted as a baby by a woman in San Francisco. And she ran away from her adoptive mom when she was eighteen."

"The mom must be pretty well off if she hired a private eye to find out about Lynn's death."

"She is."

"Wow, so I may even be a rich heir, huh?"

I couldn't tell if he were joking or seriously counting the money he thought he could get out of Laura's mom. Anyhow, under the shower I had decided to reveal as little as I could to him about the case. I had to keep him away from Marge Cunningham and her hit man if that was in any way possible.

"I can't give you any details about that. But once everything has been settled, Laura's family's lawyer will contact you if there is an inheritance."

"I was just kidding," Stu said.

And again I couldn't tell if he meant it or not.

"Were you in Afghanistan, too?" I asked.

"No, I was never deployed there."

"Did Laura ever tell you what happened to her there?"

"I heard of her injury, of course. Probably was the first one who got notified. I couldn't go see her, though. I was on deployment to Iraq. We were on the phone a few times when she could speak again. She sounded pretty normal to me. The bullet didn't damage her smarts, fortunately."

"What else did she tell you about Afghanistan? I'm interested in anything that she talked about, or maybe e-mailed."

"There wasn't much out of the ordinary. We're both soldiers. When she first got deployed I wanted to know how it felt at camp, how it was to face the enemy. But I pretty soon learned firsthand about all that myself."

"Was she friends with anybody who was with her in Afghanistan?"

"Why? Does her family think she hid a secret treasure there?

Money bags buried in the desert sand?"

I rewarded his attempt at a joke with a quick smile and repeated stubbornly, "If you know anybody who had a closer relationship with her while she was overseas, that would be of great help." And after another millisecond of thought I added, "Her mother would just love to talk with somebody who was there with her. She can't travel down here. She's ill. But she would pay for somebody to fly to the West Coast to speak with her if they really knew Laura well and could tell her mom about her experiences in the Middle East."

Stu scratched his chin in contemplation. "I could take you to the base. Some members of her old unit might be there these days. It's hard to say, though. I'd have to look into that."

"How?"

"I have to go back to Gerard's place. I can check online, make a few calls."

"Why don't you check it here? I have a computer."

"Am I *your* hostage now?"

We actually grinned at each other, amused with the absurdity of the situation.

I didn't want the man to walk around out there right now. Maybe the sniper had managed to follow me here. By now I had the suspicion there was a tracking device on the car. That's why Marge had insisted on making my travel arrangements. But how could I convince Stu to stay without telling him that otherwise he might catch a bullet to the head?

I couldn't help but check the big window front. Stu had closed the shutters. We were invisible from the outside. My breathing relaxed a bit. Again Stu gave me one of his puzzled stares, again without asking what was going on. But maybe he was just perpetually astonished.

"Why are you here in the middle of the night, anyway?" I said. "Could it be Gerard and you had a fight and you wanted to get away?"

"I just wanted to check the mail. And then I saw the lock had been changed. I decided to change it again myself. Everything took a while," Stu said with hurt in his voice.

"And your first idea wasn't to just leave it alone and call the housing agency tomorrow to ask about the lock. That would have been the easiest and most logical plan, wouldn't it?"

"Okay, Gerard and I had a fight, so what?"

"So just stay here and help me figure out some things."

Stu still looked skeptical. I pulled my last trump card. "I wonder why you still keep this place. Shouldn't you have reported to the army that Lynn is dead? Or are you collecting her veteran's pension?"

"I'm not getting her money," Stu said, clearly insulted. "It's being sent to her own account. And I'm the one paying the rent for the place. When Lynn moved to San Francisco, I asked her if we could keep the apartment, so nobody would question that we're married."

"You still should have looked deeper into your suspicion that she was dead, huh?"

"I wasn't even completely sure it was really her. I didn't want to mess around with her affairs."

I had made the guy feel guilty enough. Stu looked resigned. I began to hook up my computer to the phone line. Even in this situation, I couldn't hold back but had to check my mail. And yes, Mido had finally answered. *Dear Anna, I am holding my daughter in my arms right now. You can't imagine how wonderful that feels. Stay safe. Mido*

If only she knew . . .

The hard drive on my computer has a password-protected partition where the e-mail application and all folders are located. I opened the other partition and logged Stu onto the Internet from there. The night was advancing quickly. I brewed mugs of instant coffee, which became stronger and more lethal by the hour. Eventually, I couldn't distinguish the caffeine-induced panic from the one created by the events of the day. It felt reassuring.

Finally Stu said, "It looks as if there's only one person at the base right now who was in the same camp as Lynn in Afghaniland."

"Who?"

"Grace Lipman, a doctor. She works at the hospital down on the base."

"How do I get there?"

"You can't just drive onto the base."

"Maybe I can get an appointment."

"It's faster and easier if I take you."

I wanted to protest, but then I knew he was probably right.

"Okay," I said. "Do you have a car?"

"Sure."

"Let's go."

"We should call first, see if she's even there."

It was only four thirty a.m. Not a decent time to make a call—if it wasn't to a hospital. Stu learned that Dr. Lipman would be in by seven in the morning. We decided to take off immediately and stop somewhere on the way for breakfast.

Chapter 22

I donned Laura's down jacket against the cold early morning air and secretly thanked the dead woman for lending me her clothes. Before Stu and I stepped out of the house I said, "Get the car. Drive down to the road that leads to the highway, turn toward Biltmore Estate and pick me up at the second intersection. I should be there in twenty minutes. If you have the feeling you are being followed, don't stop, just drive by me. In that case we'll meet in the lobby of the Marriott in an hour."

"Why . . . ?"

"I'll explain later."

I asked him to wait indoors for another five minutes and left the house. I walked quickly. A bird was cackling somewhere. In the far distance a rooster crowed. A dog answered the call with a high-pitched howl. There were no human sounds to be heard, not even the purring of a car engine. I made it to the intersection, and Stu showed up a few minutes later in a gigantic cream-colored Explorer and let me hop into the passenger seat. He did a U-turn at the same spot I had the night before, and soon we were driving toward the mountains and the army base, which lay fifty miles north.

When we had reached the open road, Stu said, "Okay, and now the bloody story."

"Somebody is after me," I said. "From an old case. One less civilized than this one. A mean divorce thing. The husband got screwed by pictures I took of him with a number of hookers. He's a psychopath. He has some sort of connections here in Asheville. Last night somebody attacked me in an alley not far from the hotel. I managed to wrangle away his knife and cut him a few times. Then I ran. Laura's apartment was the only safe place I knew. So I drove there. Only later it dawned on me that they probably wired the car. That's how the hired guy found me in the first place. And I'm sure he's pretty angry right now."

"You lead quite a life," Stu said with a mix of admiration and wariness.

I did feel a little bad. This guy had been to war, and I tried to impress him with my fabricated adventure tale.

After every other curve I looked in the rearview mirror. So far, nobody was following us. We drove along the foothills. Forest enveloped the road. Every few miles ancient looking wooden houses appeared. Mirages of mist. Their gray frames seemed to have grown from the earth like the giant, gnarly trees and the tender spring grass surrounding them. Fires were burning in metal drums. I couldn't deduce their purpose apart from making this ancient land look somewhat more inhabited by man.

The sleepless night was catching up with Stu and me. We rode along in silence. After almost an hour he said, "There's a small diner two miles from here. What do you think?"

I nodded, and ten minutes later he pulled into the parking lot of Burt's Family Restaurant. We ordered eggs and bacon with grits and more coffee. After the third refill I tiredly asked Stu if there was anything he could come up with that Laura had told him and that might be of any relevance to her family. I encouraged him to mention bad stuff too—family gossip, the metaphorical and literal buried bodies.

Stu looked at me with a face that could have belonged to a ten-year old, had it not been for the red stubble, some frown lines and the moss-colored eyes that looked as if they had aged much faster than the rest of his body.

"When we got married, I asked Lynn, eh Laura, if she had any family, and she answered that both her folks had passed away. The person closest to her was Stacey, but I only saw her once, at the wedding. And that was all we ever spoke about relatives."

"And your own family?"

"They're not a pleasant topic to talk about."

"But they never met Laura?"

"Hell no!"

He wiped the grease off his plate with a piece of toast and then said, "Are you ready?"

My stomach wasn't prepared for duty again, and I had only managed to convince it to take in a small piece of bacon and half a slice of toast, mainly to soak up the coffee. I put a twenty dollar bill on the table, and we left the diner.

We drove along the wall around the army base for fifteen minutes. At a side gate we were greeted by two guards who checked Stu's ID. They cleared him and then wanted to see mine. I presented my driver's license. Stu explained I was his guest and he wanted to show me the base. A second later we were driving through the opened gate, and I was marveling over how easy it had been. They hadn't even made a copy of my ID.

We passed rows of three-story barracks, short cut lawns, the occasional bigger buildings. Some of them were made from gray rock. Others looked like nineteen seventies university architecture with ugly concrete facades and building block design.

The hospital was one of the more old-fashioned structures, a five-story, L-shaped building with small windows. It was ten past seven. Stu got me past the receptionist with his military ID. Once we had turned the corner onto a long hall, I told him I'd go see Dr. Lipman alone.

"Why?" he said.

"I'll tell you later."

"You're a pain in the butt."

My strategy worked, though. Stu was not one to ask many questions. Somebody had very successfully broken him of this vital instinct—the military or his family? I wondered while I searched for Grace Lipman.

The hospital wasn't much different than a civilian one. Its halls were probably a bit quieter, but that could be due to the early hour. And then there was the occasional person in uniform strolling by. Nobody gave me a second look. I recalled that civilians working for the military were not an unusual thing.

Finding Dr. Lipman's office was almost too easy. Suddenly there was a door whose sign read Maj. G. Lipman. It was opened a crack. I knocked. There was a short pause, then a loud, "Come in," and I entered.

"How can I help you, ma'am?"

Grace Lipman's appearance didn't support her sweet Southern accent. She was standing next to a bookshelf at the other end of the small room, a tank of a woman. Her frame was almost square, and she didn't seem to have an ounce of anything flabby or soft on her. She was all bones and hard matter with the chin of a male bodybuilder, very short salt-and-pepper hair, small, sharp eyes, thin lips and a high forehead.

"I'm a representative of Lynn Crooper's family in San Francisco. I'm not even sure if you know that she has passed away, but her family wants to organize a memorial and is looking for former comrades of hers to say a few words. Which is not all that easy. Many are deployed. I have learned that you were overseas together—"

"And so you just show up here?" the woman asked incredulously, leaning against the shelf.

"I was in the area. A friend who is stationed at this base offered to give me a ride. It's always easier to talk in person than over the phone—"

"Well," Dr. Lipman interrupted me the second time. "It's your waste of time and money. I hardly had anything to do with Private Crooper. I treated her after her injury, of course, but she was airlifted to Germany quickly. And then back to the States."

She didn't even react to the news of Laura's death.

"You were at the same camp together," I babbled on. "Even if you can't be a speaker, maybe you have an anecdote to tell that her family can incorporate in the ceremony."

"Listen, I'm an officer, she was enlisted. We didn't really mingle."

Something was wrong here. This woman's grudge against Laura sat between us like a miniature minefield underneath the linoleum.

"You didn't like her." I happily stepped on the first grenade.

"It's not about liking or not liking somebody. It's about soldierly qualities."

"Which Private Crooper didn't have?"

Boom! The second mine went off. "She actively tried to erode morale," Major Lipman said.

"How so?"

The woman shut down again. "I don't think her family would be particularly interested in hearing about the less appealing sides of their daughter. Just don't count on me to sing her praise in a eulogy."

"I've already learned from Lynn's mother that her daughter had quite a challenging personality. Her family was pretty taken aback that Lynn joined the military. It didn't seem like a natural match to them."

"Seriously, she was working on a dishonorable discharge. In this respect, her injury may have saved her."

How lucky for her, I thought sarcastically.

"What did she do exactly?" I inquired. "You know at this point her family would really want to know everything about Lynn, not only the good stuff. They miss her so much. Even hearing about her flaws will make them feel connected to her."

Dr. Lipman crossed her strong arms tightly before her chest and said, "Give her family my condolences." Then she walked around her desk and opened the door for me. I knew I was no match for her tight-lipped discipline and walked away without further protest.

Stu was waiting in exactly the same spot I had left him. When I walked up to him I thought he was just sitting upright, staring into space. As I came closer, though, I saw that he was sleeping, his spine perfectly erect, with only his head supported by the wall behind him.

The moment my shadow hit him, he opened his eyes. "Mission accomplished?" he asked and stood up.

"Not exactly," I said, and as happened many times in my life, I felt like kicking, slamming or knocking something down. I wanted to tell myself I only needed to damage inanimate objects to vent my fury, but I did sometimes fantasize about hurting somebody who would actually feel it—like Grace Lipman, for example, who had been so infuriatingly discreet.

When we were back in the car, I asked Stu if he knew why Laura/Lynn might have been dishonorably discharged from the military.

He looked puzzled, but only for a second, then he said, "There was this one e-mail. I didn't take it too seriously. I thought Lynn only needed to rant in private. But if she said those things to the wrong people a few times too often, she might have been in trouble. But why would her family want to know that?"

"What things?" I asked.

I could sense the same reluctance in Stu as in Major Lipman to spill anything internal about the military. He was the bigger gossip, though, and so he finally said, "It had something to do with their armor. Body armor, but also the vehicles. It seems they had fewer armored Humvees than needed. Lynn often went out with the medics to rescue injured comrades. As a gunner she had to defend the vehicle. But she wrote that they could just as well be riding in a cardboard box through enemy fire. That a simple bullet would pierce through their Humvee in an instant. That's all I remember. These problems exist anywhere, though. And when Lynn was in Afghanistan, the war in Iraq was already being planned and equipped. The better vehicles went there, at least in the beginning."

I had read about these allegations in all kinds of magazines. They were no real military secrets.

"Do you still have the e-mail?" I asked.

"No. I delete my mails pretty quickly. And I didn't know that Lynn would die. Otherwise I would have kept hers."

She was in a war, I wanted to yell. Wasn't it possible that she might get killed? I wondered if it was Stu's mechanism of coping with reality to deny it. Like most of us did on a daily basis, I had to admit to myself.

By now we had checked out at the gate of the base and were on the open road again.

"What kind of person was Laura?" I asked Stu. "Sorry, Lynn," I had to correct myself again. "I know by now that she must have been pretty feisty, stubborn and obviously a very loyal friend. But I'm still trying to figure out what it was like to be around her. Was she really serious and intense?" I was truly curious. In the last few days Laura had become something like a legendary figure to me. It felt like she was a kind of movie star or civil rights hero whom I had heard a lot about, but I still couldn't picture the real person.

"She was kind of . . . normal," Stu answered after a moment of contemplation. The forest had closed up around the highway again. Sprinkles of light were falling through the canopy onto the road. The reflections danced before us and turned reality into an iridescent multidimensional universe, something from an old fairy tale. "When I was with her," Stu continued, "it felt as if life was less crazy. She was just outspoken and friendly. She would say what she felt, but not in a mean way. She didn't put up any act, you know? Didn't try to be cool or anything like that. I could tell that she had been through a lot, seen a lot, but it didn't matter anymore. She wasn't cynical. It just seemed that nothing could really astonish her."

"And after her injury, was she still so laid back?"

"As I said, we didn't see each other much at that time. During her recovery I was deployed, and then she moved to the West Coast. When I was on leave, I once went to the coffee shop where she worked for a short while."

Where she and Inez had met.

"She seemed more distracted than usual, as if she had something on her mind, but then Gerard was with me—I wanted the two to finally meet—and our get together was kind of short."

"Do you remember the name of the coffee shop?"

"I passed by it the other day, but it's closed now. All boarded up."

"Do you know anybody who worked there with Lynn?"

Stu just shook his head. For a moment I had the feeling that Laura's ghost was just brushing by. "Just keep trying," she seemed to say. I couldn't figure out if she was encouraging me or mocking my attempts to uncover the mysteries of her life.

Not long after we entered the forest we passed a pickup that was driving in the other direction, a dark green truck with tinted windows. I only noticed it because I was in an acute state of paranoia and because it struck me as somehow familiar. This time when I routinely checked the mirror I saw the truck's front sneak around the bend we had just turned. It was gone the moment we entered the next curve on this winding road, but when the highway stretched out before us once more, the truck was there in the distance, about half a mile behind us.

Stu was still talking, telling me more about Laura, and I tried to focus. He told me that quite a few of the soldiers at the base were interested in her, and that it helped his reputation, as well as his immunity, when everybody learned that they had married.

"Were the people who liked Lynn male or female?"

"The ones who showed it were male, of course."

"But?"

"Before Lynn met Inez I never knew she was gay either. She never talked about her love life."

Stu had also begun to check the rearview mirror every few seconds. By now I was pretty certain that the green truck was following us. Stu was driving rather slowly, and any other driver behind us would have lost patience and overtaken our car on an empty road like this.

I frantically parsed my brain for ideas about what might happen next. Whoever was in the truck knew to look for me at the military base. It had taken him a while to get here, though, so he probably hadn't followed us on the way there. Was it a very bad sign that he didn't take care anymore about remaining invisible? Did that mean that Marge had figured out where I might have gone and had given the final order to get rid of me—and Stu? But then the green truck had been at the Biltmore Estate yesterday, and the driver had been equally careless about being seen. I had seen it there but hadn't thought anything of it.

Before I could spin my web of obsessive thoughts any further, our car suddenly jerked around. A tire has blown, I thought immediately. We are being shot at!

But Stu continued to drive in the direction we had just come from. He sped up and headed toward the truck. When he had almost reached it, he swerved over to its lane and braked just in time for the truck to stop only inches from us. Stu jumped from the car, ran around it and opened the driver's door of the truck. He was dangling from the door frame, while the truck sped backward. My own reactions were a bit slower than Stu's, but a millisecond later I was also out on the road chasing after the truck. I had no plan, no idea. I just stupidly ran toward the danger. The truck abruptly stopped, and the next thing I saw were two people dropping from it and falling onto the road. Stu's powerful frame was on top of the other person, and they were wrestling on the ground.

When I was close enough, I checked the inside of the truck to see if another attacker was lurking there, but the vehicle was empty. By now Stu had pinned the driver down, both of them panting hard. The person at the bottom was still kicking and wiggling like a fish out of water, but Stu was holding his arms down and sitting heavily on his stomach.

Finally I was close enough to see whom Stu had caught. Long blond curls were spread around her head on the pavement like a halo. But this fallen angel was no saint. It was Jasmine, the cowgirl who had kissed me so passionately in San Francisco three nights ago.

"Tell this idiot to let go of me," she gasped as soon as she saw me.

Fortunately Stu was too smart to do that. "There's a toolbox in the back of the car. Get the duct tape," he called, and I was happy to obey him.

We taped Jasmine up into a tidy package and dragged her off the road. She was bouncing and screaming—so far we hadn't gagged her—and I went to take a closer look at the inside of her truck while Stu went back to get his own vehicle off the road. Jasmine's truck was already standing on the shoulder, its rear wrapped around the trunk of a tree. She hadn't been able to steer very well during her fight with Stu. On the backseat lay a precision rifle and a pair of night vision goggles. I didn't need to see more.

"Take that darn tape off!" Jasmine—or whoever she really was—continued to scream, when I was standing next to her again. "I'm only here because I wanted to see you again."

Had the situation not been so deadly serious, I might have had to laugh. "And to shoot me while you were at it. Like you shot Stacey Schaffner and Al Burns."

The events surrounding his death became clear to me. After I had called Marge outside the shooting range, she had informed Jasmine, who had then quickly driven over and performed a little murder while I was having coffee. After that she had caught up with me again on Irving, and when I had confronted her, she had decided to come up with her infatuation story. My stomach was really not very strong these days. When the recollection of Jasmine's kiss set in, nausea attacked me like a deadly beast, and I had to bend over and throw up the meager remnants of my breakfast, together with bitter green bile. When I had caught my breath again, I grabbed the duct tape that was still lying on the road, pulled off a long strip and wound it around the killer cowgirl's mouth and head.

Stu hadn't overheard our conversation, and when he came back I quickly said, "She's the person who attacked me last night."

"Shall we call the cops?"

I shook my head. "Too much to explain. What I did during that investigation wasn't always strictly legal, you know."

He nodded as if he completely understood what I was talking about. Without further questions, he lifted the wrapped up Jasmine into her truck. I asked him to pull the keys from the ignition and make sure all four doors were securely locked. Then he threw the keys far into the forest. Next he got an emergency triangle from his own car and set it up a quarter of a mile down the road. We didn't want any poor innocent driver to crash right into Jasmine's truck.

Then we continued on our way back to Asheville.

"I thought you said a guy attacked you," Stu mused after a while.

"It was dark, and she was wearing a cap. But I recognized her smell. I was already wondering last night why a man smelled so strongly of flowers." Jasmine had in fact smelled very good again today—of roses and sandalwood. Probably quite an expensive fragrance she was wearing. But I was sure that the smell of this particular perfume would forever make me retch.

We passed the restaurant where we had breakfast. A little farther down the road was a tiny town, and I asked Stu to stop at a pay phone. I had to make a call before anybody had a chance to find and free Jasmine.

I pulled the sleeves of Laura's jacket over my hands to prevent fingerprints and dialed 911. When the operator picked up I lowered my voice to a husky rasp and said. "There was an accident on Highway 401, about eight miles south of Fort Foberland. The gun in the truck was used in a murder in Asheville yesterday. Please inform the detectives of this."

We silently drove back to Asheville. I was deep in thought, trying to come up with plans for what to do next, how to protect Stu, myself, Martha, every goddamn person I knew. And I was still tying to make sense of this unbelievably insane series of events.

Chapter 23

Stu looked pretty beat up. He had a cut on his chin, a big scratch on his forehead, and the knuckles of his right hand were bleeding.

"You might need stitches," I said.

He seemed completely oblivious to his injuries and gave me a bewildered look.

There was a first aid kit in the glove compartment, which I now got out. Awkwardly, I put disinfectant and a Band-Aid on Stu's face while he was driving. Once we had reached Asheville, I asked him if he wanted to see a doctor, but he just waved me off. "It's nothing," he said.

It was clear that the more fuss I'd make, the more I'd tear a hole in the little banner of machismo he so desperately waved, and I let it go.

Stu dropped me off at the hotel. I asked him for his address and phone number and wished him farewell.

"I'll wait here," he said.

"Why?"

"You need protection."

I sighed to myself, but then I said softly, "It's okay. I'll make it back to San Francisco without problems. I've got people there who will take care of the guy who is behind all this."

"You gonna shoot him or what?" Stu asked sarcastically.

"It will only get more complicated if I drag you into this any further. I know which strings to pull. You just watch your back for the next few days."

Again I had to remind myself to keep a serious face while all this nonsense gangster movie talk came out of my mouth like a giant gum bubble. My last warning, though, seemed to give Stu some warped pleasure. He could still feel big and dangerous and ready to get whoever wanted to get him. If only he knew in what kind of danger he might really be. And that there was no way either of us could protect him.

I had told Marge Cunningham about his and Laura's wedding picture, but she didn't know that I had actually met Stu, nor had she seen his photograph. If Jasmine was really taken into police custody and linked to Stacey's murder, it would probably take a while before she could inform her employer about Stu's presence at the scene of her defeat. If she was a serious pro, she wouldn't contact Marge ever again. There would be other precautions she'd have taken in case of an arrest, of which I had no idea, and they were nothing I could imagine with mere common sense.

I felt like a diver lost in a giant shipwreck deep in the ocean. There were countless doors and windows, but none of them led to safety, and all I could do was try every one of them, knowing my air was running low, and the more I tried, the quicker I'd be dead. If I didn't try, I'd drown, too, just slower and humiliated by defeat.

"So what will happen with Lynn's mother?" Stu asked.

I had to recall my original story, and finally said, "I'm pretty sure she'll want to meet you soon. How long will you be in the country this time?" I seriously hoped he would say that he was just in the States for a short leave and would go back to Iraq soon. My brain must have really turned into manure if I wanted somebody back in a war in order to be safe.

"For a few months, probably," Stu answered, and then his face took on this childlike earnestness again. "I can come with you to San Francisco right now. We're a pretty good team in taking out the bad guys, don't you think?"

"Make up with Gerard," I said and walked away.

In the hotel room I gathered my stuff then left the place without officially checking out. Stu's Explorer was still sitting at the curb when I stepped back onto the street. I ignored it and flagged a cab to the airport.

The earliest connection to San Francisco would take me via Atlanta and Denver. The trip would last well into the night with long stopovers in both cities, but I could leave Asheville forty-five minutes later. I purchased a ticket and gladly climbed into the small propeller plane. While we were ascending, leaving the Appalachians far below us, I felt safe for the first time since Stacey's death—which hadn't even been twenty-four hours ago.

In Atlanta I checked right through into the secured area next to the gates. While I was being patted down I wondered how the cowgirl had traveled to North Carolina, and if she had taken her gun on the plane. But then it must have been registered. In whose name? Who was she really? How many fake identities did she have? And how had she become a killer? Or had she flown into Asheville without a gun and shopped for her rifle at the local Wal-Mart?

In one of the airport restaurants I purchased a slice of pizza and a Coke, found a table and opened my laptop. I made a long list of everything that had happened in the last days, of everything I had found out, and an even longer list of unanswered questions.

Laura's manuscript! That's where everything started. Had Laura ever even written anything? Or had Marge just come up with the whole idea of her daughter being a talented writer as a pretext for sending me on my chase? Originally she had hoped that I would retrieve some of Laura's belongings, that she would find answers without having to tell me anything more about her daughter. Or had the whole buildup been part of her plan? If not, what had made her so much more aggressive between my first and my second visit in her pursuit of the mysteries of Laura's past?

My computer signaled that it had found a wireless network. I quickly checked my e-mail. Nothing new had arrived, and I read Mido's mail from last night once again. I didn't answer her. It felt like I had a contagious deadly disease which might even be transmitted through electronic contact. But looking at her mail address—*m.james@yahoo.com*—gave me an idea.

I got out my cell and dialed Stu's number. He picked up after the first ring.

"You're in San Francisco already?" he asked, sounding relieved to hear from me.

"Twenty-first century, remember? Jet planes, yes, teleporting, no." I couldn't keep myself from teasing him.

"Lynn was a Trekkie," he said.

"What?"

"She liked *Star Trek*. The original episodes, Spock and company. Told me that she even went to a convention once."

I made a mental note to add that to the biography I had just composed for her.

"What was her e-mail-address?" I cut to the chase.

"Why do you want to know that?"

"Her mother would like to find out who she was in touch with. Maybe I can get a list of Lynn's contacts somewhere online."

"You'll need her password to get in."

"Do you have it?"

"No."

Stu said that the last e-mail address of Laura he remembered had been a Hotmail account, and her user name had been *galaxybelize*.

I thanked him, hung up, entered the Hotmail Web site and typed in *galaxybelize@hotmail.com*. My next flight would take off in two hours, and for the next one and a half, I chewed pizza, bought another slice, another coffee, sipped it slowly and tried out every possible password I could come up with. I treated it as a meditative exercise—the only way to turn something mindless, boring and hopeless into a bearable activity—and almost didn't react when the mail program finally accepted my login commands and opened the *Hotmail* registered user's start page. Sometimes sitting still, only moving your fingers while trying to empty your brain by mulling over unanswerable questions does lead to enlightenment, I had to admit. The right password had been *inezspock*, and I had no idea why I had even tried this weird, unrelated combination of terms from Laura's life.

When I went to Laura's mailbox, my euphoria quickly vanished, though. There was only junk in the inbox, and the outbox was empty. Not even the address book contained any information. Just to be thorough, I opened the draft folder. I had once read that international terrorist groups used the draft folders of free mail accounts to communicate with each other without actually having to send out e-mails which could be intercepted by the mega computers of the secret services. Every member of the group could log onto an inconspicuous account from anywhere in the world, using public access.

Laura had probably not been a terrorist. By now I didn't completely exclude any possibility any more. Maybe she and Marge had planned to hijack Air Force One, and Marge was desperately trying to cover their tracks, but her draft folder nevertheless contained documents which were as interesting to me as any Al-

Qaeda correspondence would have been to the CIA.

The documents were no book manuscript. They weren't even a detailed diary or daily blog. They looked somewhat like the notes I had just thrown together. The brainstorms of somebody troubled and confused and endangered. But then they were also poetic and strangely hypnotic. I read them all within the next twenty minutes, forwarded them to my own e-mail account, downloaded them into *Outlook Express*, stuffed my computer back into its bag, ran to the gate and boarded the plane to Denver at the last moment.

It seemed to take hours before we had reached the travel altitude and I was allowed to switch the laptop back on again. There were four documents in Laura's draft folder, none longer than half a page. They had been written within days of each other, in the week between December 13 and 20, 2005, the week before her death. I read them all once more:

12/13/05

Flashbacks, still bumping over those roads, mushroom clouds of dust, and everywhere in those streets, behind the houses, in the bleak, beautiful, ancient, innocent, indifferent mountains there is destruction. Sometimes fear sucks the life from my muscles. But then the body works again, more reliable than the soul, running, shouting, shooting, ducking, carrying off somebody, his blood dripping onto our path, his brain shimmering through the bloody mess his head has become. I don't know if he's dead.

Weird moments of exhilaration, feeling useful, dashing toward an unknown cause. It's surreal. I'm a soldier. I'm in a war. It's as clear and undeniable as twelve-tone music, but I don't get it. The destiny of millions, the human lot. My life, my task, my elimination. We're completely unprotected. Nobody cares. We're the collateral, cheaper than the vehicles. The last thought before the blast. What condition will they be in? Will there be pain? Does love evaporate like a mushroom cloud, rise into the cosmos the instant you die? That's when I loved Stu, or was it Leonard? He was with me all that time. I left him behind. Abandoned him. Like he abandoned me. That's all they taught us. The only beautiful thought—I love.

12/15/05

I shot somebody. He just appeared before me. The other end of a gun, the tiny, black hole that sucks you up. I shot. That's all I ever learned. That's how far I came, hunter and prey, prey and predator. He was the enemy. That's what I can do. That's what I am capable of. That's what this animal is capable of.

12/17/05

Leonard was there. I made him promise to never ever come close to them. But then he touched her. And what does Stewart need? He needs something. Poor man. I have to ask L. He'll tell me. Otherwise I'll tell. But whom? I have to know. I have to know more first. Blood. It all comes down to blood.

12/20/05

Now there's Inez. She's all and everything. I can't leave her. Can't abandon her, like I abandoned everybody else. I want to curl up inside her and sleep. That can't be. If she finds out, she can't love me anymore. I'm not worthy. I have to go. I have to go.

For the rest of my trip I read the notes over and over again. I wanted them to tell me what to do next. Wanted Laura to tell me what in the world to do, what had been on her mind, what she knew.

❧

Back in San Francisco I went to the Hertz counter and requested a wheelchair accessible minivan. They referred me to a company that specialized in such vehicles. I called them and a woman told me I'd have to pick up the van at her house in the Excelsior, as it was already after regular business hours. She sounded friendly, and I told her I'd be there in half an hour.

I entered BART and once the train was moving, turned on my cell. It was almost ten p.m., far beyond the time I was supposed to perform my daily call to Marge. When she picked up, I quickly said, "I've found out some really interesting things. But I'm in a rush to a late-night meeting with one more source here in Asheville. I'll catch the first plane tomorrow morning back to the West Coast. Can I brief you in person tomorrow evening?"

"Be here at eight," she said.

Martha had left me a message. Mainly she wanted to know if I was still alive. She'd find that out soon enough, so I didn't call her back but checked the other two messages on my voicemail. The first one consisted of static. Caller ID had been blocked. I thought I heard some hectic but very low breaths, then came the click that marked the end of the call. The second message started out in the same fashion. Static, almost inaudible breaths—but then there was a new noise, as if a door was being closed somewhere in the background. There was a little gasp. It almost felt like a word. With a lot of imagination it could have been the word *Help*.

I had received a call like this the night before my departure to Asheville. They didn't sound like the anonymous hauntings of a pervert.

The train pulled into Glen Park station, and I grabbed my belongings and got off. On the platform I turned off the cell. I didn't want to have anything on me that could be electronically traced. There was no cab to be seen, and after a half hour foot march, I finally reached the house of the van rental company's owner—a bubbly woman in her late thirties who seemed pleased to conduct business at this hour. She was heavyset like Martha and a wheelchair user herself. She showed me how the automatic ramp of the van and the tie-downs worked. I signed a few papers, swallowed the info about the exorbitant rental fee with what I hoped was inconspicuous outrage and drove off in a black Ford Windstar.

Chapter 24

Martha had locked the office door from the inside and left the key inserted. I was glad she had taken at least this small precaution to protect herself and called her from the other side of the door. After she had let me in she studied me from head to toe and said, "No Cheney holes in my chicky."

I bent down and gave her a bear hug. Partly out of true fondness and relief to be back in Martha's overbearing but protective dark aura, partly to shut her up.

"We have to go," I said. "I rented an accessible van."

"I love road trips," my partner said, and her face lit up so brightly I swore to myself that if we survived this case, I'd take her on a really fabulous, harmless vacation somewhere in the beautiful wildernesses of this country.

We went to Martha's apartment, where she packed an overnight bag. On top of her underwear and toiletries she laid her beloved Sig-Sauer 9mm and tucked some extra clips of ammunition in at the side.

Then we were ready to go, and I tied down Martha's chair inside the van the way the rental lady had shown me. It was fifteen minutes after midnight when we crossed the Golden Gate bridge. There was one more call to make, and I stopped once again at a pay phone along the way.

Rita was still up and so happy to hear from me that I instantly felt bad for having to keep our conversation short.

"Have you been followed in the last days, or have there been any strange cars or people close to your home?" I asked her.

"I don't think so."

That was good news, but it didn't remove any of the boulders that were crushing my chest.

"Now you're going to tell me to be really careful, keep my eyes open and if possible move in with a friend for a few days," Rita teased me. She sounded somewhat worried, though. The last time I had given her a similar kind of warning, she fortunately hadn't been attacked, but the story behind it hadn't been pretty, either, and it had ended with Mido and me almost being killed.

"Is there anybody you could stay with?" I asked hopefully. Ideally somebody on another continent, or even better, another planet.

"It's fun and exciting being friends with you," Rita said. "But I can't go into hiding whenever you're working a dangerous case."

"Not always," I begged. "Just this time."

Rita had been to the prison with me. She had also been at the bar where I had noticed Jasmine for the first time. It wasn't far-fetched to imagine that a paranoid killer might be afraid I had shared crucial information with her and that she had to be silenced.

"Okay," Rita finally said. "I'll call up a few friends and see if I can stay with them. But you owe me a mah-jongg night for this. Oh, what am I saying, four mah-jongg nights."

Rita loved playing mah-jongg, and she couldn't always get the necessary four players together. I wasn't into the game all that much. It was too nerve-racking for me. But I now promised her a whole year of mah-jongg nights.

When I was back in the car, Martha, of course, demanded to hear the whole nasty story of the last days. We slowly rode into the night while I brought her up-to-date. For the first twenty minutes I had no real plan where to go, but then I got an idea, and I turned the van onto a northbound road.

For many miles the fog was so dense we couldn't even see the ocean, which I knew was crashing against the cliffs on whose edge we were riding. The night closed in on us like a cosmic wormhole. Only when we reemerged in a small town twenty miles from Aldridge, did we believe we hadn't landed in a different millennium, but were still stuck in the same old century, decade, year, month, day . . . The car's clock showed 2:24 a.m., and we checked into a Holiday Inn where we got a wheelchair accessible room with two queen-size beds. Spilling my guts to my partner had made me weirdly hungry, and we quickly walked to a twenty-four hour supermarket across the highway and purchased fruit, chocolate bars, fried chicken and some red wine. While we were picnicking in our room I felt almost giddy, as if this were, in fact, already our Girl Scout weekend and the world out there a big harmless playground. We giggled senselessly over a stupid TV show, clearly trying to push aside the fact that we had to come up with some kind of plan.

"Let's sleep, chicky," Martha said when I tried to get back to the case. "We'll have enough time tomorrow to fight for our lives."

And with this, we turned off the lights, rolled over in our respective beds, and a few minutes later Martha was snoring loudly and peacefully. Her snore neither bothered me nor kept me awake. On the contrary, it was reassuring to hear the sounds of a living being so close to me who was clearly on my side.

I was awakened by a whisper somewhere close by. Somebody was calling for help. Sleep had me in such a tight grip I couldn't open my eyes. I struggled to find the source of the whisper. Finally, I realized it was coming from inside my own mind. And then my heart jump-started with a jolt of energy that raced through my chest with the force of a freight train—or rather a wheelchair speeding down a steep hill out of control.

The echo of Kali's calls for help when I had been running after her chair rang in my ears. Then there was the message from last night—the second one where there had been the low whisper that had sounded like the word *Help*.

It was five a.m. I didn't want to wake Martha and tried to go back to sleep, without success. At seven I couldn't stand it anymore. I got up, showered, and when I came back into the room, Martha was already sitting in her wheelchair, her hair in a long braid, ready to go. She had taken a bath the evening before and didn't want to bother with the shower, so she just brushed her teeth, washed her face, and we could leave. We crossed the street, found a table at an IHOP, ordered breakfast and went into the details of Laura's story once again. I let Martha listen to the call on my voicemail and told her about the connection my over-exhausted subconscious had come up with.

"Laura must have had a very good reason to run away from home," I said. "And now there is another young girl living with Marge, one who doesn't speak English, who can't see or walk. Maybe she even pushed her wheelchair down the hill herself, in order to get my attention."

"And now she's calling you, you think?" Martha asked.

"She has to do it secretly, when nobody's around. And that doesn't happen very often. I've seen how protective Marge is of her. She hardly lets her out of sight."

"Which might be necessary if her trip down the boulevard

was an indication that she's accident prone. How would she know your number, anyway?"

"She could have listened when Marge called me. Could have just pressed redial or memorized the touch tones."

"You think there's nobody else around she could confide in?"

"I have no idea what her life is like. Leonard seems to drive her places. I think he mentioned hospital visits. Apart from him, I don't know if there's anybody she could reach out to."

"What is Marge doing to her?" Martha said. "What do you think?"

"I have no idea. Maybe Laura was molested. Maybe beaten, maybe emotionally abused. I still have no clue. She never talked to anybody about it. Nobody I've found so far, anyway."

"And you think Kali is going through the same thing now?"

Our breakfast plates arrived, a gigantic portion of buttermilk pancakes for Martha, and a four-egg, bacon, cheese, tomato omelet for me. Thinking about Kali's possible demise wiped out my appetite, but I knew I had to somehow calm my angrily growling stomach, and devoured the food without tasting much.

"If Laura was molested and Kali is subjected to the same thing now, by the same person, what happened in all the years in between?" Martha brainstormed. "Child molesters don't stop what they're doing for almost fifteen years."

"The Cunningham Foundation is involved in so many charities. Leonard said his aunt almost always has a child who needs medical help staying with her."

"We have to find the other children."

"Good luck with that," I replied full of frustration. "They are probably long back in their countries. Probably they did receive medical treatment and will keep quiet forever about the other treatment they were subjected to in the U.S."

"Or they do speak about it, but their families either don't believe them or are too scared to confront a powerful organization like the Cunningham Foundation," Martha said. "If we can't get to the abuser through the victims, we have to get to him through himself."

"What do you mean?"

"We have to find out who the driving force in the family is. It might be Marge herself. There certainly are female sexual predators around, but they are fewer in numbers. More often they are the facilitators. Mothers who look away when their boyfriend rapes their children on a daily basis, for example. I once worked a case where wealthy pedophiles courted young single moms, started relationships with them and then molested their kids. But they didn't just do it at home, alone and in secret. They took the children on so-called camping weekends where they hooked up with their pedophile friends, who paid well to have the kids all to themselves for days in a row. It was a whole ring of pedophiles, and they were involved in everything: trading child pornography online, making videos of the kids and selling them off, and organizing molestation package tours to somebody's hunting cabin."

"And the moms?"

"They didn't want to see it. They thought they were living with those great, generous, rich guys. Couldn't get themselves to burst their own bubbles."

"How did you get involved?"

"It was a concerted police effort. One of the cyber cops got hold of a video where a child was being killed on camera. Some of the ugliest monsters get off on that, and these clips sell for incredible sums. So homicide got involved. It was a crazy investigation, but we had clues that the film had been produced in the Bay Area. We caught the moviemaker. Never found the dead child nor the mother, but the videographer fingered a few of his connections in order to save his deranged hide, and we arrested a number of the esteemed citizens he was selling to. In a cabin that belonged to one of them, we found traces of what kind of hunting party was usually meeting there."

I couldn't swallow a single bite anymore. Of course I had heard what sexual predators were doing, but most of the time I pushed the full realization far away. Martha's story made this impossible.

Martha had also abandoned her plate.

"So you think Marge may be selling off the children in her care to some pedophile she knows or a whole pedophile assembly?" I said when I had collected myself.

Martha looked at me with deep sympathy. "I have no idea what she's really doing. I'm just saying it's a possible scenario where the pieces you've gathered may fit the mosaic."

"Kali is disabled," I said. "Would pedophiles be as attracted to a blind Middle Eastern child in a wheelchair as to a nondisabled Goldilocks?"

"Pedophiles have quite idiosyncratic tastes. Remember, some get off on dead children. It's about weakness and dominance. They need to victimize the child to feel in charge. The big papa caring for the weak little creature. It's very twisted. Some of these guys actually believe they are protecting the children, initiating them sexually, while all they do is prey on a kid's innate defenselessness. Kali doesn't speak the language. She can't run away. She can't even visually identify them. How perfect can a victim be in a pervert's universe?"

I had to get to Kali, at least to find out if she was indeed the anonymous caller.

But right now we were far away from San Francisco and close to the town where Inez was. I pulled out Laura's murder book and opened it for Martha. Then I showed her the photos and pointed out the ideas they had given me.

My partner studied them for quite a while. Her face with the high cheekbones and the olive-colored baby skin took on the expression of a black panther, poised, focused, ready to jump from a tree and drive her fangs into an unsuspecting neck.

"You're right," she finally said, and it was one of the biggest compliments I had ever received from her. "There's something wrong here. The boys should have checked why somebody cuts her veggies with a hunting knife."

"And a professional chef especially."

For the next twenty minutes, Martha was on the phone. Then she had worked her magic and had gotten me another visitation date with Inez. She was still in the prison ward of Aldridge hospital, but she was better and ready to see a visitor.

"Don't you want to come with me?" I asked my partner.

"The DOC allows only one visitor at a time, and you've already established rapport with the inmate. You'll do fine."

I hadn't asked Martha because I particularly wanted her to accompany me. I was mainly amazed that she didn't seize the chance to exercise control. I had to admit that working in the field with her felt much better than I'd have ever imagined.

I had to be at the hospital in two hours, and Martha and I spent the time in a coffee shop next to the IHOP, continuing to discuss the case. Martha had contacted Marcus Robinson's parents right after I'd alarmed her with my call from the bathroom of Laura's Asheville apartment. She told them she was organizing a class reunion—at this point I had to laugh hysterically. We really had to develop a few better pretexts for the future, or at least different ones. His parents had given her his number at the military base in Texas to which he had returned. Martha had reached him there, had claimed she wanted to sell him life insurance and hung up after he declined.

He was probably safe for now. First, he was far away in a guarded and armed environment, and second, he'd seen Laura last when they were in high school. So far, only the people who had spoken with her in the months before her death had been killed. What a consolation!

Chapter 25

Inez had been the person closest to Laura in the months before her death, and she was probably in the gravest danger. Suddenly, the thick, bulletproof sliding glass doors she was kept behind at Aldridge hospital's prison ward seemed reassuring rather than depressing.

A nurse inserted a pin card at the first door. It glided open, and she let me pass through. She stayed behind when the door closed after me, and for a few minutes I was trapped alone between the transparent walls. Then a guard appeared behind door number two. She pushed some keys into locks and opened it. I had to step into a small room and hand over the contents of my pockets, along with my cell phone, wallet and car keys. The correctional officer locked them in her desk, looked me up and down—I was wearing my natural colored brown eye, black corduroys and a green sweater—and led me down another hall. She was as detached and matter of fact as the COs I had encountered in the prison during my visits there. At the end of the corridor was a barred door, much like the ones in the actual penitentiary. The guard unlocked it, and we entered the next hall which looked like a regular hospital ward. A broad-shouldered male nurse was slowly walking toward us, and when the CO explained who I wanted to visit, he nodded and took me over from her. Finally, we reached the door behind which Inez was kept. It wasn't even locked. The man just opened it and let me enter.

It became clear at first glance why the door didn't need to be locked. Inez was sitting up in her bed, her legs on top of the sheets. She was wearing one of the prison quality blue shirts and matching blue cotton pants. She was the only patient in the room, although there were two empty beds next to hers. Her left hand was cuffed to the steel frame of the bed. Had she tried to run away, she would have dragged the heavy, cumbersome hospital bed with her.

Inez looked different than on my first two visits. She was still pale, but the dull film over her eyes had vanished, and she greeted me with a broad smile which opened up her whole face.

"How are you doing?" I asked her, awkwardly shy. The door to the room remained open, but the nurse hadn't come in with me.

"Much better," she said. "It's strange. I always thought that it was just the fact that I was in jail and everything that happened that made me feel as if I had an iron cage around my heart. Now that the medication is kicking in, I feel quite a bit less stressed."

"That's great," I said, distracted already. I didn't know how much time we had and I needed to ask her the most crucial questions.

"Listen," I said and sat down on the edge of her bed, as there was no chair available and the other beds stood too far away from Inez's. "I don't think you killed Laura."

Immediately, her face closed up like a mimosa leaf that had

been touched and rolled itself up in protection. Before she could cut me off, I continued. "I think you're trying to protect your father, but I'm rather certain he didn't do it, either. The evidence doesn't support it. But you have to be honest with me and tell me what really happened on that day."

"You don't think dad did it?" Inez whispered frantically. "How can you prove that?"

"Your whole story doesn't work out."

She turned her head away from me, stared at the wall as if she was hoping to burn a hole into its bricks. Her face was gorgeous, her eyes clear and narrowed in concentration. She was a woman who had fought for her life, and who had made it. Her soul was conflicted but ready to continue to hold on to what she believed in. She looked extremely lonesome, and I longed to touch her, to convey some human loyalty, but I didn't dare.

"The person who killed Laura must have hurt himself, or he must have worn thick gloves, which I don't think your father did."

"He didn't wear gloves," Inez said, barely audible, still looking away from me.

"I saw his hands. He doesn't have scars on his palms."

Inez opened the palm of her right hand, stretched it out for me to take a good look. There were three long, deep red scars on it and a crisscross of smaller ones. "And how do you think I got these?" she asked me defiantly, as if I would turn on her the next second, ready to cross over the line from supporter to prosecutor.

"You tell me," I said.

"He must have done it. He was holding the knife. He was all bloody, and Laura was just lying there. She was dead."

"Where were you when it happened?"

"I wasn't there. I didn't protect her. She was sometimes scared that she wouldn't be able to deal with dad when he had one of his bad moments. I shouldn't have left her alone with him."

"So you weren't even in the house?"

Inez shook her head. "I had a job, a corporate Christmas party in the early evening. I'd usually do all the preparations for jobs in the afternoon, then pick up dad. Laura and I would have dinner with him, and I'd take him to bed, give him his sleep aid and leave again once he was fast asleep. That usually worked out fine."

"But that day it didn't."

"The company wanted the food at an unusual time. I wanted to decline the job, refer them to somebody else, but they were such great clients and they insisted I do it. Laura said it would be okay. She could pick up dad and handle him until I came home."

"And when you came home, she was dead and your father was holding the knife."

Tears were streaming down Inez's cheeks, but she didn't sob. She sounded clear and strangely monotonous, like the automated voice of a call center phone menu. "He was pointing it at me. He was very confused and agitated. He didn't even recognize me at first. I had to struggle with him before he gave me the knife."

"And that's how you got cut?"

Inez nodded.

I pictured the scene. The frantic, confused man. Inez facing the mutilated body of her dead lover. Her father pointing a knife at her. She must have grabbed at the bare blade in order to wrangle it out of his hands. She was most likely in terrible shock, unable to feel any pain, unable to manage any clear thoughts. It's a wonder our heart doesn't just explode in such a moment, but continues to pound at a deadly speed.

"Did the knife belong to you, your father or to Laura?"

"It was a weird knife. I remember that. It had such a strange hook thing on the blade. When I was finally holding on to it, I was thinking I'd never seen a knife like that before. But dad sometimes manages to get a hold of stuff. He steals it or finds it.

It's not always easy to trace back to the rightful owners."

"So Laura was probably cutting the veggies in the kitchen," I pondered. "For some reason, she must have left the house and wandered into the front yard. Because there was no blood in the house and no signs of a struggle."

"The kitchen faces the front yard," Inez said.

Laura could have seen her attacker approach the house and gone outside to meet him. He could have brought the knife, killed her and fled, leaving the weapon behind. Inez's father either witnessed the whole scene or just walked out himself, found Laura, found the knife, and when Inez came back from her job, she found him.

I had no idea how any of this could be proved, if there could be a new trial, if Inez could revoke her confession, so that the investigation would be opened all over again. I had nothing to promise her, no hope to give. Still, she looked at me with a gaze of true amazement and the most profound relief.

"I don't know what I can do," I said. "But I'll try everything to get you out of here, out of jail."

"That's okay," she said. "Don't do anything that would endanger dad. I read an article where they've convicted an Alzheimer's patient who killed somebody and sentenced him to life in prison, although he was clearly demented when he did it."

"That's why you tried to cover for him."

"He wouldn't survive being incarcerated."

You almost didn't yourself, I thought.

As if a long, sharp object had just pierced her chest, Inez suddenly pressed her eyelids down as if in severe pain. Oh no, not another heart attack, I thought, and shot up to find a doctor. But then she said, "Who killed her? I was just so relieved that dad probably didn't do it . . . but that means that Laura's murderer is still out there."

"He is," I said.

The nurse came back in and told us that we only had another

three minutes. I began to plant as many questions in Inez's mind as possible and made her promise to think about everything Laura ever told her that might give us a clue as to who could have wanted her dead and why. Inez seemed somewhat confused, but she was eager to rack her brain for whatever important information might be buried there.

We agreed that she would use her phone privileges as soon as possible to give me a collect call. I asked her in a low voice not to accept any other visitors and to complain about a few more health problems so she could stay in the hospital as long as possible. For now she was more protected here than on the outside or in the regular prison.

Before I left, I leaned down to her and gave her a hug. The nurse, who was standing in the door, whistled sharply as if I were a dog in need of discipline, and I let Inez go. She grinned at me, showing laugh lines I hadn't seen on her face before. An impish spark was dancing in her eyes, and it wasn't hard to imagine why Laura had fallen so deeply and truly in love with her.

Brooding over my new findings, I drove back to where I had left Martha. Inez's father had probably not witnessed the actual murder, or at least the killer hadn't seen him, otherwise he wouldn't still be alive. Inez had an alibi, which had never been checked by the authorities due to her confession. If she had catered an event, many people must have seen her there. On the other hand, it probably just proved that her confession wasn't completely accurate. If Laura had been killed only minutes before Inez arrived at the scene, Inez could still be tied to the murder. But if we showed that there were inconsistencies in the original confession, maybe that could lead to a reopening of the case.

Chapter 26

Martha was waiting for me in a coffee shop in the mall close to the hotel. My laptop was sitting on the table before her, and she was reading Laura's notes.

"We have to talk to Susan Bradley," she said before I could even say hello. "We need inside information on the Cunninghams."

Susan Bradley was Big Susan, Mido's former boss, owner of one of the biggest advertising companies in the city, and scion to a clan at least as rich and powerful as the Cunninghams, and she was the person who had referred Martha and me to them.

"I'll call her," I said, a bit hesitant. I was doubtful that Big Susan would be anything but her usual super-discreet self. Maybe the story I had to tell her would break through the shell of upper class solidarity, though.

On the way back to San Francisco, I asked Martha what she

thought about Laura's outrage over the unarmored Humvees they had to use in Afghanistan.

"Sounds outrageous to me," she said. "But not more so than weapons of mass destruction dreamt up by the White House's personal tarot card expert."

Martha was balancing my laptop on her knees, still trying to make sense of Laura's notes. "Isn't the Cunningham Corporation into producing armored vehicles?" she then said.

I told her I had made the Cunningham Corporation's Web site available offline on Internet Explorer, and she opened it.

"So now we have two theories," she said, after perusing the site once more. "They either killed Laura because she wanted to rat out their child pornography business, or they stabbed her because she got in their way of selling dysfunctional armor to the military or vehicles which were supposed to be armored, but in fact weren't. That's quite a range."

"What do you make of Laura's writings?"

"She was pretty messed up."

"She had a head injury, she was traumatized as a child, lived a life on the fringes of society, then went to war. I think she was as sane as can be under the circumstances. We just have to listen to what she's really saying."

"Well, you listen hard and let me know when she's told you," Martha said, clearly offended that I had lectured her.

"I just have the feeling there's something in her notes, something she wants us to know."

Martha read Laura's last letters out loud. By now I almost knew them by heart. And maybe they hadn't even been just letters to herself. I would send them to Inez as soon as possible. They were Laura's heritage. And hopefully her lover would be able to understand them.

"Laura killed somebody," Martha said.

"I think so, too. She probably shot someone in Afghanistan."

"She loved Stu. She loved Leonard. She loved Inez," Martha

listed. "She pities Stewart. That's not Stu, is it?"

"I don't think so. There's a Stewart Cunningham mentioned in the family history."

Martha fell silent for a few minutes, reading the computer screen. Then she said, "Stewart Cunningham: Marge's brother, Leonard's father, Alcott's son."

"Leonard was there," I quoted Laura's note. "And Stewart wants something. Laura doesn't know what he wants. But she is willing to tell something if Leonard doesn't tell her what she wants to know. Also, she made Leonard promise something. Not to touch them. Who is them? And why does it all come down to blood?"

Suddenly I remembered the blood test Stacey had given me. After her murder I had forgotten all about it. Martha found it in my bag, and I told her the relevance of the piece of paper with the Arabic letters.

"So it's a blood test for somebody but not Laura, and Stacey doesn't know where Laura got it from?"

I nodded. None of this added up.

"Laura believed there was something she had done that would stop Inez from loving her if she found out." Martha continued to interpret the notes. "She thought she had to take action in order to deal with whatever that was."

"Maybe the fact that she killed somebody?"

"If she killed somebody in combat, there wasn't much she could do about it later. And don't you think Inez would have understood that?"

I didn't even know if Inez was aware that Laura had been a soldier. I hoped I'd have time to ask her when she called me. And was it important that Laura had written that she had loved Stu? Had there been any misunderstanding between her and her husband? False hopes on her side? But then she had fallen in love with Inez. Wouldn't that have solved possible complications between her and Stu? The fireworks of unanswered questions were dancing wilder and wilder.

"Stay on Bay Street," Martha said after we crossed the bridge back into the city. We soon reached the Embarcadero, and I realized what my partner's plan was. *AdUp*, Susan Bradley's company, was located in Pier 3. I parked across the street, helped Martha out of the van, and we ventured over to the luxurious offices of Big Susan's advertising agency.

I had once worked here as a security guard, and a former coworker who was staffing the security post in the lobby greeted me warmly and let us pass without questions. Inside *AdUp's* quarters—they consisted of a gorgeous spacious main office overlooking the bay and a few smaller offices belonging to the managers, as well as the owner—I spotted Peter, Big Susan's assistant, and asked him for a spontaneous audience with the queen.

"Let me ask her," he said and walked off.

He never returned, but suddenly Susan Bradley was standing next to me. She must have come from behind us. Big Susan was a petite, elegant woman in her fifties. As usual she was wearing a gray pantsuit and white dress shirt. Her spiky red hair was her most colorful feature, together with the serious green eyes. There was something inconspicuous about Susan Bradley. Or maybe everybody would have seemed unimpressive in person if you knew that she was really royalty. And Susan was just that, if not in the blue-blooded, but the green-billed sense.

"Anna," she greeted me coolly but kindly. "Are you looking for me?"

"We need your help," I said.

Susan Bradley welcomed Martha then led us into her office, whose decoration repeated the aqua and silver of the iridescent water outside the big window. We arranged ourselves around a low table. Susan pressed a button, asked an anonymous entity at the other end of the intercom for refreshments, then comfortably leaned back in her chair and crossed her legs.

"I spoke with Marge a few days ago. She is very happy you have taken on her case and has been impressed already with your first results."

"Well, since then we've had a few problems," Martha said.

I didn't even know where to begin. I didn't think Susan Bradley was in any way involved in the Cunninghams' scheme. But I also didn't think she would necessarily believe our story over theirs.

"What problems?" Susan asked.

"What can you tell us about the Cunninghams?" Martha asked. She sounded quite like a cop performing an interview, and immediately Susan Bradley shut down.

"Nothing that Marge wouldn't tell you herself if it were important for the case," she said.

Martha realized the effect she had caused and continued in a much milder voice. "I appreciate your discretion. And Anna and I are, of course, grateful that you recommended us."

Her verbal curtsy was doing its trick. Susan Bradley's features lightened up a bit. She leaned forward, her stance more open, unprepared for the next onslaught of Martha's innate bad cop routine.

"But now people have been killed," my partner thundered. "By a sniper. A hired gun. And we have every reason to believe Marge Cunningham has hired her. We have to know why. There are many signs that Laura was abused when she was living there."

Susan Bradley didn't look as shocked or angry or even incredulous as I was sure she would be. "That sounds like a rather wild story," she just said, stern, matter of fact, almost emotionless. "Are you really certain of this?"

I nodded. When are you ever absolutely certain of anything? One of the reasons I had once chosen to become a scientist was that I wanted to be able to verify what parents, teachers and other authorities were serving me as truths. That the earth was orbiting the sun, for example. As a little girl I had been obsessed with disproving it, had forever observed and calculated the movements of the stars, and finally had to admit that it was almost certainly true.

Martha looked at me and nodded, too. Susan Bradley would tell us what she knew, and we hardly dared to breathe so she wouldn't change her mind.

"I really don't know why Marge would hire a killer," she said, her eyes locked on mine. "Where would you even find somebody like that?"

"There are ways," Martha said quietly.

"Such as?"

"You ask around. Hint at it. Very vaguely, of course. Innocent people, such as yourself, would never get such a hint. You'd think somebody is looking for a good florist, or menswear supplier. If you ask around long enough, in the right circles, you'll eventually find somebody who can decode your hint, who will hint back."

Susan was a creative person. I knew her imagination was at work coming up with all kinds of scenarios. I was getting impatient, though. My leg was moving up and down of its own volition. Susan stared at it. I tried to sit still.

"There have been rumors," she said. "A long time ago. Before Alcott became so frail he didn't leave his house anymore."

"What rumors?" I asked.

"That you didn't want to leave your children unobserved when he was around. When I was growing up, my mother told me I shouldn't be in a room with him without another adult present. To politely excuse myself if a situation ever occurred where he would try to talk to me alone."

"Were there many occasions when he would have had a chance to do that?"

"There were parties. Our families were acquainted. Alcott's wife and my mother were bridge friends."

"But nobody ever did anything, at least cut him off, to get him out of the vicinity of their children?"

"My parents grew up in different times. Sexual molestation wasn't treated the way it is nowadays."

Which didn't do much to stop pedophiles today. But she was right, the public awareness of the issue had become more heightened.

"Weren't people worried for his own children?" Or grandchildren, I thought.

Susan didn't answer this question. It was obvious nobody had ever been worried enough to do anything. Alcott's children were Marge and Stewart.

"When did you last see Alcott?" Martha asked.

"That was many years ago. I believe it was at his wife's funeral. She had been sick for a long time. A quiet little lady. It's strange, I can hardly recall her face. My mom asked me to accompany her. Alcott must be over ninety by now. I've heard he's bedridden."

"How close are you to Marge? Did you ever suspect her father molested her? Or Stewart, or Leonard, or Laura?"

Susan became paler when I listed all these people who were possible victims of her parents' good old pal Alcott.

"I have to admit I blocked out the whole thing after I had grown up. And Marge and I were never intimate friends. Good acquaintances, yes. She's a few years older than me."

"Stewart must be closer in age to you," Martha cut in. "Did you two ever hang out the way teenagers do at boring family gatherings?"

My partner had hit a vulnerable spot with Big Susan. The billionaire closed her eyes for a millisecond as if to hide the expression in them. Then she caught herself again, pressed the intercom button once more and said, "We're almost done here. If the coffee doesn't show up in the next thirty seconds, you can pour it down the drain."

Susan Bradley had the reputation of being a tough but fair businesswoman. Her employees respected and feared her. Now I could see where the fear part came from.

"Stewart is very ill. Something heart related," she said, and she sounded as if this fact was somehow our fault. "But I can't tell you exactly what it is. I haven't spoken with him since he broke off our engagement over thirty years ago."

It was very clear that this was the last we would ever hear from Big Susan on this particular topic. She opened the door for us, silently and determinedly accompanied us all the way to the main lobby of the pier building and stepped back into the realm of her agency with the most fleeting of good-byes.

Chapter 27

Back in the van, I tried to convince Martha that I wanted to keep my appointment with Marge Cunningham at eight o'clock tonight. It was almost five by now, and I was becoming increasingly nervous, tortured by the fact that Kali had probably called me for help yesterday, and so far I had done nothing to respond.

"There's a chance that Marge really doesn't know I've witnessed Stacey being shot," I said. "And if Jasmine has been arrested and hasn't had a chance to contact her, she may still believe that I'm working for her. If I don't show up, though, I'm blowing a great cover."

"There's also a chance that your mother had you through immaculate conception," my partner bitched. "But that doesn't make you a virgin."

"That may sound funny, but it doesn't make any sense whatsoever," I bitched back.

"Okay, chicky," Martha said more peacefully. "Let's think it through."

I believed in Martha's peacefulness about as much as I believed in nuclear warheads as peacekeepers. I nevertheless turned around. "Okay. Let's say she knows that I know. What's our alternative? If I don't show up, she'll begin to hunt me down at around five past eight tonight, anyhow. But if I go there, I may have a chance to check a few things out."

"Or she'll greet you right at the door with a loaded Beretta."

"Marge isn't the type to do the dirty work herself."

"But she's the type who has already hired the next killer to do it for her."

"I can let her know that if I don't leave her house unharmed by eight forty-five at the latest, you'll have the police department at her doorstep."

"And do what? Engage in polite chitchat on the porch while her janitor is driving away with your body through the back gate?"

"There is no porch and no back gate, and it's not that easy to get rid of a body without leaving any evidence. Also, I'm telling you, she won't do anything while I'm on her estate. She's too tidy for that. Too anal."

"You said that Leonard is driving the girl to the doctor on a regular basis. Why don't we just surveil the house and wait until Kali is on neutral territory? You should be able to approach her in a hospital surrounding."

The desperate gasp for help resounded in my head and grew into the louder but still suppressed calls Kali had made when she was speeding down the hill. When had that incident taken place? I calculated backward. Last Friday. It was Wednesday now. Five days ago Kali had been in such distress that she had possibly pushed her wheelchair down a deadly incline just to get my attention. How long had she been suffering to be willing to risk her life just to get me—to get anybody—to notice she needed help? I couldn't wait any longer. I had to find her today.

"I'm going," I informed Martha.

She looked strangely relieved. I had no idea why. "I'll wire you good then," she said.

We drove to an electronics supplier in the Mission. The shop was huge and crowded. In a back corner they had a big assortment of everything a spy wannabe could dream of. I let Martha pick out what she needed and marveled over the mini cameras hidden in eyeglasses, pens, ties and even a wig. I was wondering if there was a camera I could hide behind one of my eye patches, or an artificial eye with a camcorder built into the pupil. Maybe one day I'd patent the idea.

When Martha was done, we drove back to the office. She had more devices there that she wanted me to carry. We pulled down the blinds. I took off my T-shirt and let Martha tape a mini microphone right beneath my collarbone. She used an old fashioned Band-Aid for that, the flesh-colored kind with the white spots for air to get to the wound. It was supposed to camouflage the device at least somewhat, in case somebody took a closer look at my cleavage, and the air holes would let enough sound through. The mic had its own battery and built-in transmitter. I would carry a voice-activated mini tape recorder in my bag which the mic would transmit to. It looked like any other dictaphone, so if somebody searched me, it would be a pretty inconspicuous tool for a PI. The mic would also broadcast to a second recorder, which Martha was carrying. She would wait not far from the house. The mic's transmitter was probably not strong enough to deliver very good results to her device, but we wanted to give it a shot.

Next, Martha placed two tracking devices on me. A stronger, bigger GPS device I could carry in one of the front pockets of the cargo pants I was wearing. It was disguised as a key ring mini flashlight. I attached a weaker, tiny positioning bug to the inside of my panties. Again, Martha would be holding on to the receiver for this device. Last but not least, I would leave on my cell phone as another device with which my position—or at least the position of the phone—could be triangulated.

I didn't feel much safer with all the technological knick-knacks, but they'd make Martha feel that she did everything to protect me, and in case I really got busted by Marge's henchmen, that would make her a less guilt-ridden widow. Or at least I hoped that'd be the case.

Lastly, she wanted to supply me with a weapon. I strictly declined taking one of her guns. She had made me practice shooting a few times, but I didn't feel I was really in control of the thing yet. I possessed a long, strong hunting knife, which I had bought in Reno during another adventure, and I agreed to take it with me. Once again, I exchanged my artificial eye for a patch, so not to be bothered by a potentially itching object in my orbit, and was ready to go.

At seven ten, I drove us up to Pacific Heights. Martha had suggested I show up fifteen minutes before the agreed time. She wanted me to be in charge from the get-go, and showing up ear-lier was a little distraction intended to throw Marge off just the tiniest bit.

We approached Marge's neighborhood from an unusual direction, came down a steep side street from the north, turned the last corner at an angle invisible from the house, and I parked the car beneath the Cunningham mansion, out of sight from the windows of the building and next to its lower foundation.

Martha would be trapped if she stayed in the car, so I helped her out as quickly and quietly as possible, and she pushed away in the opposite direction from which I was walking. She would find a driveway or other hidden space to wait for me. Her Sig-Sauer was secured in its holster.

Marge opened the door after my second ring.

"You're early," she said, stating the obvious.

"On my watch it's exactly eight," I said and looked at my wristwatch, which I had set ahead. I made sure Marge could see the watch's hands as well.

"If you're not ready, I can wait," I offered.

"Come in," she commanded, and I followed her into the hall. "I'm impatient to hear what you found out."

We walked into the same salon where we had spoken during my two previous visits. It was almost dark by now, and the lights of the city beneath the windows were glistening like an ocean of stars. Again Marge offered me a drink from the carafe, which I declined. Then she took a cigarette from a box sitting on the same table and lit it. I had never seen her smoke before, and the nicotine seemed to immediately redden her cheeks and focus her gaze, which she now threw directly at me like a punch in the face.

During my last two visits, Marge Cunningham had displayed various personas, from the maid to the uptight aristocrat to the grieving mother. She had always seemed neurotic to me. Unpredictable, smart, but weirdly one-dimensional. She was not a bad actor. Her roles held up for a while, but then it became clear that there was this whole complex human being firmly hidden behind the mask. Today, for the first time, she appeared to be a truly feeling, loving, suffering, hating person. Her thin lips were tensing and flexing nervously between the drags on the cigarette. She seemed agitated, and at the same time, full of anticipation. I wondered for what.

Her pupils were wide, opening the gates to a dark, cavernous space full of turmoil. It was hard to tell if there was danger lurking at the bottom or pain. Even Marge's hair was different, I realized, less coiffed. It fell to her shoulders in a natural wave of bright white. She was wearing a pair of designer jeans and an ironed but still casual white tunic accentuated with Belgian lace. Her feet were clad in expensive suede hiking boots, comfortable and practical, yet stylish.

"I will be sending you a complete report tomorrow," I said. "I've almost completed it. I just wanted to wait until after our meeting. There are a few loose ends I'd like to tie up, and I want my partner to go over it and give me her input. She's not in town today, but I've e-mailed her the file."

If Marge had only the slightest idea about electronic communication, she would now believe that I had laid out one more of those sticky virtual slime tracks. Just what she thought Laura had left, too, and what she wanted to erase so badly, together with every human in whose brain the same info might be stored.

She didn't show any sign of worry, though, and just said, "I'm mainly interested to learn what you found out in Asheville, and who, apart from Stacey, you've talked to. Laura seemed to have lived there for a long time."

Since I'd entered the house, I'd been looking around to find out if Kali was anywhere near. So far I hadn't seen any sign of her.

"I told you I've found out Laura was in the military. She was a gunner and deployed to Afghanistan," I said. Martha and I had decided I should stick as closely to the truth as possible, without giving any information about real people I'd met.

Marge had once more placed herself in the comfortable armchair. Now she got up, walked over to the picture window and stared out into the vast space of the city below her feet.

"Laura received a head wound when she was riding in an unarmored Humvee during her service. After that, she suffered from headaches and memory loss." I freely made up the memory loss.

I also rose from the chair on whose edge I had been hovering.

"That's terrible," Marge said in a low voice and turned around to face me.

"I know. You'd think with all the money that's being blown up in those wars, we'd at least protect our soldiers better."

"Did you speak with any of Laura's fellow soldiers?"

"I tried. I even went to her army base. But none of them were there. Some were deployed, others discharged due to injury, or their contracts were up and the military wouldn't release their names to me."

"And the picture you talked about. Do you have it with you?"

I tried to remember what I had told her exactly about Laura's wedding picture. I was carrying it in my bag. If I gave it to Marge, she'd know what Stu looked like, but I couldn't come up with a good reason to hold back the picture. So I handed it to her.

She studied it closely, and when she lifted her head, her eyes were shinier than before, as if a thin film was covering them.

"Who is the man?"

"I have no idea."

"Didn't you ask Stacey about him? After all, she's in the picture as well."

"She wasn't very forthcoming. Of course I asked her, but she said that Laura had invited her to some kind of military function, and she was never really introduced to the guy in the picture. That he didn't seem close to Laura, though."

"It looks very different here. From what I can see, Laura and this man could be getting married. Look at the flowers she's holding."

"That's just what I said to Stacey, but she told me Laura had received some kind of medal on that day—for brave conduct—and that's why she got the flowers."

Marge stared at me as if she was trying to hypnotize me. I stared back. For some people, it's unnerving if they are being stared at by just one eye. I've been told by friends who hated me doing that to them. If it had any effect on Marge, she didn't show it. It would now be the time when one of us should talk about Stacey, suggest that Marge or I try to contact her again, wonder why she had been so unforthcoming, muse over the friendship she had with Laura, what else she knew about her friend. Of course I didn't say anything. Neither did Marge.

There were no uncertainties between the two of us. We both knew that the other one knew. From here on we were two predators staking each other out. Unfortunately, I felt like the much smaller cat to the saber-toothed one before me.

"You said you had interesting news for me," Marge said.

Wouldn't it have been really interesting—albeit disturbing—for many mothers to learn that their daughter had suffered severe head trauma in a war?

"That depends on what you want to know," I said. A wicked cold chill was suddenly creeping down my spine. Every instinct told me to run now if I wanted to have any chance to run at all. But I had to find out if Kali was anywhere in the house.

"I didn't find any manuscript," I said. "Nothing that Laura wrote. Stacey lost all the e-mails Laura ever sent her."

I was wondering if I should mention that Stacey knew Laura had fled from the Cunninghams. There was a small chance that Marge might lose her composure and involuntarily reveal something that'd help me solve the puzzle. The result would be that she'd be absolutely sure that I was after this secret. Somehow I felt that my death sentence had been signed by her anyhow, so I was getting ready for my own last verbal attack—when the telephone rang.

"I have to get this," Marge said and grabbed the receiver of a cordless phone lying on the armrest of her chair.

My thoughts were performing somersaults. I badly wanted to listen in on her phone conversation. But even more, I wanted to seize the chance to explore the house. So I mouthed the word *bathroom* to her and walked to the door of the salon.

"One second," she said to the person on the other end of the line, then she covered the phone's mouthpiece and explained to me that I'd find a restroom next to the front door.

I closed the door of the salon behind me and rushed into the hall. The house was really not much bigger than a regular single-family home. There was a kitchen next to the hall, a big living room, a formal dining room, and a small extra room decorated with boring drawings of ancient columns, typical guest room design. A child's clothes were hanging over a chair. Kali was staying here, I guessed. It was empty, like all the other rooms which I checked out quickly but thoroughly. The girl was nowhere to be seen. The restroom, which also contained an accessible shower, was empty as well.

Next to the salon door was a staircase. I put my ear on the door and heard Marge's subdued voice inside. I slipped up the staircase, tiptoed from room to room on the second floor. There were two more guestrooms, a master bedroom, which looked like a giant Victorian suite—all dark woods and flowery designs—a few closets. And again no sign of Kali. A very narrow staircase led up to another floor, probably the attic. It was too tight to carry Kali's wheelchair up. I was just about to climb it, nevertheless, when I heard Marge's voice sounding from the hallway.

Slowly I snuck halfway down the stairs, hoping she would go back into the salon, and I could enter it in a few seconds, pretending to come back from the bathroom.

"Yes, he picked her up," Marge was saying, softly, with a most striking tenderness. "And he'll come to your place later . . . Everything as planned . . . I love you, too, Stu . . . I'll be there, don't worry."

She walked into the hall, laid down the phone on one of the small rococo tables and looked at the closed bathroom door. For a second she seemed hesitant, battling the impulse to knock at the door. But then she turned away and finally walked back into the salon.

As silently as possible, I dashed down the rest of the stairs, through the hall and into the bathroom, where I flushed the toilet and walked out again. On my way back to the salon, I couldn't resist the impulse to oh so quickly check the caller ID status on the phone. I was holding the receiver when the salon door opened and Marge emerged. She gave me a look. I looked back and didn't even bother to come up with an excuse. I just laid the phone down again.

"You better leave now," Marge said.

I just walked to the door. We might not be equal opponents—she knew what all this was about, while I had no idea—but we met at eye level when it came to our dislike of continuing a tedious game.

Chapter 28

I made it back to the car unharmed. Martha emerged from the shadows in which she had been hiding and pushed up toward the van. We drove off knowing that the farther away we got from Marge's neighborhood, the likelier it was that we'd get attacked by whomever chased after us. I soon realized we were being followed. A car had pulled out of a parking spot a few yards down from ours. When I turned into a quiet side street, it was still behind us. Far behind us, but it was there. Martha understood without explanation why I was curving around quiet Pacific Heights for a while, trying to make completely sure the headlights would stay on our tracks. They did. Sometimes it took a while before they appeared again in the rearview mirror, but as soon as we hit a longer, straighter stretch, they lit up in the distance.

"That's not a pro," Martha said. "We wouldn't be able to spot him that easily."

"Jasmine was not much better," I said. But then I wasn't even sure Jasmine hadn't remained so visible on purpose, to unnerve me, or rather to further the stalking game she was pretending to play.

"I wonder where Marge found her, anyway. You say she was a good markswoman, but she was definitely not an experienced contract killer."

"Well, you can't always pick and choose," I replied dryly. "Sometimes you have to compromise on your job description."

The headlights were there again, two blocks behind us. I'd had enough of riding around this residential neighborhood, testing our shadow. Where were we going next, anyway?

"Marge was on the phone with somebody she called Stu," I said. "It could be Laura's Stu, but I doubt it."

"Then it's probably her brother."

"She told him that somebody—a he—had already picked *her* up. And would come over to his place, as agreed."

Before I had finished my sentence, Martha was already dialing 411. But Stewart Cunningham's number and address were unlisted.

"What's Big Susan's number?" she asked me impatiently.

I handed her my cell which had *AdUp's* number programmed. I didn't have Susan Bradley's private data. Fortunately, she was working late. Martha asked her for Stewart's information. My partner silently moved her lips, memorizing an address, thanked Susan and hung up.

"She's not sure where her former fiancée now lives. But when they were together, he had his own apartment within the family mansion. She thinks he might still be living there."

Martha directed me to Sea Cliff, a neighborhood on the edges of the Golden Gate. We drove down Clement Street, passing through an inconspicuous Chinese middle-class neighborhood, and I was astonished when Martha said I should turn right at the next intersection. But in fact, two blocks down we entered a different universe. Carved stone pillars announced the area's name, and then we were passing houses and yards which seemed to grow slowly, becoming more luxurious the closer we got to the ocean. Most of the residences were clearly extremely expensive, but nevertheless, they displayed openness. The front doors were only yards from the street, the windows huge. Through some you could see into the rich spaces behind and right through another window at the other side, onto the wild sea, which at this hour was illuminated by the bright lights from the ships approaching the Golden Gate Bridge about a mile to the east.

Alcott Cunningham's mansion was invisible from the street, though. A high brick wall separated the estate from its surroundings. There was an iron gate topped with spikes that rose like daggers into the night sky. The wall was studded with glass shards. Bushes and trees created a dark boundary which sucked up every bit of light that might be emanating from a residence behind them. We were facing a fortress. I didn't even dare to park in front of the entrance too long. A police car was patrolling the area and was already passing by us for the second time in five minutes. The next time the officers would knock on our window and demand to know what we were doing here.

Our follower had either lost us or was hovering somewhere in the background. After we'd entered the neighborhood, I hadn't spotted the headlights again.

We drove around the next corner, but of course the property was situated right on the cliff so that we couldn't circle it. There were basically three ways to enter the grounds apart from just ringing the doorbell: climb the ten foot glass-sharded wall, enter the daggered eight foot gate or put on mountain climbing gear and go up the cliff.

"I don't have mountain climbing gear," I said to Martha.

"I knew you were wondering where the next outdoor store

was," she joked.

By now we weren't able to have a reasonably serious conversation anymore. When the world turns surreal on you, the best way to test your sanity is to laugh about it.

"I'll ring the bell," I said.

Martha nodded as if she was truly considering this option. "Look," she said suddenly.

We had parked on a street adjacent to the estate, still in sight of its entrance. A white minivan was now approaching the gate. The driver leaned out the window and spoke to somebody over the intercom built into the wall.

I looked at Martha. Again she nodded, assertively this time. "But you . . . ?"

She quickly patted her chest, caressing her Sig-Sauer. The next moment, I was out of the car and dashing down the sidewalk in the shadows of the great trees lining it. I crossed the street, trying to stay within the blind spot of the van's mirrors. The gate opened slowly and automatically, the minivan pulled in—with me in tow.

As soon as I had made it onto the grounds, I jumped into the cover of the vegetation bordering the driveway. The van slowly took off, its driver obviously unaware that somebody had come in behind him.

The underbrush was dense, and I pushed through it trying to stay parallel to the driveway to my right. Twigs snapped against my face, and for a moment I wondered if poison oak only grew right above the ground or if it could hit me at head level as well.

Then there was a weak light gleaming through the foliage. A dark structure arose before me. The reflection of the moon from the ocean's surface revealed that the house crept down the cliff over four floors toward the water's edge. On the land side, where it had two floors, a weak light was coming from an upstairs window. Two downstairs windows were somewhat more illuminated, and a yellow lantern, reminiscent of an eighteenth century gaslight, hung over the entrance. It was too dark to make out the details of the house, but I could see that it was a heavy, graceless brick building, clinging to the cliff's edge like an overweight climber to the rock face of El Capitan.

The minivan was parked right before the entrance. A stone stairway led up to the front door. It looked oversized even for this kind of structure, as if the house were sticking out its ugly tongue to greet its visitors.

I bent forward in order to stay out of sight from the mansion's downstairs windows, raced across the driveway, snuck up to the corner of the building and crept over to the entrance along the wall.

I wanted to get into the house. I had to find out if Kali was here and what was happening to her. I was hoping there would be some kind of side entrance, a cellar door or window, something that I could open—if necessary with force—and climb through.

When I came closer to the front of the building, I thought I saw a tiny door in the outer wall of the staircase. It would probably just lead to a storage space for gardening tools underneath the stairs, but maybe there was a connection to the house.

The door's knob was sturdy. I couldn't move it. The wood panels of the door were thick and impossible to break without making noise.

I was just about to round the stairway to see if there was another option on the back side, when a door opened and voices sounded from the top of the stairs.

"Okay," somebody said with an artificial cheer. "I'll help you to the car first, then I'll get your chair."

I pressed myself against the wall, trying to emulate a dark, flat moth, a night creature, invisible in its element.

There was low panting on the stairs above my head, heavy but weak breathing and the steps of two people, slowly and irregularly descending.

225

When they had made it down to the van, they walked up to the passenger door which was situated only six feet to my left. I turned my head, certain they would see me, ready to jump forward and run.

But the two men were too caught up in their own exhausting endeavor. A large African-American guy was holding on to a tall, extremely thin white man. The thin guy's arm was wrapped around the shorter man's shoulder. The big guy had opened the passenger door, trying to help the thin man, whose breathing was unnaturally labored, and whose legs looked as if they would buckle beneath him any second, into the van. There was equipment tethered to the man. A cable emerged from beneath his jacket, leading to a kind of suitcase. I had seen such a device in a hospital lab I once worked in. It had been bigger than this one, though, a more old fashioned thing, but together with the information Big Susan had given us, I could identify it. It was the external unit of a VAD, a Ventricular Assistance Device—basically an artificial heart.

A VAD can help a patient heal after heart failure. But if the heart is destroyed beyond healing, it is also used as a bridge before a transplant becomes available. Patients can live on such devices for quite a while, but complications can occur, infections, and, of course, the machine itself can have technical problems. All in all, it was a difficult state of existence.

Once the big guy had managed to place the thin man in the passenger seat, he carefully lifted the heart's power unit into the foot space and closed the van door. Then he disappeared from my sight again.

The man inside the van leaned his head back and closed his eyes. He had a long face, many wrinkles and full white hair brushed back from his forehead. Despite his bad state of health, the sunken features, the gray skin tone, it was obvious that in an old-fashioned way he was a beautiful man. He reminded me of a wrecked Cary Grant. I knew his real name was Stewart

226

Cunningham.

The man who had helped him into the van came down the stairs again. He was carrying something heavy and metallic, and there was a clanking sound when the object hit the stone. I slowly came out of my hiding place and crept around the front of the van, making sure to stay so low the man in the van couldn't see me.

The big man was heaving the seat of an electric scooter into the back of the van. He was sweating profusely. More large parts were lying at the top of the stairs. I waited in the cover of the van for him to walk up again, grab the next piece—the base of the scooter—and carry it down. For an instant, I wondered why they weren't just using a manual wheelchair which would have been so much easier to transport. Probably Stewart didn't have enough strength to push such a chair himself. In a power scooter he would still be in control and not have to be pushed around.

The driver had trouble getting the cumbersome scooter base into the van. This was the little chance I had waited for. While he was bending down, trying to get a better grip on the scooter, I snuck through behind him, made it up the stairs and into the open front door. Inside the house, I rushed through the entrance hall and into a dark hallway to the left.

I was trembling, trying to catch my breath. I let all my systems calm down so no part of my body would make an involuntary sound. Then I waited for the click of the front door as it closed, and for the van's engine to start and then for the van to drive away.

All of this happened in the next five minutes. My surroundings became quiet. I waited another seemingly endless amount of minutes, probably about three, then I slowly walked into the front hall.

In a corner, a small staircase lead up to the second floor. It looked inconspicuous. The more obvious feature of this giant room was the gallery at the ocean side of the building from which you could see two stories down. A gigantic window front covered the whole of these floors, an open staircase led down on each side of the gallery into a main room, which reached up all the way to the hall through which I had entered. Again, only the reflection of the moon on the waves illuminated my surroundings. The signal from a lighthouse in the distance was twitching like the dot on a medical monitor.

I had no idea where to begin looking for Kali in this big dark place. On impulse, I walked down the stairs into the vast room. A crystal chandelier was tinkling a little. There was heavy old furniture strewn everywhere, and worn out rugs covered the floor. Hallways led off the main room into the back of the house. I wandered into them, opened doors and whispered "Kali?" every now and then.

The rooms smelled dusty. Some reeked of wet fireplaces, and there was a humid, salty stench everywhere. Eventually, I realized that the downstairs of this house hadn't been used in a long time. A thick layer of dust covered every surface, and the fabrics smelled moldy. Even the floors were covered in dust. When I came closer to the window, I could see my own tracks on the floorboards along its edge.

I climbed up to the front hall again. A wheelchair lift was attached to the staircase, which led up to the next floor. Silently, I walked up. Light shone from a hallway. Again I whispered "Kali," this time even lower. I sensed the presence of a human being somewhere on this floor and hoped that it would be the girl and that I could grab her and rescue her from whatever it was that scared her so immensely.

A door stood open at the end of a narrow hallway. I ventured toward it.

"You're late," a voice suddenly sounded.

I almost shrieked with panic. It had been a male voice. Brittle, impatient, extremely old.

I turned around. I wanted to run, but a shadow appeared

before me.

"Who are you?" the man demanded.

He was as tall as Stewart, also very thin, upright, ancient. Alcott Cunningham, the man Susan Bradley had been warned about as a child. The man you didn't want to leave your children alone with.

"Where is she?" I demanded.

"Huh?" the man only answered.

"Where is Kali?" I said again, it almost came out as a whisper.

"You have to speak up. I don't hear well," Alcott Cunningham responded. "Did Joanne send you? You're late."

Whoever Joanne was, I was willing to play along. "Yes, she sent me. I couldn't find the house. She told me to take care of Kali first."

"I have no idea what you're talking about. I want my dinner."

I walked up closer to the man. He was holding on to a door frame with disfigured, arthritic fingers. Had I breathed only a tiny bit stronger, I would have knocked him off his feet.

The doorway opened into a salon not unlike the one in Marge's house. It was darker, though, like an old fashioned smoking room. Alcott Cunningham slowly walked to a big chair positioned by a cold fireplace. He lowered himself carefully into the chair. He was wearing formal pants, shirt, vest and tie. On his shirt were food stains.

I stepped up to his chair, remained standing before him. "I want to know where the girl is who lives with Marge, your daughter," I said.

"I know who my daughter is," Alcott said impatiently. "I just don't know what you're talking about. If you're not here to prepare my dinner, I guess I will call the police and have them arrest you."

A cordless phone lay on a table next to him. I quickly snatched it and held on to it.

"You've guessed correctly. I'm not here to fix your meal.

229

Where has Stewart gone?"

"I have no idea. I don't care what he does. His days are numbered."

Alcott didn't strike me as demented. His features were sharp, his eyes clear. His skin was so wilted, it seemed as if something cancerous was eating at it, but his gaze was steady. It was something else that made him talk incoherently. A lifelong fix of too much power, I guessed. The knowledge that he was the sun in the universe of everybody he knew and that it was the natural task of the people around him to make sense of whatever he was saying even if he was talking gibberish.

"You don't seem to care very much for your son," I said.

"Stewart is an idiot," Alcott said nonchalantly, which made this damning parental statement sound particularly cruel. "A weakling. He should have married that Bradley girl. Fuse our two good names, two great fortunes."

"Why didn't he?"

"Didn't want to ruin her life, he told me. As if our family was something to be ashamed of. Then a few months later, he gets this girl pregnant. I don't even know where he met her. She just dumped the baby on our doorstep and disappeared."

"Leonard?"

"Of course Leonard. Stewart never had another woman after that. He was always like that, always made bad decisions. He wasn't fit to take over the corporation. He likes the firewater, you know?" Alcott actually pretended to knock back a drink. What a comedian! Then he continued to babble. "Neither was Marge. She's good with the charity work. But Stewart? He's completely dependent on me. And will be until his death. Marge, maybe I'll put her into my will, make her a board member at CBM." Alcott gave an evil chuckle. "But maybe I won't. I'll decide that on my deathbed."

"So you're still fully in charge of the corporation?" I asked. CBM, Cunningham Beams and Metal, I recalled. Alcott may not be demented, but he also didn't look as if he could still lead a global corporation. He smelled of unwashed skin and old food, and he was very pale. He looked as if he hadn't left the mansion in a while. There was something supremely insane in the way he just spilled his guts to a complete stranger who had broken into his house.

"No," he said. "The board is. Good men. But I still hold the majority stock. They can't bypass me when it comes to top personnel decisions."

An idea shot through my mind like a flare. "Did Laura visit you lately? To talk about the corporation? The armor they produce for the military?"

"Laura. That little bitch. I told Marge she shouldn't adopt a stranger just like that and pass the family name to a little yellow brat. Wasn't it enough we took her in, rescued her from a terrible destiny? But no, Marge became all mommy over the little thing. Wanted her to be entitled."

"When did you see Laura last?"

"She came here. Although I told her never to come before my eyes again." The hoarse, breathless, disgusting chuckle came from his mouth once more. "I gave her quite a scare. She could have ruined us. I had to protect the family. Of course I never looked for her after she was gone, didn't even think of her, but I know she's been running ever since. I was sure she wouldn't dare to ever show up again."

"But then she did."

"She came in here, all crazy eyes and loud mouth. She used to be such a little darling. And then she grew up into such a bitch. I told Marge that gun practice thing was nonsense. Who wants a little cutie pie swinging a weapon? She should never have allowed it. And then the brat just shows up with a pistol one day. All shaking, but threatening to shoot me. She didn't even notice Eberhard standing right behind her."

"Eberhard?"

231

"My man servant, bless his soul. Long gone now. But he had connections. And he was indebted to me. I knew all about him. You have to know people if you want to succeed. Their secrets, what they try to hide, what they love most. Laura never had a chance against me. She knew I would find her wherever she went. I planted the fear of the devil in her."

How true, I thought and probed, "But then she came back and threatened to expose everything. The dirty deals with the military, what you did to her as a little girl . . ."

Alcott looked at me with almost sentimental longing. "No, she was looking for Leonard. She didn't have to yell at me like that. I told her he was probably at Marge's place. Then she calmed down a bit."

"You have a visitor, Mr. Cunningham," a woman's voice sounded from the door. "You should have told me. I would have prepared more food." A short Asian woman came into the room.

"This young lady was just about to leave, Joanne," Alcott said, reaching for the phone I was still holding. I had to hand it over to him if I didn't want to raise the housekeeper's suspicions. Alcott grabbed the receiver with his claw-like hand, and I couldn't shake off the image of these fingers touching a child's skin, viciously digging into it like the talons of a bird of prey.

"That's right," I said and walked to the door. Joanne left the room ahead of me. When I turned around a last time I saw Alcott was dialing a number. A short one, consisting of only three digits.

I had to be out of the house before the cops showed up. The front hall was lit up. From somewhere came the sounds of dishes being moved around.

Now was my last chance to get whatever kind of information I could. I wondered if I should ask Joanne where Stewart might be. Then I spotted a Rolodex sitting on a telephone table. I grabbed it, ran out of the house, jumped once more into the shelter of the bushes and threaded my way back to the front gate.

Indeed, a cop car was standing in front of the gate and an officer was pressing the intercom button. My trick worked a second time. The moment the vehicle made it onto the property, I came out of my cover and slipped through the narrow crack of the closing gate.

Chapter 29

"Are you sure Kali is nowhere in the house?" Martha asked after I had jumped back into the car.

"For all I know, she could be shackled and gagged, lying in a dungeon underneath the mansion," I said, still out of breath from my escape. "But I don't think so."

I quickly told Martha about my encounter with Alcott and handed her the Rolodex. She flipped through it, and I drove us away from Sea Cliff, down Clement, again without a plan where to go next.

"So you've finally met the infamous Alcott," Martha said.

"Yes, and his son Stewart, who must have had a hell of a life with that kind of father."

"Well, he could have left."

"Maybe yes, maybe no. Anyhow, now he's in really bad shape. I saw him when he left the house. He can hardly move. And he's using an artificial heart."

"Something like that exists?"

"They've been around for a while. The heart is basically a pump, so researchers have been eager to find a way to replace it with a mechanical device. Unfortunately, it's a pretty complex pump, and our bodies never love foreign objects being stuffed into them. That's why patients don't survive forever on these machines. They are used to buy some time in case a transplant becomes available."

"And many patients die anyway while they're waiting."

I nodded. A crazy idea was forming in my head. It must be terrible to be waiting for a heart transplant. The demand is so much higher than the available amount of donor organs. And if you have any other condition that drops to the bottom of the donor list, or a rare blood type, it can be a completely hopeless wait.

"So you're saying Stewart didn't look as if he was driving off to have some perverted fun with Kali somewhere on neutral territory," Martha said.

I knew she needed to talk like that in order to be able to bear all she had already seen in her career, her life. Still, I cringed at her lingo.

Around us were restaurants, cafes, a buzzing city life. It must be hard to see all these things when you couldn't enjoy them any more, when you were terminally ill, and knew you'd be gone for good soon. When I had cancer myself, I was only a little kid. I didn't remember much of it. Were it not for the missing eye, I'd probably have forgotten the experience. I had never been scared. But now I wondered how it must feel when life was slipping through your fingers, when you couldn't muster the strength to hold on to it anymore.

"Is there a hospital number in the Rolodex?" I asked Martha.

"I'm already looking," she said, and I knew that we had the same completely wild, but somehow also very logical thought.

"No number that is obviously linked to a hospital or doctor. But there is a number in red tagged *Only in emergencies*."

Martha was already dialing it. "It's a voicemail," she said when she hung up. "Of somebody called Vince." She continued to go through our stolen address pool. "Vince al Rami," she then said.

"Automated message," she sighed after dialing al Rami's number. But then her voice lit up. "Marin Cardiology Center. In Tiburon, 93 Bay Drive."

I was already changing lanes, turning the van onto Park Presidio, in the direction of the Golden Gate Bridge.

"You have to wait until somebody dies who has your blood type so that you can get a heart transplant, is that right?" Martha asked.

"Yes. But then there are other factors, too. It's not only the blood type that decides if you're a candidate. If you have a condition that might affect your new heart as well, you're excluded. Age is a criteria, too. Donor organs are too valuable, so transplant teams are looking for the most promising candidate."

"It's like a lottery."

I nodded. It did resemble a medical lottery overseen by destiny. An available donor also had to have died at a distance not too far, so the organ could be airlifted to the recipient before cell death of the transplant organ became too severe. The donor had to have agreed to organ donation before his death, or his relatives must agree to it once brain death was determined by the doctors. Then, the donor had to be reasonably healthy himself, and in the case of a heart transplant, the organ, of course, had to be undamaged.

"What a temptation for a desperate heart patient when your sister is in charge of a gigantic foundation with access to power-less folks all over the world who could be looted for their organs," Martha said.

"I've long heard stories of rich patients traveling to poorer countries to buy organs from people there, a kidney or even a piece of liver," I said. "I've even read an article about transplant trips to China. It appears that the government there is selling the organs of executed prisoners to wealthy Americans. That way you can buy yourself a new Chinese heart, involuntarily donated by a political prisoner."

"Yuck," Martha said, and nothing further needed to be added about the ethical implications of the practice.

"But you still need to be in shape to travel if you want to go that route," I said. "A heart won't survive the flight from China to the U.S."

"So you think Stewart went on the lookout for a heart that could be brought right to him, nicely wrapped in a living little girl."

"Martha, you have to stop doing this," I groaned.

"What?" she asked, clearly clueless about what was bugging me.

"If our suspicion is true, then they are planning to murder Kali in order to harvest her heart. Maybe they've already done it . . ." We had only just passed the toll plaza to the Golden Gate Bridge. It would take us another twenty minutes to get to Tiburon, and I was feeling nauseous, imagining this unbelievable nightmare might be true and we would be too late. "I can't take the way you're talking about it."

Martha nodded slowly. Then she continued, "Wouldn't it be rather hard to pull off? You'd have to have doctors testing probably thousands of children in their countries of origin. Then you'd have to find a transplant team here who is willing to commit murder."

It sounded completely implausible. But as we were soon to learn, it had happened. You just needed the resources and the cash to make it happen. And Marge Cunningham had both.

When we finally reached the Marin Cardiology Center, I was close to a nervous breakdown. Our shadow had picked us up

237

again, all the while we were curving around picturesque Tiburon, trying to find 93 Bay Drive, his headlights appeared on and off in the rearview mirror. At one point I had to stop at the side of the road, open the door and puke on the shoulder. A black cloud rose from my brain. I had to hold onto the van frame so I wouldn't fall forward. Martha gave me a worried and at the same time challenging look. She didn't look too peachy herself, though. She was pale, with coal black circles underneath her eyes. When was the last time we had eaten anything? I wondered and took it as a bad sign that I couldn't remember.

The clinic looked dark and uninhabited. But then we turned the next corner, and there was the white van that had picked up Stewart. Or at least a very similar looking van.

"Couldn't we just call the cops and ask them to stake out the building?" I asked. "We could tell them we've heard shots from inside."

"I doubt they'd go in if they don't hear or see anything themselves," she said. "It's not a private home where somebody might be battering his wife. If there are no signs of forced entry on any of the doors or windows, they'll leave the building alone. Too much trouble for them if they break down a door."

"Then I'll have to go in," I said.

"I'll come with you," Martha replied.

I gave her a questioning look.

She pointed at the front entrance to the clinic, "Ramp," she said.

"Locked door," I answered.

"It's an automatic sliding door. I can show you how to break the circuit."

She told me to park our van right in front of the entrance parallel to the ramp and the sidewalk. It was not an official spot, of course, but there was enough space, and this way we were hidden from the street while breaking in. The van might even deflect a sniper's bullet, but I didn't count on that too much.

Right now, I didn't see our follower's headlights and decided to ignore the probability that he was somewhere close by.

We walked up the ramp, and I almost shrieked when the automatic door opened automatically before me. Martha grinned viciously. "You can always rely on people's negligence," she said, and we entered the building.

The street front of the clinic was only about ten yards wide, but the building stretched far back. We passed a dark reception area and wandered down a faceless hospital hall, whose only unusual feature was its plush carpeting. The carpet made it harder for Martha to push her chair, but it also allowed us to proceed very quietly. We had almost reached the back end of the building when the corridor forked.

"Where to next?" I whispered.

She pointed at a narrow bar of light painting the floor at the end of the hallway to the right. The light crept from underneath a door almost at its very end.

We snuck up to the door. Low sounds came from inside, a beeping, then a clanking. There were footsteps.

I looked at Martha and she nodded. I slowly pressed down the door handle and pushed against the door. It wasn't locked. I pulled out my knife and wielded it like a sword while I slowly opened the door wide enough for Martha and me to fit through.

We entered a small operating room. A surgical table was standing in the middle. A glaring light illuminated the person lying on it. It was Kali. She didn't move when I stepped up to her. Nobody else was in here, but there was a door to the adjacent room. It was slowly closing on its own with a low whoosh, as if somebody had just passed through it without shutting it completely.

Kali had an IV catheter in her right arm. No drip was connected to it yet. When I approached her, she didn't respond. Her eyes were closed. She was covered with a thin sheet. I pulled it away from her chest. Her skin was unharmed. She was completely naked. I checked her pulse. She was alive.

I made sure there were no other tubes going into her body. Then I wrapped her in the sheet, grabbed her and carefully laid her over my shoulder. She was tiny, very light for her age, which I estimated at thirteen or fourteen. Nevertheless her weight was almost too much for me to carry.

Martha held the door open, and we left as fast as we could, my partner pushing hard against the resistance of the carpet, me struggling with the load on my shoulder. I was waiting for agitated voices behind us, running feet, shots, but we made it to the van undetected.

I had to lay Kali on the blacktop next to the van while I opened the door to get the ramp out. Suddenly there were quick steps behind us. They came from the street and came closer fast. I dropped the ramp with a loud bang and bent over Kali to shield her. Martha turned her chair toward the steps. The sturdy, muscular shape of a man emerged before us. Martha pulled her gun.

Chapter 30

"Stay back," Martha ordered.

The man came closer. It was too dark for me to see him clearly. He was blond with a round face. When he opened his mouth I recognized him.

"I'm so glad you found her," Leonard said and pointed at Kali. Then he raised his hands, showing us they were empty, signaling he was coming in a peaceful mission.

"I didn't know what to do," he continued. "I had promised Kali to take her to a concert at the symphony tonight. When I went to pick her up, Marge said she had become sick and was taken to the hospital. But then I couldn't find her there either, and nobody knew where she was. I was so scared my grandfather might have gotten a hold of her."

"We have to leave," Martha said. "We can't hang around here and chat." She moved her chin from Kali to the van, indicating I should carry the girl into the van. I followed her order, laid Kali on the backseat, and got ready to push Martha in.

"I'm coming with you," Leonard said. "I'm not letting you take her to God knows where. I know you're Marge's hired hands. I read the notes that you dropped in front of her house."

"You can follow us in your car," Martha said. "That's how you found us, anyway, isn't it?"

"And risk that you'll get away?" Leonard was already climbing into our van.

I wouldn't be able to carry *him* out, and Martha couldn't shoot him just for trying to hitch a ride. She let me help her into the van, turned her chair so that she was sitting backward facing Leonard and Kali. Her hand was firmly holding on to the gun resting in her lap, and our most unlikely travel group took off. We had just turned the corner when the clinic doors behind us opened and a man in scrubs stormed out. I sped up, dashed around the next corner and drove toward the freeway as fast as possible.

"What's wrong with her?" Leonard asked. I adjusted the inside mirror so I could see him. He was sitting beside Kali, holding her hand.

"I hope she's just heavily sedated. She should regain consciousness in a while," I said.

"What were they doing to her in there? And why are you abducting her now? Maybe she needs an urgent medical procedure!" Leonard had clearly joined our club of people so filled with unanswered questions we were about to explode.

"You know that your father needs a new heart," Martha said.

"Yes, but it looks pretty bad. He has an unusual blood type. He also has a drinking problem. That's what destroyed his heart to begin with. And he can't dry out. So he's at the bottom of the transplant list."

I doubted that Leonard's father was on any transplant list at all. Active alcoholism is a strong contraindication for an organ donation—booze being too potent a cell killer. *Poor Stewart*, Laura's words resounded in me.

"You can't seriously believe that Kali needs a procedure at the private cardiology clinic we just came from. Is anything wrong with Kali's heart that has to be fixed today, in the middle of the night, in all secrecy? What do you think?"

It took a moment for Leonard to process the information, just as it had taken Martha and me quite a while before we had come up with the reason for Kali's fear. I suspected that her English was much better than everybody thought, and that she had overheard what Marge and Stewart were planning for her.

"How do you communicate with Kali?" I asked Leonard.

"I speak some Dari."

"Never in English?"

"She doesn't speak English. It's hard for her to learn. She doesn't know Braille."

It wouldn't have been all that hard. Kali had all the time in the world, and her ears and mouth worked perfectly fine. Nobody had gone to the trouble to teach her, but I was sure she had learned it, anyhow.

Something in Leonard's story didn't add up. If he had gone to Marge's place to pick up Kali and then driven to her usual hospital, who had followed us after my own visit to Marge's mansion?

"Where did you start to tail after us?" I asked. "And why did you follow us here?"

"When I came to my grandfather's place, I saw the police enter the premises," Leonard said. "I thought . . . I was afraid . . . I just hoped if he was doing something to Kali that they had been notified, maybe by the housekeeper, and that they would come and get him. I didn't want to be seen there when that happened. Then I saw you drive away. I thought you may have called the cops on him, and . . . I don't know . . . I wasn't thinking clearly . . . I just followed you on impulse . . . thought you could give me some answers. I know that Marge hired you to find out why Laura disappeared."

"You were both molested by Alcott, weren't you?" I said gently.

"He made me watch," Leonard finally whispered. "When he raped Laura. I couldn't do anything to help her. Later, he wanted me to touch her, too. We were in love, you know. And he had found out about it. Then he wanted to watch . . . when we . . . did it. After that . . . I couldn't . . . I mean, I still loved her . . . but I couldn't be with her, couldn't touch her. I didn't know how to protect her."

What Leonard wasn't saying told even more of a story than his words. A horrifying story. I didn't have the heart to press him for more details. He would probably have to give a statement to the cops sometime soon if this whole mess was ever to be sorted out. In order to free Inez. To finally make Alcott pay for what he had done. I suspected Marge and Stewart had already gone through the same torture when they had been children.

"Do you think your grandfather had Laura killed? In order to shut her up after she had resurfaced and probably threatened to expose him?" I asked.

"I'm not sure," Leonard mumbled. "Didn't her lover stab her?"

Behind me there was a shuffle. I couldn't turn around. We were in the middle of the Golden Gate Bridge. A low moan came from the backseat. Kali was waking up. As soon as we had passed the toll plaza, I pulled over, stopped at the shoulder and moved around in my seat.

The girl was struggling to sit up. Her eyes were wide open, unfocused. She had pulled her hand out of Leonard's.

"Don't be scared, Kali," I said. "Remember me? I'm Anna. We met the other day when your chair went down the hill. And then you called me, right?"

Kali nodded. She understood exactly what I was saying. I continued, "Martha is here, too. She is my partner. We're both detectives, and we're trying to help you. And then there's Leonard. He's your friend."

Big tears started to run down the girl's cheeks. In the orange lights from the toll plaza, her eyes glowed like giant amber pearls. She looked as if she had just woken up in this foreign place for the first time, a peaceful, terribly scared creature from a different universe.

"They take my heart," she said.

"They didn't." Martha smiled. "Your heart is still where it belongs. We'll take you to the doctor now, but just to get you checked. Don't worry, you're safe. And then the police will have some questions. But we'll stay with you. Nobody will harm you."

Maybe my partner's verbal outpouring was frightening the girl. She was probably just still in shock from all she had gone through—the terrible fear of the past weeks, the cruel loneliness—but she didn't stop crying. She still looked scared out of her mind.

If Leonard was her friend, why had she never told him about her fears? Was he too connected to Marge? Too much a member of the Cunningham family for her to trust him? And why had she not confided in anybody at the hospital where he took her for treatment?

"Who is her doctor?" I asked Leonard.

"She's being treated at California Pacific Medical Center on Buchanan. There are a few specialists who deal with her injuries, an ophthalmologist, an orthopedic surgeon. They're probably not on duty right now," he said.

"We mainly need a tox screen for her. To see what they've given her for sedation," Martha said.

"Do you usually stay around when she's being examined?" I asked Leonard.

"Of course. To translate. And so that she doesn't feel scared," he said, somewhat impatiently. We were still sitting on the shoulder, and I didn't make an effort to start the van.

Kali might not be able to stand or walk, but she could move pretty well while she was sitting. She had managed to slide away from Leonard on the back bench as far as possible, wrapping her sheet tightly around her. Something was weird here. Maybe Martha and I scared Kali. We were strangers, after all. But why wasn't she relieved to see Leonard, her protector? *Leonard was there . . . He touched her*, the imaginary voice I had assigned to Laura reverberated in me. That's what she had written in her notes.

I had to speak with Kali alone, without Leonard present, or have a psychologist talk to her.

"Let's go," Leonard said. "Let's get this over with. Can't you see she's deadly tired?"

"Dead," Kali suddenly said. "The lady dead."

"Nobody's dead," Martha tried to comfort her. "Everything's fine. Don't worry."

"Laura," Kali continued. "Laura. Scream. Dead. Make her dead."

Kali had overheard Marge and me speak about Laura's death. But nobody had mentioned any screams.

Leonard stared at Kali. Then he reached over to her and grabbed her hand. He spoke to her in a language I didn't understand.

"What are you saying?" Martha demanded. "Kali, listen, when did you hear screams?" My partner looked at me. "We have to find a Dari interpreter."

I was still marveling over the meaning of Kali's words. Before my train of thought had reached its final destination, before I could draw the last and brutal conclusion myself, or could react to it, Leonard was reaching for Martha's gun. Her fingers were wrapped around it firmly, and he struggled to get it away from her.

Martha would never ride around in a car with an unsecured gun in her lap. But somehow Leonard managed to cock it. There was the telltale clicking sound. Martha's fist was around the barrel. Leonard tugged at the handle. Kali shoved herself forward and rammed her small curly head into his side. I was still trying to get my knife out of my pocket, when a shot sounded. There was a piercing scream, a loud moan, and then Leonard fell forward toward Martha, whose chair got knocked into the van's console. She almost toppled over backward. Kali was lying on the backseat. Silence befell us.

Chapter 31

"Martha!" I heard myself scream.

Kali was sobbing loudly. Leonard had slid to the floor of the van. He was lying in a weirdly twisted position, a big red spot spreading on the front of his sand-colored T-shirt.

Martha moved her head, shook her arms, looked down at her lower body. Her torso seemed unharmed, but she wouldn't have felt an injury to her legs. She touched them, then said in the lowest tone I'd ever heard from her, "I'm fine. Take care of the girl."

Kali was sitting up again, huddled in the furthest corner of the seat.

"Do you hurt?" I asked her. There was blood splatter on the light green linen of the sheet around her, but no bigger splotch.

"I fine," she said.

I got out of the driver's seat, rushed around the van, opened the side, and pulled Leonard down the ramp. I kneeled down beside him. He was unconscious, his breathing flat, the blood stain on his T-shirt growing.

Martha was sitting in the open door of the van, dialing a number on her cell phone. Minutes later sirens began to howl in the distance.

My partner was carefully examining Kali to make sure the shot had indeed not injured her. People ran over from the toll booths. Somebody gave me a piece of cloth, which I used to press down on Leonard's abdomen. But blood kept pulsing underneath my hand, pumped out by his weakening heart. He was drifting in and out of consciousness. His eyelids were fluttering. "I loved her," he whispered.

"I know," I said.

He was dying. I believed Kali, believed that Leonard had killed Laura, his reaction had completely given him away. From Laura's notes it sounded as if he might also be a pedophile, since she had made him promise never to come close to *them*. I suspected she meant children. And she had seen him with Kali, had probably confronted him about it. Maybe he had molested Kali all along.

But he was dying, and I didn't have the heart not to comfort him. "She loved you, too," I said to him softly.

For seconds he was passed out, then he whispered again with his eyes still closed, "She made me promise . . . and then she didn't believe me . . . she didn't trust me."

"Did you touch Kali?" I asked.

He didn't answer. His eyes remained closed. His breathing became raspy, labored, then it stopped. I touched his neck, unable to feel a pulse anymore. When the paramedics arrived, he was dead. They took Leonard with them.

Half a minute after the ambulance, the cops showed up. They found me crouched on the blacktop next to the van. I was crying so hard I couldn't stand up. Kali was quiet and collected. Martha had a look of shock on her face, but she was able to answer the questions of her former colleagues concisely. Half an hour later the three of us were sitting in the back of a black-and-white, on the way to General Hospital for an assessment of our physical and psychological conditions.

The hardest part of the next few hours was being separated from Martha and Kali. As soon as we had been admitted to the ER, we were each taken in different directions. My physical checkup was over quickly. I hadn't been injured. The nurse mainly needed to collect my clothes and hand them to the waiting officers so they could be processed by trace. She also took off the mic I was still wearing, sending it along with my clothes. It would be useless to the investigators, but maybe the recorder in Martha's purse had been able to catch the conversation in the van prior to Leonard's death. I doubted that what had been said would make any sense out of context, though.

I had long since stopped crying and explained to the doctor who finally came to see me that I had just been momentarily traumatized but that I was fine now and able to speak to the police if only somebody could provide me with something to wear. I was sitting on the side of a bed, dressed in one of those skimpy hospital gowns that are open at the back. The physician, a tired-looking, skinny Asian woman in her late fifties, nodded. She looked at my chart, where the nurse had jotted down blood pressure and temperature, and said, "She can go. Give her something from the closet."

A while later the grumpy nurse came back, threw a heap of fabric on the bed, and left again. I chose a faded black T-shirt, a pair of raggedy jogging pants, a washed-out pink sweater and some rubber clogs and walked into the hall. A policewoman was sitting on a bench reading a magazine. She looked at me questioningly when I emerged, and I said, "We can go. Where are my friends?"

"Ms. Bega is already at the station."

"And the girl?"

"I don't know. Child Protective Services will probably take care of her."

The officer was a quiet African-American woman in her twenties, her partner an older, pretty worn out looking white guy, equally as taciturn as she. As I had been involved in an as-yet unresolved shooting, they put handcuffs on me before they placed me in the back of their car.

On our way to the hospital Martha had already bugged the officers to contact all kinds of people: her former captain, some friends at the squad. When word came back over the radio that she was in fact a still respected ex-cop, she had been able to convince the officers to contact their Marin colleagues and get them to drive to the clinic in Tiburon. I wanted to know what they had found there, but nobody gave me an answer. I had already been part of this game before during another case. For the next few hours I wouldn't be the one asking anything.

At the station I was taken to a drab interview room and began to wonder if I needed a lawyer. I wished fervently that Martha were with me, but when I asked for her, the detective who would be performing the interview told me my partner was being interviewed separately.

I had never touched the gun. Before bringing me to the room, trace had swabbed my hands for gunshot residue. Even though my hands had been washed at the hospital—they were covered in Leonard's blood—the CSIs would still be able to find burnt-in specks of gunpowder—if there were any.

I wasn't worried they would try to nail me for Leonard's death. My main worry now was to solve this crazy mystery, have the right people arrested for the right things and have Inez's case taken up again. So I agreed to cooperate fully with the police. The detective, a tall, athletic woman with curly brown hair and a broad, open face, introduced herself as Sergeant Luanne Silver. She sat down opposite me, and for the next three hours asked questions, sometimes interrupted me, but all in all, let me tell her the whole story.

"We need the girl's testimony," Detective Silver finally said. "To even begin sorting all of this out."

By now she had received word that I had no GSR on my hands. When the interview came to an end, she told me not to leave the county until further notice, and to keep myself available in the next days for questioning. Then she gave me a long, investigative look and said, "I'll have a squad car drive you home."

I was more than grateful for this offer. Twenty minutes later I exited yet another police car and thanked the officer for taking me. When he had driven off, I was standing in front of the door to my apartment building, wondering how I would get in without keys or any tools to pick a lock. Only now did I realize that my personal stuff was still in the minivan and I had no idea when I would get the laptop, my wallet or any of the other things back.

It was just after four a.m., and I was so tired I couldn't even come up with some good curses to yell into the early morning darkness. I got ready to spend the next two hours, until the doughnut shop next door opened, on my own doorstep like a homeless person. All I could do was pray for a neighbor to enter or exit the building so I could sneak in. I'd even risk breaking my shoulder, trying to knock down my apartment door if only I could get into bed.

Fifteen long, desperate, damned minutes passed. Then another cop car pulled up. A uniformed officer got out, unloaded a wheelchair from the trunk and helped Martha out of the back of the car.

"Do you have your keys?" I called.

She nodded and grinned, forever amused by the little stupidities of her chicky. I had never even thought to ask at the station for my belongings.

We took the elevator upstairs, entered Martha's apartment, and she insisted on making some coffee and shaking me down for everything that had happened since we had last seen each other. The coffee rush worked its magic, but only for a little while. For half an hour, I was more alert, able to talk, to sit upright on a kitchen chair. Then I crashed, curled up on the floor, unable to keep my eyes open.

"Okay, chicky, I get the message. Let's break into your place," Martha said and went looking for her lock picks.

She had told me that the Marin cops had found Dr. Vince al Rami at the clinic. The door had still been open, so they were able to enter. They overheard the doctor arguing with a team of nurses over their pay for a night shift. There were no grounds for the cops to arrest any of them. Stewart Cunningham had been on the premises as well, his sister nowhere in sight. The doctor said he was preparing to perform an emergency surgery related to the VAD on Stewart. That's why he had called the surgical staff in. But then the patient had unexpectedly become better, so he wanted to wait until morning.

It was unbelievably frustrating and hopeless. In my mind I could piece together the whole scenario. Heart transplant surgery was a lengthy, intricate, but also rather straightforward procedure. An experienced surgeon could perform it with the help of an anesthesiologist and two surgical nurses. Under normal circumstances, he would ask another surgeon to assist, but it was possible without. I guessed that Vince al Rami had hired a surgical team of people he knew, and who probably were in desperate need for money. It can happen to anybody. You gamble, or get divorced, or have a car accident that proves to be much more expensive than the insurance coverage, and all of a sudden your house—or clinic—is in foreclosure. Credit bureaus hunt you down. Life becomes a hell of nonexistent dollar bills fluttering before your eyes at every waking hour and into your dreams.

Then a respected surgeon asks you to help out with a transplant procedure, and promises to reimburse you to a degree that will wipe out all your money worries in one night. He will probably have you on call, tell you he has a patient who is not topmost on the official recipient list, but who is incredibly wealthy. The doctor will also tell you that he has somebody paid off at UNOS, the United Network for Organ Sharing, which coordinates all official transplants, and that an organ will be made available for his patient. To the transplant team it will sound as if the doctor is just bribing a few people in the right places. He will never tell them that he is in fact killing the donor. He will do the harvesting of the heart alone. I suspected that was why the doctor didn't cause a greater ruckus when he realized we had taken off with Kali. He couldn't have his whole team run after us when he hadn't told them about the girl's existence to begin with.

Was he rationalizing the whole scheme by telling his own sick conscience that Kali's life wasn't worth living anyway due to her disabilities? Because she came from a poor, war-ridden country? That he deserved the money because he was such a great helper of humankind? Or was he just plain unscrupulous and didn't even need such pitiful excuses?

I had told Martha what I was thinking, and things fell into place, down to the amount of time that had passed since Kali had entered the country a few months ago, not long before Laura's death. They probably hadn't performed the transplant earlier, because the preparations had taken longer than expected. And then somebody—maybe the doctor, maybe Stewart, probably Marge herself—had become increasingly nervous about some comments Laura had made. Or maybe it had just been the fact that Laura had stolen Kali's blood test either when she had visited Marge or when she was at Alcott's mansion looking for Leonard. The more realistic it became that Stewart would in fact receive Kali's heart, the more important it also got for him, and Marge and Vince al Rami to make sure everybody whom Laura might have told about her suspicions would be silenced.

Leonard was there, it had said in Laura's notes. Had she seen Leonard in Afghanistan? He had told me he was accompanying children from there to the United States on behalf of the foundation. *I made him promise to never ever come close to them.* If Laura had suspected that her cousin, and teenage sweetheart, was a pedophile himself, she might have made him promise to stay away from kids. And when he broke this promise, she confronted him. He showed up on her doorstep with a knife, and Kali waited in the car, heard their altercation, Laura's screams . . . and then later the conversations about Laura's murder in Marge's house. Kali had learned more English, made more sense of things and pieced information together.

"Your castle is open." Martha's voice broke through my twilight musings.

I was still lying on the floor of her apartment, eyes closed, thoughts racing through a consciousness ready to go black. I struggled to sit up.

"Great. Thank you," I muttered, slowly rose to my feet and walked into the hall.

The lock to my apartment was an old thing that I had wanted to change for a while, but tonight it had proven practical that it was so easy to pick. At least that's what I thought in the moment before I stepped into the living room. It was a terribly stupid thought, as it turned out.

Chapter 32

I closed the apartment door behind me. All my instincts told me to lock it, but I couldn't without the key. Maybe I should have asked Martha for a quick lesson in how to reverse pick a lock, but then I was tired beyond fear and stumbled rather than walked through the living room to the kitchen. I was thirsty, craving a few gallons of water before lying down. While waiting for the water to run through the filter, I stood in front of the sink, staring out the window into the early morning gray zone at the backs of the neighboring buildings.

"Welcome back," a voice sounded behind me.

When I turned around I was looking into the one black eye of a silencer attached to a heavy handgun. It was aimed at my chest, tilted upward just a bit. At such proximity, the shooter wouldn't even have to take aim. She was holding it at hip height, nonchalantly, like a water gun at a summer street fair. Her face looked equally cheerful, long blond hair tied back in a ponytail, one eye steady, the other one a bit out of focus, her pretty mouth in a wide smile.

"Jasmine," I said weakly.

"You didn't count on the friendliness of a stranger, did you?" she asked, and I was nonplussed until she explained. "The next car that came by stopped and checked on the poor victim of a highway robbery tied up inside. Southern charm and hospitality, I'm telling you. The good Samaritan freed me from your duct tape. My skin is still sore from it."

In fact, she had an angry red stripe around her mouth and cheeks, contributing to the insincerity of her happy expression.

"It took a while to convince the man not to call the cops. I promised I would report the incident to the police in the next town, and then he let me take off. By the way, the rifle you saw on the backseat is resting in a deep lake. And this gun will be lying at the bottom of the Bay soon, after it has fulfilled its purpose, of course. I have to say, it's getting pretty expensive, this job for Mrs. Cunningham. I may have to ask for a raise."

"I thought a self-respecting contract killer would never reveal her employer." It felt as if my survival instincts had been turned off. I almost wished for the shot to sound, the punch in the chest, the darkness, and peace, and the end to all the riddles and worries and grief. All I wanted before the cowgirl would kill me were a few answers, my curiosity outweighing every other drive by now.

"I think you deserve to know who really wants you dead," Jasmine said. "You humiliated me, I have to admit. I would have loved to kiss you longer. You are very beautiful. But then you and this baby GI Joe showed no mercy. I wanted to kill you in that moment. But I don't carry a grudge very long. I would have been willing to make up, to make out some more." She chuckled diabolically. "But I have to stay loyal to my employer. It's all word of mouth in this business. And Mrs. Cunningham wants you dead. She just asked me to make sure it doesn't happen close to where she or her family live. So I had to wait a bit."

She had been following us around the night before. "Tell her it will be quite conspicuous one way or the other, after all that happened tonight," I said. "After the statement I gave to the cops. You may want to take off now, Jasmine, look for another profession. And let the distinguished Mrs. Cunningham take care of her own dirty work."

"Oh no," Jasmine said. "It will look like a very convincing robbery and rape by one of the junkies from the neighborhood. Your place will be vandalized, you will be strangled to death, and your private parts will be mutilated by a blunt object. I'm only holding this gun to keep you in check while we're talking."

Then why the need to drop it into the bay later? I wondered, forever a slave to logical thinking. "If I move now and try to attack you, you'll have to shoot me, and that will destroy your neat little plan, won't it?" I said. And with these words I propelled myself forward, trying to stay out of the range of the gun. Adrenaline had finally kicked in and jump-started my survival mode.

Jasmine avoided the attack, swerved around, the gun once more trained on me. I ducked, dashed into her knees and managed to destabilize her. The only chance I had was to take advantage of her hesitance to shoot me point-blank. She was still trying to knock me unconscious with the barrel of the gun. She bent forward and tried to take a good hit. I rammed my head into her crotch, and she fell over.

We were wrestling on the floor. I focused on keeping her gun arm immobile, clinging to it with both hands. But Jasmine was stronger and heavier than I was. Soon she had managed to roll on top of me and sat down on my hips, pinning me to the floor with her face hovering close to mine. She was sweating, but her triumphant grin had become even wider. Her right hand was holding my left arm down. Her left hand was clasping the weapon, and she stretched high in the air. I tried to reach for it with my own free arm but couldn't get a hold of it.

Jasmine was truly flexible. She bent her head, her lips coming

258

close to mine. I lunged up, knocking my forehead into her teeth. She started to bleed from a small cut to her mouth. Her smile turned into a grimace.

"Drop the gun!" Martha yelled from behind us.

Jasmine hardly even looked up.

"Drop the gun! I mean it. I have you in clear range."

And I knew my partner was not lying.

Jasmine's gun arm jerked in Martha's direction. For the second time tonight a shot sounded. A gun dropped to the ground with a loud bang. Jasmine sank onto me heavily, holding her hand. Blood dropped onto the pink sweater I was wearing.

With my arms free I could push her off me. I had almost managed to sit up when something hit my face. My eye was being driven out of its socket. I fell back. My head hit the ground, and suddenly I couldn't feel my body anymore. Then I sank forever into a swirling Milky Way of iridescent stars.

The pain in my face made me realize I was regaining consciousness. I tried to open my eye, but didn't see anything. I began to panic. My nightmare had come true. I was blind.

I was lying on my back. There was an acceleration and then an abrupt stop. I was in a car. I tried to speak, to move my head. A narrow window of vision opened, a dark shape was hovering above me.

"Where . . ." I muttered.

"Hey, chicky, you're back!" Martha's voice was so full of relief that I felt a pang of love for her so strong I wanted to hug her. But something was holding me down.

"You're in an ambulance," she explained. "You were out for almost twenty minutes. I got worried."

In the hospital it turned out I had a bad concussion, whiplash and a black eye. The eye itself wasn't injured. The reason I couldn't see much was because it was swollen shut. The injured, bleeding Jasmine had taken one last good punch at me and had knocked me out before she collapsed herself. Martha had shot her right through the wrist.

My partner told me—with considerable pride—that before the cops and two ambulances arrived, she had made the cowgirl tell her once again that Marge Cunningham was her employer and that she had shot Al and Stacey on her behalf.

"I threatened to blow out her shriveled little heart," Martha said sitting next to the hospital bed where I would have to stay for the next twenty-four hours. I was already drifting in and out of sleep listening to my partner's story.

She had heard the noises coming from my apartment where Jasmine and I were fighting. She had been on the phone with her former captain, who had called her after hearing about tonight's events, and had asked him to stay on the line while she was checking on me. It had been an official line, directly from the precinct. So the cops now had Jasmine's confession on tape.

"Have I ever told you you're a genius?" I asked.

"You told me not too long ago you loved me," Martha said. "Maybe we should go out on a date. I know you're looking for a smart femme to come and rescue you whenever you get your pretty butt in trouble."

"My butt is not pretty," I mumbled, wondering where I'd heard this exact exchange not too long ago. I couldn't come up with it. Sleep was getting the better of me. The last words I could mumble were, "And you're not a dyke."

"Next lifetime then, chicky," Martha said.

I fell asleep, welcomed by Laura's face looking down on me. She had a serious, extremely sad expression, but there was also a sense of relief. Even asleep I knew her image was a figment of my imagination, but I felt comforted somehow as I watched her walk away from me, her voice becoming lower and lower. The last words I would ever hear her say were, strangely enough, "Live long and prosper."

Chapter 33

Mido looked happier than I had ever seen her. She had invited me to come over to her house and meet her daughter, Esmeralda. They had been able to travel back from Guatemala sometime earlier than planned. The little girl had taken to her faster than usual, and the bureaucratic process had been completed in record speed as well.

The bruise around my eye hadn't completely vanished. It still shone in all colors of hematoma's rainbow. It was a great April day, the sky a bright, almost violet azure. It was windless, and when I walked up to Mido's house, I enjoyed the heat of the sun on my still somewhat stiff and hurting neck.

Mido had set a table in her yard. A swing set was standing in a corner, a sandbox next to it. The little girl was playing in the box. When I entered the yard, she looked up at me with big, earnest, hazel eyes. She was just a toddler, fourteen months old.

She studied me intently while I studied her, too.

Rita came out the back door. Mido was standing at the kitchen window, keeping an eye on her daughter. I hugged Rita, then walked over to Mido. She smiled at me broadly, leaned out the window and kissed me on the cheek.

"She's really cute," I said.

Rita had crouched down in the box, helping Esmeralda fill a tiny red bucket with sand.

"I'm sorry, Anna," Mido said.

"Don't—"

"I was just so confused before I left, terribly nervous—"

"And feeling alone, and disappointed in me—"

"No—"

"Yes! And you had every right to be."

Mido was gorgeous. She had spent some time in the sun. She was slightly tanned, her eyes glowing as if there were a candle lit behind them, her mouth more than ready to smile. I wanted to grab her, and kiss her, and make long, wild and explosive love to her.

Esmeralda was giving off a little scream. Mido's eyes shot over to her. The toddler began to cry without an obvious reason, the way little children do when they want their mommies to pay attention to them. Mido disappeared from the window, came out the door a second later and rushed over to her daughter. Rita looked at her, perplexed. Mido grabbed the girl, lifted her up and cradled her. Immediately Esmeralda calmed down, wiping her eyes with her little fists.

"She's just hungry," Mido said. "Let's sit down. I'll feed her. Coffee is almost ready."

I walked into the house, watched over the coffeemaker and brought out the pot as soon as it was ready, and then we all placed ourselves around the table. I had purchased brownies. Rita served us ice cream, and Mido fed her daughter banana chunks and tiny bits of the pastry. It was a peaceful afternoon. I could feel the parts of my body that were still damaged heal.

Maybe Mido and I could get back together. She seemed to have forgiven me. I still loved her, desired her. She was a cute mother, and her daughter was adorable. Many afternoons like this would be waiting for us—struggles too, of course, childhood ear infections, temper tantrums, but also a lot of fun and good times.

When Esmeralda had completely calmed down, Rita said, "I want to know all about this last case of yours. After all, you made me go into hiding again, so I deserve to hear every gory detail."

Mido looked surprised and displeased. It was news to her that her best friend had been once again affected by one of my adventures.

I tried to make it short, to give just the raw skeleton of the story. Too many loose ends were still open, and the destinies of the people involved weren't coffee talk. Mido hardly looked at me throughout the whole narration. She was busy stuffing little pieces of fruit into Esmeralda's heart-shaped mouth. I knew her well enough, though. She was closing down. Only her politeness kept her from asking me to leave and relieve her forever of everything I had seen.

And that's when I knew we had no chance. Sure, we could try it with each other once again. We'd have some good weeks together, possibly. But Mido would never forget what I'd been touched by, shaped by, just as she wasn't able to forgive herself for what she had been through. Mido had worked hard to get her life back together, and I would be a constant reminder of how fragile her own existence was. She averted her gaze, trying not to let my soul touch hers, slowly detaching herself from me, and I could sense my own feelings for her receding. We were falling out of love with each other.

"So what have the cops done now?" Rita asked.

"They are still sorting out all the crazy evidence," I said, a little absentminded. "Kali has given an official statement with the help of an interpreter. They've run DNA tests on the knife that was used to kill Laura, and have, in fact, found Leonard's blood on it. The autopsy showed that he had a scar from a deep cut between the palm and wrist of his right hand. He must have worn thick gloves when he stabbed Laura, but he still cut himself above the cover of the gloves."

"So it was premeditated," Rita said.

"You're watching too much *Law and Order*," Mido cut in, her lips tight. "You even know the whole vocabulary."

"It sounds like it," I said, trying to keep my voice level. Remembering the incidents on the night of Leonard's death still made me tremble. "But as he is dead, it won't make a big difference."

"What do you think happened between him and Laura?" Rita asked, ignoring Mido's obvious disapproval of the topic.

"Nobody will ever know for sure if Laura really saw Leonard in Afghanistan, but there are records that he was picking up children at a hospital in Kabul at the same time she was stationed there. Also, the cops have found another e-mail account with a few more notes that seem to indicate that Laura saw her cousin from a distance with a young girl here in San Francisco a few weeks before her death."

Martha was squeezing her sources at SFPD for updates about the case whenever possible.

"But there is no manuscript?" Rita asked.

"Inez doesn't think Laura was working on a book. She was quite affected by her constant headaches. She told Inez she had received the head injury in a work related accident and was receiving worker's comp. When she could, she helped Inez with her business, doing bookkeeping, et cetera."

Inez was now working with the cops, trying to help them piece everything together. But I had also visited her again, and she had told me what she knew.

"Then it's not even clear who really invented the manuscript story, Laura or her mother?"

"I think it was probably Mrs. Cunningham's idea to come up with this fictitious manuscript. She was paranoid about anything Laura might have found out and written down."

I didn't want to admit that I still hadn't given up hope that despite all this information, there might be a book somewhere in the world that Laura had written, and that would give me more insight into her life. I was secretly contacting publishers and agents, in search of the manuscript, summarizing Laura's adventures, hoping they might recognize parts of it and remember that it was buried in one of the piles of unsolicited texts they had received. One of the agents had even suggested I write the book, and we'd sell it as Laura's. She was intrigued by the whole story.

Laura had once told Inez that her first love was a boy who left her when she was growing breasts. They were talking about coming out, and Inez suspected that maybe the boy had found out he was gay. In the new light it was possible it was Leonard, and he realized he only liked preadolescent girls. It looked as if Laura had that suspicion, too, especially after what she and Leonard had gone through with their grandfather. She may have made Leonard promise that he would never get close to children. And then she saw him in Kabul or back in San Francisco together with one or more young kids.

"What did Kali say?" Rita asked. "Did he molest her?"

"It seems that he hugged her a lot and told her he loved her, but that's all she has revealed so far. It's possible she is too ashamed to say more. She might even be afraid of her family's reaction back in Afghanistan. It could also be that's all that ever happened, which would still be confusing and invasive to a young girl."

Rita nodded in contemplation. "So Laura went back to see her family because she was looking for Leonard. And somehow she found out what Marge and Stewart were up to."

"She probably didn't even know exactly what they were planning. She stole Kali's blood test, though. She must have had a suspicion that they were up to something unsavory and tried to find out what it was."

"This family is seriously twisted," Rita said. "Why did nobody ever go to the cops about the pedophile grandfather?"

"Power, I suspect. Money. Fear. He frightened the wits out of Laura when she was younger. She must have threatened to tell on him. And she was very courageous to begin with. Still, he made her run for most of her life. In one of her notes the cops found, it says that she had nightmares about killing Leonard. Maybe that was one of Alcott's threats, that Leonard would die if Laura told on him."

I was on the right track. But soon I would learn even more details of the Cunninghams' secret. For now, Mido interrupted Rita's and my speculation by saying, "I have to put Esmeralda to bed." The little girl had fallen asleep in her arms. "And I'm pretty tired myself. She still doesn't sleep through. The trip has gotten her circadian rhythm confused."

Rita and I got up, cleared the table, washed the dishes, then wished our friend good-bye. And I knew that was what Mido would be for me. A friend. I couldn't tell how close this friendship would be, if we would drift apart, become distant acquaintances, or if we could remain confidantes. Time would tell. When I walked away from Mido's house, I felt incredibly sad. Tears were once more streaming down my face, but I was also somewhat relieved, in a mood to look forward and explore what life had in store for me in the days beyond tomorrow.

Chapter 34

Inez never moved back into the house of her childhood, the place where she had lived with Laura and her father and where Laura had died. When she finally got released from prison, more than two months after the night of Kali's rescue and Leonard's death, she stayed in a small apartment not far from where Martha and I lived. I had found it for her while she was still in Aldridge, and had furnished it minimally. We didn't see much of each other in those first weeks of her regained freedom. She was busy putting her life back together. She managed to sell the house to an old client of hers for a much better price than the realtor had asked. The buyer was a former world class heavyweight boxing star, now the owner of a successful boxing stable, who wanted his young talents to live in the house. Inez had provided the catering for many a victory party for one of his champs, and when she asked him to tell his boxers to keep a close eye on their neighbors, Lucy and her husband, he was delighted to promise such protection. Lucy's husband wouldn't be a very happy abuser as long as Mario's heavyweights stayed next door.

And then, another two months after her release, Inez was finally able to move into a condo by the ballpark with a great view of the Bay Bridge and the water. She had to accept that she couldn't take care of her father on her own. He was quickly deteriorating, but she was able to get him into a smaller facility specializing in the care of Alzheimer's patients that was not far from where she lived. Not long after her release she received a very generous check, issued to her by the Cunningham Foundation.

It bugged me that Vince al Rami, the doctor who would have performed the heart transplant on Stewart Cunningham, thereby killing Kali, wouldn't be charged. Fortunately, he didn't have a chance to harm the girl, but that also meant that there was no proof of his intent, and his team were keeping their mouths shut, sticking to the story that they had only been called in to do emergency surgery on Stewart Cunningham. The sedatives that the tox screen had revealed in Kali's blood weren't enough to prosecute him. After all, we could have given them to her, al Rami's lawyer claimed. Even worse, though, was that the DA hadn't been able to indict Marge for the deaths of Al Burns and Dr. Stacey Schaffner. Despite Jasmine's confession, Marge had wiggled out of the charges with the help of an army of lawyers. There was no clear evidence that she had hired Jasmine or given her the order to kill anybody. And even Jasmine wasn't being punished for the murders. There was nothing to prove that she had been at the scene of either of the attacks. Nobody had really seen her there, and she had revoked her confession as soon as she was in police custody, claiming the pain and shock from the injury to her hand, as well as Martha's pressure, had made her say what she did that night. The only charges against Jasmine were the break-in to my apartment, as well as the punch she had given me. She was treated like the random junkie she had planned to blame for my murder. A tox screen revealed she had cocaine in her system, together with the remnants of beta blockers she probably had taken to keep a steady hand when she committed her precision killings. She ended up being sentenced to eighteen months in a medium to high security women's prison. She virtually took over Inez's cell in Aldridge.

Stewart died only four days after his son. The check Marge sent Inez was made out in the name of a Stewart Cunningham Memorial Fund. Inez asked Martha and me what to do with the money. She felt it was dirty and had qualms about cashing the check. I could fully understand her feelings, but ever practical Martha said she should keep the money under all circumstances. It was the only indemnification Laura ever got, and she would have wanted Inez to have it. Inez finally decided to open a restaurant with it, where she would serve excellent food for very low prices. I thought it was a marvelous way to relieve her conscience and was excited when she invited Martha and me for the opening party at her new place, Laura's Delights.

Many of Inez's former clients showed up, as well as some close friends who had stuck with her throughout the terrible times, and people from the neighborhood. Inez was busy whirling around, and Martha and I didn't know anybody apart from her. We were happily sitting at a small table in a corner of the beautiful establishment, enjoying the hors d'oeuvres of wasabi oysters, and caviar blini, and the most excellent tuna tartar I had ever tasted. Inez had decorated the place in bright ochres, blues and some stark white. It looked like a cross between a lively Mexican hacienda and a Japanese temple. Martha sighed deeply after finishing her sixth blini and said, "On days like today, it's wonderful to have an insatiable appetite. I wonder what she has for entrees and desserts."

I stuffed myself with more raw fish, completely agreeing with my partner. While we were waiting for the next course, we couldn't help but talk about the Cunninghams once again. We had long taken on new cases. More deadbeat dads and children abducted by one of their parents in ugly divorces who needed to be found, and jobs were trickling in slowly but steadily. We had kept the money Marge Cunningham had originally paid for our services. We had worked hard for it, after all, albeit not according to the wishes of our client. It made me feel uneasy sometimes, thinking that the woman who had wanted me dead was still out there, free and loaded like a hand grenade with the pin pulled. In spite of the havoc she created, she hadn't achieved her goal. She hadn't been able to save her brother.

"Why do you think Marge and Stewart and Leonard always stayed around, letting Alcott destroy them as children, and then they just stuck it out with him?" I asked Martha, still unable to comprehend the zillion ways this family was twisted in and around itself.

"Trying to figure out the mechanisms of abuse within families is much like trying to get a clear view by looking through a crystal prism," Martha said. "However you turn it, emotional facets light up in bright and weird colors, while the reflections from the other sides break and distort your perception over and over again. It's no wonder molested children sometimes develop multiple personalities. Often, they originally love the abuser. He tells them how much he loves them, how wonderful they are, while he devalues them, tramples on their trust, violates their bodies. It's a truly insane system, where common sense, clear emotions, intuition, the integrity of the victims' whole self are being vandalized. Marge and Stewart may have stayed close to their father because they wanted to participate in the family riches. But I don't think so. Stewart broke off his engagement to Susan. He and Marge were clearly closer than usual siblings. He was such a heavy alcoholic that he practically drank himself to death. Marge has a very violent streak herself, but she also seems to have loved Laura in her own way. But then she didn't protect her from Alcott. Leonard appeared to be put together and kind, devoted to his cousin, and then he killed her in a violent rage, probably driven insane by his own feelings for children he knew he shouldn't have."

"Laura was the only one who broke away from the family," I said.

"Yes, and she was the only one who could clearly tell herself that she didn't really belong, that she didn't share with them the *Cunningham blood* or whatever. That was probably her chance. The others were stuck even more in the family scheme."

"But then Laura came back," I said.

"She couldn't completely escape her past," Martha said. "You never can. Especially when you've seen what she has. And when you have a sense of responsibility."

I looked at my partner, who reshifted her attention to the food on her plate. Inez had personally brought us samplers of the entrée choices. I was just about to again stick my fork into the piles of wonders, when I realized Martha wasn't eating. Her gaze was directed inward. I knew better than to ask her what she was thinking about. While she'd been talking, I had only peripherally sensed that she knew very personally what she was referring to. Now I understood that her insight into the Cunninghams stemmed from more than just professional police experience.

"Are you okay?" I asked softly and reached for her hand.

She looked at me directly with one of her typical shotgun glares and said, "I am, chicky, don't worry." Then she attacked her plate with the force of a ravenous army, devouring every last crumb, finally soaking up the sauce with big chunks of bread.

"Go over and flirt with the ladies," Martha encouraged me.

Inez was standing in the doorway to the kitchen chatting with some of her guests.

"I'm too shy," I said. "You know that I'm no party chicky."

Martha chuckled. Then she rolled off and made her way over to our host. Soon she was engaged in a lively chat with a few women. Inez broke away from her friends and wandered over to me. When I looked up into her smooth cocoa eyes, she caught my gaze and said, "Tonight it's going to stay hectic, but I'd like to talk with you in quiet. Can you come over on Monday?"

On Mondays the restaurant was closed, and in the early evening I punched the door code at Inez's condo which was located two houses down from Laura's Delights. Inez greeted me with a hug and led me to the dining room table situated by a huge window, high above the Bay. It was almost September. The days were getting shorter, but in San Francisco the warmest part of the year had only just begun. A mild breeze blew in through the open window. Inez served me all kinds of cold delights, and we ate quietly, enjoying the view, both shy around each other.

"I'm still trying to figure so many things out," Inez finally said.

She was looking into the distance, over to the misty Oakland hills, her long legs stretched out, leaning back in her chair. I knew by now that she was a few years older than I was, just past forty, but since her release she had looked younger each time I saw her. She told me her hair had turned from dark brown to bright white in the days after Laura's death, and she had decided to leave it that way, but her features were relaxed today, her olive skin clear and soft. Her wide upper lip gave her the look of a determined, courageous, yet quietly amused fighter.

"It seems that I hardly knew Laura at all," she continued. "I sometimes wonder who it was that I loved, who she really was, and what was a lie and what was the truth."

"Her love for you was the truth," I said.

"But why didn't she ever tell me what had happened to her?"

"She wanted to protect you. Her whole life she felt that she needed to protect the people she loved from her grandfather, and consequently also from herself." I had wondered for a while why Laura had used her real name with Inez, but then when she had met Al, her old trainer and friend, she had pretended not to know him and had resorted to being Lynn Crooper again. I guessed now that she had planned on finally being open with Inez, the woman she loved, but when she had begun to discover what Marge and Stewart were planning, the old fear had once again emerged, and she had decided to shield the people who were in touch with her. Martha's image of the crystal prism came to my mind again. Laura herself had been quite a prismatic person, forever changing, forever breaking the light people tried to shed on her.

I showed Inez the newspaper I had picked up on the way over. Marge had tried to stay out of the news as much as possible. But a reporter from the *Chronicle* had been provided with allegations about Alcott and his family on a regular basis and had published the occasional article about the Cunninghams. I knew that Martha had his name and e-mail in the address book of her Outlook Express. He had written a human interest story about Laura's life, from her disappearance, to her military stint, to her murder at the hand of her cousin. It was the stuff fairy tales were made of these days. The journalist hadn't been able to openly imply that Alcott was a molester, but it was clear that Laura had gone through traumatic experiences which had led to her flight from the family. Today the *Chronicle* was following up on the story with a piece about a woman who claimed she had been molested by Alcott while her mother was a housekeeper for the Cunninghams after Laura had left. The woman was a young ADA in Seattle, and her allegations would be treated with great seriousness. Alcott was old and frail, but he was healthy enough to be tried in a court of law.

When she had finished reading the article, Inez looked at me in amazement. In this instant it was as if the very softness of her gaze touched me like a swift, comforting caress. I couldn't help but smile—so strong was the sensation—and Inez smiled back.

"What I wanted to talk about with you," Inez then said, her

voice a bit raspy. "You know that Kali and I get along pretty well."

I nodded. For months Kali had been at California Pacific Medical Center, receiving the multiple surgeries she needed for her eyes, her spine, her legs. Then she had been transferred to a rehab facility for children in the Central Valley. Inez had wanted to meet her, so I took her with me on a visit. She and Kali liked each other immediately. Since then, Inez and I visited her separately. We wanted Kali to have as many days with visitors as possible.

"She will be ready to be released next week, but it seems that nobody has been able to locate her family in Afghanistan. Kali's parents are dead. She has an older sister, but she and her family must have moved, and nobody knows where. Now Child Protective Services are looking for a place for her to stay."

I knew that, too. Martha and I had wondered if she could live with one of us, but when we asked the authorities, they said that our apartments were too small. Kali needed her own room.

Inez continued. "I've offered to take her in. I have enough space, and I can take her to school and pick her up. She can reach me any time at the restaurant, can easily come over . . ."

"That sounds like a great idea," I said.

"I wanted to talk with you first, though. Kali adores you, and she would have loved to stay with you. And I do have long hours . . . I was just wondering, if . . . if we . . ."

"I'll be there for you and Kali."

Inez reached for my hand, and again we fell silent. The sun began to set at the edge of the water, its light breaking on the waves, changing from dark blue to pink and violet, subdued and mysterious. Its rays glowed in the mirror of the bay, then sank into the waves, shimmering from below the surface, before it seemed to drop off the horizon. It was good to know it was still there, still one hundred million miles away, still keeping us alive from the farthest distance.

I didn't dare move my hand in Inez's. Her long fingers were lightly wrapped around mine. There was the roughness of her palm which stemmed from many scars, as I knew. Slowly our hands acquired the same warmth, melted into each other, until we let go, knowing that the time would come when we would touch again, tenderly, timidly. We weren't there just yet. We were both still watching another star vanishing into the distance. Laura's light would never disappear from our lives. The love Mido and I had shared still glowed in me, only slowly retreating, but then we were such small creatures on this great planet racing into infinite space at tremendous speed, and it was right to hold on to each other, if only for a moment, then leave some warmth behind and the hope that eventually we'd find one another again.

ROMANCING THE ZONE by Kenna White. 272 pp. Liz's world begins to crumble when a secret from her past returns to Ashton . . .   1-59493-060-0 $13.95

SIGN ON THE LINE by Jaime Clevenger. 204 pp. Alexis Getty, a flirtatious delivery driver is committed to finding the rightful owner of a mysterious package.

1-59493-052-X $13.95

END OF WATCH by Clare Baxter. 256 pp. LAPD Lieutenant L.A Franco Frank follows the lone clue down the unlit steps of memory to a final, unthinkable resolution.

1-59493-064-4 $13.95

BEHIND THE PINE CURTAIN by Gerri Hill. 280 pp. Jacqueline returns home after her father's death and comes face-to-face with her first crush.

1-59493-057-0 $13.95

18TH & CASTRO by Karin Kallmaker. 200 pp. First-time couplings and couples who know how to mix lust and love make 18th & Castro the hottest address in the city by the bay.   1-59493-066-X $13.95

JUST THIS ONCE by KG MacGregor. 200 pp. Mindful of the obligations back home that she must honor, Wynne Connelly struggles to resist the fascination and allure that a particular woman she meets on her business trip represents.

1-59493-087-2 $13.95

ANTICIPATION by Terri Breneman. 240 pp. Two women struggle to remain professional as they work together to find a serial killer.   1-59493-055-4 $13.95

OBSESSION by Jackie Calhoun. 240 pp. Lindsey's life is turned upside down when Sarah comes into the family nursery in search of perennials.   1-59493-058-9 $13.95

BENEATH THE WILLOW by Kenna White. 240 pp. A torch that still burns brightly even after twenty-five years threatens to consume two childhood friends.

1-59493-053-8 $13.95

SISTER LOST, SISTER FOUND by Jeanne G'fellers. 224 pp. The highly anticipated sequel to *No Sister of Mine.*   1-59493-056-2 $13.95

THE WEEKEND VISITOR by Jessica Thomas. 240 pp. In this latest Alex Peres mystery, Alex is asked to investigate an assault on a local woman but finds that her client may have more secrets than she lets on.   1-59493-054-6 $13.95

THE KILLING ROOM by Gerri Hill. 392 pp. How can two women forget and go their separate ways?   1-59493-050-3 $12.95

PASSIONATE KISSES by Megan Carter. 240 pp. Will two old friends run from love?

1-59493-051-1 $12.95

ALWAYS AND FOREVER by Lyn Denison. 224 pp. The girl next door turns Shannon's world upside down.   1-59493-049-X $12.95

BACK TALK by Saxon Bennett. 200 pp. Can a talk-show host find love after heartbreak?   1-59493-028-7 $12.95

THE PERFECT VALENTINE: EROTIC LESBIAN VALENTINE STORIES edited by Barbara Johnson and Therese Szymanski—from Bella After Dark. 328 pp. Stories from the hottest writers around.   1-59493-061-9 $14.95

MURDER AT RANDOM by Claire McNab. 200 pp. The Sixth Denise Cleever Thriller. Denise realizes the fate of thousands is in her hands.   1-59493-047-3 $12.95

THE TIDES OF PASSION by Diana Tremain Braund. 240 pp. Will Susan be able to hold it all together and find the one woman who touches her soul?
1-59493-048-1 $12.95

JUST LIKE THAT by Karin Kallmaker. 240 pp. Disliking each other—and everything they stand for—even before they meet, Toni and Syrah find feelings can change, just like that.   1-59493-025-2 $12.95

WHEN FIRST WE PRACTICE by Therese Szymanski. 200 pp. Brett and Allie are once again caught in the middle of murder and intrigue.   1-59493-045-7 $12.95

REUNION by Jane Frances. 240 pp. Cathy Braithwaite seems to have it all: good looks, money and a thriving accounting practice . . .   1-59493-046-5 $12.95

BELL, BOOK & DYKE: NEW EXPLOITS OF MAGICAL LESBIANS by Kallmaker, Watts, Johnson and Szymanski. 360 pp. Reluctant witches, tempting spells and skyclad beauties—delve into the mysteries of love, lust and power in this quartet of novellas.   1-59493-023-6 $14.95

ARTIST'S DREAM by Gerri Hill. 320 pp. When Cassie meets Luke Winston, she can no longer deny her attraction to women . . .   1-59493-042-2 $12.95

NO EVIDENCE by Nancy Sanra. 240 pp. Private investigator Tally McGinnis once again returns to the horror-filled world of a serial killer.   1-59493-043-04 $12.95

WHEN LOVE FINDS A HOME by Megan Carter. 280 pp. What will it take for Anna and Rona to find their way back to each other again?   1-59493-041-4 $12.95

MEMORIES TO DIE FOR by Adrian Gold. 240 pp. Rachel attempts to avoid her attraction to the charms of Anna Sigurdson . . .   1-59493-038-4 $12.95

SILENT HEART by Claire McNab. 280 pp. Exotic lesbian romance.
1-59493-044-9 $12.95

MIDNIGHT RAIN by Peggy J. Herring. 240 pp. Bridget McBee is determined to find the woman who saved her life.   1-59493-021-X $12.95

THE MISSING PAGE A Brenda Strange Mystery by Patty G. Henderson. 240 pp. Brenda investigates her client's murder . . .   1-59493-004-X $12.95

WHISPERS ON THE WIND by Frankie J. Jones. 240 pp. Dixon thinks she and her best friend, Elizabeth Colter, would make the perfect couple . . .   1-59493-037-6 $12.95

CALL OF THE DARK: EROTIC LESBIAN TALES OF THE SUPERNATURAL edited by Therese Szymanski—from Bella After Dark. 320 pp.
1-59493-040-6 $14.95

A TIME TO CAST AWAY A Helen Black Mystery by Pat Welch. 240 pp. Helen stops by Alice's apartment—only to find the woman dead . . .   1-59493-036-8 $12.95

DESERT OF THE HEART by Jane Rule. 224 pp. The book that launched the most-popular lesbian movie of all time is back.   1-59493-035-X $12.95

THE NEXT WORLD by Ursula Steck. 240 pp. Anna's friend Mido is threatened and eventually disappears . . .   1-59493-024-4 $12.95

CALL SHOTGUN by Jaime Clevenger. 240 pp. Kelly gets pulled back into the world of private investigation . . .   1-59493-016-3 $12.95

52 PICKUP by Bonnie J. Morris and E.B. Casey. 240 pp. 52 hot, romantic tales—one for every Saturday night of the year.   1-59493-026-0 $12.95

GOLD FEVER by Lyn Denison. 240 pp. Kate's first love, Ashley, returns to their home town, where Kate now lives . . .   1-1-59493-039-2 $12.95

RISKY INVESTMENT by Beth Moore. 240 pp. Lynn's best friend and roommate needs her to pretend Chris is his fiancé. But nothing is ever easy.   1-59493-019-8 $12.95

HUNTER'S WAY by Gerri Hill. 240 pp. Homicide detective Tori Hunter is forced to team up with the hot-tempered Samantha Kennedy.   1-59493-018-X $12.95

CAR POOL by Karin Kallmaker. 240 pp. Soft shoulders, merging traffic and slippery when wet . . . Anthea and Shay find love in the car pool.   1-59493-013-9 $12.95

NO SISTER OF MINE by Jeanne G'Fellers. 240 pp. Telepathic women fight to coexist with a patriarchal society that wishes their eradication.   1-59493-017-1 $12.95

ON THE WINGS OF LOVE by Megan Carter. 240 pp. Stacie's reporting career is on the rocks. She has to interview bestselling author Cheryl, or else!

                                                                                1-59493-027-9 $12.95

WICKED GOOD TIME by Diana Tremain Braund. 224 pp. Does Christina need Miki as a protector . . . or want her as a lover?   1-59493-031-7 $12.95

THOSE WHO WAIT by Peggy J. Herring. 240 pp. Two brilliant sisters—in love with the same woman!   1-59493-032-5 $12.95

ABBY'S PASSION by Jackie Calhoun. 240 pp. Abby's bipolar sister helps turn her world upside down, so she must decide what's most important.   1-59493-014-7 $12.95

PICTURE PERFECT by Jane Vollbrecht. 240 pp. Kate is reintroduced to Casey, the daughter of an old friend. Can they withstand Kate's career? 1-59493-015-5 $12.95

PAPERBACK ROMANCE by Karin Kallmaker. 240 pp. Carolyn falls for tall, dark and . . . female . . . in this classic lesbian romance.   1-59493-033-3 $12.95

DAWN OF CHANGE by Gerri Hill. 240 pp. Susan ran away to find peace in remote Kings Canyon—then she met Shawn . . .   1-59493-011-2 $12.95

DOWN THE RABBIT HOLE by Lynne Jamneck. 240 pp. Is a killer holding a grudge against FBI Agent Samantha Skellar?   1-59493-012-0 $12.95

SEASONS OF THE HEART by Jackie Calhoun. 240 pp. Overwhelmed, Sara saw only one way out—leaving . . .   1-59493-030-9 $12.95

TURNING THE TABLES by Jessica Thomas. 240 pp. The 2nd Alex Peres Mystery. *From ghosties and ghoulies and long leggity beasties* . . .   1-59493-009-0 $12.95

FOR EVERY SEASON by Frankie Jones. 240 pp. Andi, who is investigating a 65-year-old murder, meets Janice, a charming district attorney . . .   1-59493-010-4 $12.95

LOVE ON THE LINE by Laura DeHart Young. 240 pp. Kay leaves a younger woman behind to go on a mission to Alaska . . . will she regret it?   1-59493-008-2 $12.95

UNDER THE SOUTHERN CROSS by Claire McNab. 200 pp. Lee, an American travel agent, goes down under and meets Australian Alex, and the sparks fly under the Southern Cross.　　　　　　　　　　　　　　　　　1-59493-029-5　$12.95

SUGAR by Karin Kallmaker. 240 pp. Three women want sugar from Sugar, who can't make up her mind.　　　　　　　　　　　　　　　　　1-59493-001-5　$12.95

FALL GUY by Claire McNab. 200 pp. 16th Detective Inspector Carol Ashton Mystery.　　　　　　　　　　　　　　　　　　　　　1-59493-000-7　$12.95

ONE SUMMER NIGHT by Gerri Hill. 232 pp. Johanna swore to never fall in love again—but then she met the charming Kelly . . .　　　　　1-59493-007-4　$12.95

TALK OF THE TOWN TOO by Saxon Bennett. 181 pp. Second in the series about wild and fun loving friends.　　　　　　　　　　　　　　1-931513-77-5　$12.95

LOVE SPEAKS HER NAME by Laura DeHart Young. 170 pp. Love and friendship, desire and intrigue, spark this exciting sequel to *Forever and the Night*.
　　　　　　　　　　　　　　　　　　　　　　　　1-59493-002-3　$12.95

TO HAVE AND TO HOLD by Peggy J. Herring. 184 pp. By finally letting down her defenses, will Dorian be opening herself to a devastating betrayal?
　　　　　　　　　　　　　　　　　　　　　　　　1-59493-005-8　$12.95

WILD THINGS by Karin Kallmaker. 228 pp. Dutiful daughter Faith has met the perfect man. There's just one problem: she's in love with his sister.
　　　　　　　　　　　　　　　　　　　　　　　　1-931513-64-3　$12.95

SHARED WINDS by Kenna White. 216 pp. Can Emma rebuild more than just Lanny's marina?　　　　　　　　　　　　　　　　　　1-59493-006-6　$12.95

THE UNKNOWN MILE by Jaime Clevenger. 253 pp. Kelly's world is getting more and more complicated every moment.　　　　　　　　　1-931513-57-0　$12.95

TREASURED PAST by Linda Hill. 189 pp. A shared passion for antiques leads to love.　　　　　　　　　　　　　　　　　　　　　　1-59493-003-1　$12.95

SIERRA CITY by Gerri Hill. 284 pp. Chris and Jesse cannot deny their growing attraction . . .　　　　　　　　　　　　　　　　　　1-931513-98-8　$12.95

ALL THE WRONG PLACES by Karin Kallmaker. 174 pp. Sex and the single girl—Brandy is looking for love and usually she finds it. Karin Kallmaker's first *After Dark* erotic novel.　　　　　　　　　　　　　　　　　1-931513-76-7　$12.95

WHEN THE CORPSE LIES A Motor City Thriller by Therese Szymanski. 328 pp. Butch bad-girl Brett Higgins is used to waking up next to beautiful women she hardly knows. Problem is, this one's dead.　　　　　　　　　1-931513-74-0　$12.95

GUARDED HEARTS by Hannah Rickard. 240 pp. Someone's reminding Alyssa about her secret past, and then she becomes the suspect in a series of burglaries.
　　　　　　　　　　　　　　　　　　　　　　　　1-931513-99-6　$12.95

ONCE MORE WITH FEELING by Peggy J. Herring. 184 pp. Lighthearted, loving, romantic adventure.　　　　　　　　　　　　　　　　1-931513-60-0　$12.95

TANGLED AND DARK A Brenda Strange Mystery by Patty G. Henderson. 240 pp. When investigating a local death, Brenda finds two possible killers—one diagnosed with Multiple Personality Disorder.　　　　　　　　　1-931513-75-9　$12.95